THE ALLARDS

BOOK FOUR
THE VOYAGEUR

Wilmont R. Kreis

THE ALLARDS

BOOK FOUR

THE VOYAGEUR

By Wilmont R. Kreis

Port Huron, Michigan
2009

ISBN: 0578000997
EAN-13: 978-0-578-00099-2

Library of Congress control number: 2008911170

Dedicated to the three French-American women who helped to form my life:

Philomene-Sue* Forton-Forton, my great grandmother who often cared for me during the first six years of my life. She spoke French to me and took me fishing on her son's dock on Lake Saint Clair. There I caught my first fish, a perch.

Julia-Philomene* Forton-Allard, my grandmother who lived with my family until I left home for college, she served as my second mother, filled my brain with wisdom and stories of her ancestors, and held me on the backyard swing for hours.

Gladys-Genevieve* Allard-Kreis, my mother who continued my grandmother's stories into my adulthood and more than anyone, made me who I am.

Acknowledgements

As before I would like to thank Susanna Defever who has provided enormous assistance in editing my books as well as Karen Allard who has provided excellent editorial assistance and Carrie McLean for help with maps.

I would also like to thank Lorelei Rockwell and others who have been very supportive of my work, and especially my wonderful wife Susan, without whom I could not have done this.

PROLOGUE

The fourth book in a series about my Allard ancestors, <u>The Voyageur</u>, continues as a form of historical novel, a type of *Les raciness canadiennes française* or French-Canadian roots. The period encompasses Pontiac's Rebellion and the American Revolution, including time from 1781-1796 when Détroit, although part of the United States, remained under British occupation.

As in the first three books the story is that of my mother's actual ancestors and the people with whom they lived. The dates of birth, marriage and death are a matter of record. The story is set in the events of the period. The book tries to be faithful to history and the historical personalities. "Blanks" have, however, been filled in when necessary with my own conception of what could have happened. This is foremost a story and not a historical document. Do not reference it on a history term paper without first checking your facts..

<u>Names:</u> As before, the French have very few first names. As the book concerns actual people, there are frequently several Pierres, or Jean-Baptistes. Last names are frequently used to keep characters straight, and asterisks* are used after the first name of all direct ancestors, helping to keep Jacques* Allard separate from the many other Jacques in the story.

<u>Maps:</u> Maps are included in the text before the appropriate chapter.

A list of main characters as well as a brief summary of book three is included at the beginning of this book. A family tree of the Allards to 1804 is provided at the beginning. At the end of the book, a more complete list of descendants of Pierre* Allard, Jacques* Allard's father, and Henri, the patriarch of the Algonquin family who follows the Allards through the books is found.

THE ALLARDS
To 1804

François* Allard~1671~Jeanne* Anguille
Québec
1639-1725   1647-1711
Normandie, France   Loire Valley, France
I
Jean-Baptiste*Allard~1705~Anne-Elizabeth* Pageot
Québec
1676-1748   1686-1748
Québec   Québec
I
Pierre* Allard~1743~Marie-Angelique* Bergevin
Québec
1716-1759   1722-1788
Québec   Québec
I
Jacques* Allard~1780~Marie-Genevieve * Laforest
Détroit
1746-1814   1764-
Québec   Détroit
I
1) Archange* Allard
1789-1810
Détroit

2 Louis-Pierre* Allard
1793-1832
Détroit

THE ALLARDS
BOOK THREE: PEACE AND WAR
A SUMMARY

After the Peace of Utrecht, life in Québec is tranquil. Pierre* Allard and Toussaint, his Indian friend, who compete in local canoe and sled dog races, invent a sled that sails on ice. Pierre*'s father, Jean-Baptiste*, loses the three oldest of his seven sons in the plague. Toussaint, also a wood carver, carves their likenesses as well as Pierre*''s iceboat.

Jean-Baptiste* and Toussaint's father, Joseph, take their sons, Pierre* and Toussaint to Détroit. En route they visit Niagara Falls with Pierre* Saint-Aubin and Nicolas* Reaume. In Détroit, the boys meet Pontiac, the son of the Ottawa chief and Samuel Price whose aunt had once possessed the Allard medallion.

Returning to Charlesbourg, Pierre* falls in love with Marie-Angelique* Bergevin. Promising to wed her when he returns, he and Toussaint accept an offer to travel West with the old voyageur, Pierre Roy, and others. The trip involves a passage through the lakes of Canada to the plains and eventually the mountains. Trying to find the passage to the sea, they spend the winter in what is today Yellowstone National Park. Returning to Québec, the two young men marry and move to the Allard compound.

The Peace of Utrecht slips away and the hostilities begin over the land west of the Appalachian Mountains. The men are in the militia and involved in several battles. Eventually Québec falls to the British in 1760, Pierre* dies of wounds from battle, and Toussaint moves his family to Détroit. Pierre*'s widow remarries Pierre*'s old friend, Louis Jacques. They move the family to an island close to Montréal. As the story ends, Jacques* Allard, to whom Pierre* has given the medallion and the wampum, leaves – still a boy – to become a voyageur.

THE ALLARDS: BOOK FOUR
MAIN CHARACTERS

In order of appearance

Jacques* Allard: Boy who leaves his home in Québec at the age of fifteen to work as a helper for the great voyageur, Jean-Baptiste Charbonneau. Jacques* becomes a voyageur in his own right and later a landowner and citizen of Détroit.

Jean-Baptiste Charbonneau: Voyageur who pushes the limits of the frontier trying to find the Northwest Passage.

Henri-Pierre de Baptiste: Jacques*'s life long *métis*, or mixed blood, friend.

Joseph de Baptiste: Henri-Pierre's grandfather.

Toussaint de Baptiste: Henri-Pierre's father.

Jean-Baptiste Rivard: Long term resident of Détroit. He runs a trading post and is the conduit of information in the French community.

Pierre* Saint-Aubin: Long term wealthy and influential resident of Détroit.

Jean-Baptiste* Laforest: Friend of Jacques* who joins him as a voyageur. His father Guillaume* runs the mill in Détroit at Windmill Pointe.

Pierre Drouillard: Voyageur friend of Jacques* who is an Indian interpreter.

Quiet Stream: Flathead Indian maiden Jacques* meets in the west. She dies of smallpox.

Samuel Price: British colonist and American patriot whose father and aunt were kidnapped by Indians and sold to the nuns in Québec. Because of his French-Canadian connection, he and Jacob Andrews are sent to Détroit to quietly form American alliances with the French citizens.

Genevieve* (Jennie*) Laforest: Younger sister of Jean-Baptiste* above. She marries Jacques* Allard.

Jacquot Allard and Louis-Pierre* Allard: Two of their sons.

THE ALLARDS
BOOK FOUR

Chapter 1

<u>Mitchell Bay, Lake Saint Clair, Walpole Island, Ontario - November 2007:</u>

Staring at the dark sky, Lucien reflected how wonderful a gloomy day could be; surprisingly warm for November with a light southwest breeze barely rocking the boat. The heavily overcast sky brought the birds in low. The radio had called for a big front this afternoon. Then all hell would break loose. This would probably be the last good day this season.

A small low flying flock caught his attention, and he gave a call. Turning, they swept in toward his blind. He remarked calmly, "Looks like another good shot, ma'am." His client stood slowly, and took aim. A single shot was followed by a splash. Eight shots today and eight ducks, this girl could shoot as good as she looked. Lucien wondered if Mr. Cabela had ever thought anyone could look this good in a pair of his canvas pants. The blond pony tail exiting the Ducks Unlimited hat was also a nice touch.

Quickly entering the water, the dog returned with the duck. Lucien liked this dog almost as much as the client. He belonged to Jim Trombley who was hunting from another boat. A black and white mixed breed, he was mainly standard cocker spaniel. The doctors and dentists that made up much of Lucien's current business had black labs or golden retrievers. They worked reasonably well but none were as good as the standard cocker that was once the stock and trade of local hunters.

"That makes eight, ma'am. That's a full bag for you. Not bad for eight shells."

She replied, "My Daddy always said, 'Only take as many shells as you want birds plus one.'" Then with a wink, "Just in case one of the shells is bad."

Lucien started his outboard and slowly made his way to the next blind where two men sat in a second boat. Coming aside he shouted, "Miss Becky's got her limit. From the look of the sky, I think we should be heading in."

A chagrined Ben Champine replied, "Jim and I have been much kinder, we have two each. Maybe we can take a few of yours in our boat and Becky can continue her attempt to render the canvasback extinct."

The guide returned, "Probably a bad idea today. The Ontario game warden has been watching. Also I suppose Mr. Trombley neglected to call customs when he landed his boat on the island."

The other man called back, "It's the only civil disobedience I have any longer." Just then there was a piercing clap of thunder. "Maybe you're correct, Lucien." Jim Trombley started his motor and the two boats started for shore. They made their way carefully through the marshy shallows of the bay until they reached the entrance to the canal running through the reeds called "bull rushes" by the locals. As they headed north along the island, the wind shifted suddenly and violently to the north. Lightning strikes began and the rain came down in sheets.

"Good thing we made the canal!" Lucien shouted. Becky simply looked up and forward letting the rain and wind hit her face. Lucien marveled at the sight. This young lady loved this as much as he did. In his fifty years guiding he could not recall a man or woman who was a better shot. And certainly no one as beautiful as this client.

Becky Gauthier had come to Detroit from her home in New Orleans where her Cajun father ran a dive service. Becky grew up the son he never had. Her mother was descended from early Dutch colonists to the islands. Becky worked as a reporter for the *Detroit Free Press*. She had met Ben Champine, who rode in the other boat, when she interviewed him for an article on iceboats. They were now engaged to be married in the winter.

As they reached Lucien's dock, the wind had become fierce. Hollering to be heard above it, "I think you folks should come in until this dies down." Scarcely able to stand, the threesome agreed. Lucien's house was larger than most of the small residences on the Chippewa Reservation of which Walpole Island was part. The yard was neat and did not contain the usual collection of small boats and motors under some theoretic repair which littered many of the other yards on the reservation.

The interior of the house was also nicer than the neighboring homes, but it did have the smell of wood, newly cut, wet, or burning, typical of island buildings. Lucien's wife, Angela, had fortunately started a fire in the wood stove. With a typical warm island greeting she said, "Come in quickly and get out of those wet things." She gave Ben a hug and kiss and was introduced to the others.

Lucien had guided Ben's father and his grandfather. In fact Lucien's father had guided Ben's great grandfather. Ben had been a boyhood friend of their son, Francis, but he had left the reservation for the University of Western Ontario in London and now lived in Toronto. Angela taught at the reservation school and the family was more educated and reserved than most of the local tribe. After some small talk with Becky, she excused herself to make tea. Becky walked around the room looking at Angela's collection of native art.

As Angela returned with the tea, Becky's eye caught a wooden board with a carving of a young girl. Her mouth dropped open and she said, "Ben! Come look at this." Ben Champine came over and immediately recognized what had caught her interest. Coming over to offer them tea, Angela remarked, "My granny gave me this. It was done by one of her ancestors."

Becky asked, "Do you know what the initials are?"

"TdB? I believe they are the initials of the artist."

Hearing this Jim Trombley sprang from his seat and came over, "My God! It is the same person. The style is the same. What else do you know about this?"

Angela thought, "Only what I told you, other than it has been around forever. Granny has some more of these, I think."

Trombley looked puzzled, Angela had to be well into her fifties, "Your grandmother is still alive?"

"No my grandmother died a few years back. Actually 'Granny' is my great grandmother."

Trombley did the math, "But she would have to be…"

Angela smiled, "That's correct, very old. I'm not certain how old but well over one-hundred years."

Trombley stuttered, "Does she, can she uh…"

"Still talk? Oh my yes. The question is always: can she shut up? Would you like to meet her?"

"Boy would we ever."

Angela set her tea cup down, "She no longer lives on the reservation. She moved down to Belle River a few years ago. The tribe has a retirement home there they fund with U.S. casino money. It's quite nice and there are a lot of activities. In addition many of the ladies speak French. She never cared for English."

"When do you suppose we could meet her?"

"Well, as I said, they have lots of activities. I think she bowls today." The threesome looked at each other mouthing, "Bowls?"

Angela continued, "I'll call her tomorrow. Leave me your number and I'll give you a call."

The weather had improved as quickly as it had deteriorated. There was a brisk northeast wind, but the rain had stopped and the sun was coming out. The temperature had, however, plummeted from 65° to near freezing. Lucien drove them to the marina where Jim Trombley had left his boat. "I'll have your ducks cleaned and frozen for you the next time. Have a safe trip home." Ben paid Lucien for the day and they boarded the boat.

Trombley owned a thirty-four foot Chris-Craft with a fly bridge. Fortunately it also had an inside driving station.

When they entered the cabin, he said, "I think I've only used this lower station twice before but it will be nice for today." The group was obviously anxious to discuss their find. So he continued, "Why don't we stop at Brown's Landing for something to eat?"

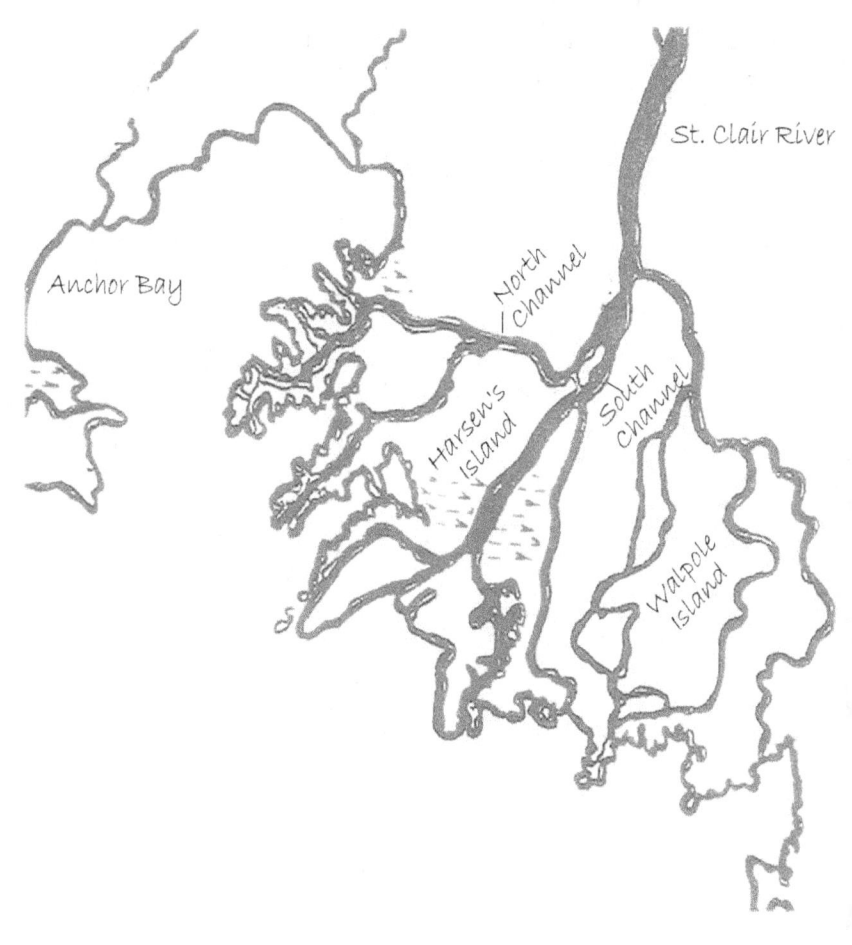

SAINT CLAIR FLATS PRESENT DAY

Chapter 2

Connecting Lake Huron to Lake Saint Clair, the Saint Clair River runs downstream from north to south with strong currents, often as fast as ten miles per hour. It separates Canada on the east from the United States on the west. At the southwest corner of Lake Saint Clair is the city of Detroit where the Detroit River continues to Lake Erie. If one considers the marshland, Lake Saint Clair is almost a square, thirty miles on each side. Only eighteen feet at its deepest natural point, a dredged channel has facilitated shipping. Due to its size and depth Lake Saint Clair has always been a haven for fish, birds and other wild life.

The Canadian shore is shallow and often marshy, lined with small villages and cottages. The American side is deeper and is lined with suburbs of Detroit, originally lines of cottages but now a "gold coast" with homes of ever increasing size and value. Before reaching Lake Saint Clair, the Saint Clair River turns west, splits into a north and a south channel. Soon after, the north channel splits and its southern branch is called the middle channel. These form a delta of several islands and interspersed marsh that occupies the northeast corner of the lake. It is referred to as the Saint Clair Flats.

From the marina on Walpole Island, Trombley headed east up the South Channel, "I think we better avoid the lake with this wind. As long as we're protected from the wind, we'll have a pretty ride." As he entered the Saint Clair River proper, they could see the village of Algonac on the American shore in the final days of autumn color.

Trombley made a careful U-turn and headed west down the North Channel. He soon veered left into the Middle Channel with Harsens Island on his left and Dickinson Island on his right.

The coast of Harsens Island was idyllic with occasional docks and boathouses in front of well tended cottages and homes. They were separated by lines of trees with many willows whose yellow leaves wept to the water leaving their reflection in the sunlight. Ben remarked, "It never ceases to amaze me how quickly the weather can change on the flats."

His fiancé replied, "Just like back home. It's the same in any bayou, Sugah."

Around a curve they came to a faded sign that had apparently come loose in the storm. Now vertical, it read "Brown's" with an arrow pointing directly down. Trombley chuckled, "I hope this isn't a bad omen." They entered a small harbor with twelve docks, all of which were vacant. Trombley chose a slip close to the entrance of the harbor, "We can walk from here. I don't want to risk going aground this late in the season."

Sitting on a slab, Brown's was an old frame building with a low flat roof. The windows contained neon signs that, had all their letters functioned, would have said, "FOOD, DRINK, DANCING". The interior was classic flats: multi-colored square linoleum tile floor, knotty pine walls covered with various fish and animal trophies, tables with hard, shiny linoleum tops and shiny aluminum borders, and aluminum chairs with cushions of shiny vinyl in various non-matching colors.

The long bar was backed by a mirror and the obligatory bottles of liquor as well as the usual cutesy signs such as "NO SPITTING OR FIGHTING WITHOUT PERMISSION OF THE MANAGEMENT" and "IF YOU DON'T SEE WHAT YOU WANT, THE NEXT FERRY IS IN ONE HOUR". As they passed the bar Ben said softly, "I see they still haven't gotten into single malt scotch." In the corner there was a digitalized version of an old juke box. If one bothered to look, it held artists from Perry Como to Slipknot.

There were three other occupied tables. As the threesome sat at their selection, Trombley noted, "These are all locals up to close their cottages for winter. I think Brown's closes right after Thanksgiving." The waitress came by and they ordered a pitcher of beer. Soon the owner, Bobby Socia, came over and greeted Ben and Jim and was introduced to Becky. Ben asked him, "How's the perch?"

Socia replied, "Great, Lucien's cousin was just here."

After he left Ben explained, "The Indians on the reservation bring their fresh catch to the smaller private bars. It's quite illegal, but no one seems to care, and it's much better than the fish you find in the good Detroit restaurants." Then looking around slowly, "This place was built after the depression by a guy named Earl Brown. His mother was an Allard from Grosse Pointe. They all loved to hunt, trap and fish up here, so Earl opened this place. He lived out in back until he died a few years ago. My dad used to tell great stories about coming here with his father. You still find Allards on the east side of Detroit, but around

23

here most are called Allor. Like Champine and Trombley and many other French names, some of them changed when the English came and started writing them down."

Changing the subject, Trombley asked, "What do you think about this wooden plaque?"

Ben answered, "I know that Angela would never bull-shit me. It must be on the level."

Becky added, "You know, it's funny; isn't this how we all met?"

The previous winter, Ben had shown Becky an old carved picture of an iceboat in conjunction with an article she was doing. It had been given to him and he knew little else about it. They contacted Jim Trombley who was interested in early American History and its native inhabitants. He taught at Wayne State University and worked with the Burton Historical Collection at the Detroit Public Library. Trombley believed the carving was from Québec of the seventeenth century. It contained the initials TdB. Sometime later they discovered the same initials in a surveying plate from the same period found at the junction of the Missouri and Yellowstone Rivers in the west.

Trombley concluded, "Well, we shall just have to wait to hear from Granny, the bowling centenarian."

The group retuned to the dock. Trombley's bird dog sat patiently on the back deck waiting. As they stepped aboard, Trombley said, "Good boy, Antoine!"

Becky interrupted, "Why did you call your dog Antoine?"

"Actually he is Antoine Cadillac de Trombley. He has no legitimate pedigree, but with some training and grooming, he passes himself off as something exceptional."

Jim Trombley's boathouse was at his summer cottage a short way up the middle channel. When they landed in the boathouse, he announced, "I think I'll spend the night so I can go see Heck Allor at the marina in the morning to have him come and winterize the boat. I think I'm through for this year. I'll be in touch as soon as I hear from Angela."

Ben and Becky drove to the west side of the island where they took the ferry to Algonac. They headed south on the river road toward their house in Saint Clair Shores. As they crossed the wetlands area known as the Saint John's Marsh, illuminated only by street lights, Ben remarked, "You know, I guess it is a bayou, *Sugah*."

Chapter 3

Jacques* Allard

<u>The Niagara River - June 1761:</u>

Although not yet sixteen years old, Jacques* Allard had spent a good deal of time in a canoe. Until this voyage, he had thought himself expert, but the past month had proved him woefully incorrect. Today he did not think he could manage the canoe if Joseph had not been in the back. It wasn't merely a question of strength but knowledge of currents, the subtleties that made one part of the river easier or gave one the ability to float *upstream* with no effort in the proper conditions.

However he was learning, and rapidly, not only the canoe but all aspects of the back country, as well as language. Certain nights he felt his brain was going to burst from new knowledge. Today he very much wished he was a better paddler. Charbonneau had warned the boys that today would be the hardest between Montréal and Détroit. He had further said that this part of the journey was unnecessary but was being done for Jacques* and Louis*.

The noise of water was becoming overwhelming; the men had to shout loudly to be heard within each canoe. Communication between the crafts had become impossible. As they came around the turn, Jacques* jumped with fear. In front was a whirlpool many times larger than anything he had ever seen. Joseph called out calmly, "Go far to the right." As they moved to the right bank, Jacques* realized that they were being pulled upstream. As they passed the pool Joseph called out, "Now stay hard to the right and paddle like hell!" After several strokes, the current became very weak although it was obviously ferocious in the center and on the other side.

When they came around the next bend, Jacques*'s mind was still on the whirlpool. He didn't look up until the spray hit his face. Like all the young voyageurs before him, he could not have been prepared for this sight by the tall tales. The falls at Montmorency in Québec were higher, but the length and power of this was inconceivable. The first falls were straight, then a large island with a small falls reminiscent of Montmorency; finally the last falls which formed a crescent, almost a horseshoe.

At this point, Jean-Baptiste Charbonneau took the lead. The voyageur was more skilled than even old Joseph. In fact sometimes, Jacques*thought that he could probably make the canoe fly. With young Louis* Renaud in the front, the Charbonneau canoe made its way to the end of the last falls. They went carefully under the edge of the water and actually behind the falls. Jacques* and Joseph followed. They had been warned the night before to stay close to the rock wall, for the force of the water would crush them like a bug if they went under it. They came from behind and went to the center of the horseshoe where it seemed that the falls were on all sides.

Jacques* became worried when he realized in the dense mist, he could not tell which way led away from the falls, but they followed Charbonneau who brought them out of the mist intact. Finally Jean-Baptiste signaled, and they headed back. Before the whirlpool he came abreast and warned, "Remember to stay tight to the wall at the whirlpool and paddle as hard as you can when you come out, or you'll be sucked in and down.

The return around the whirlpool was definitely more difficult than the entrance. Jacques* was certain that he could not have done it without Joseph. After the whirlpool, the ride became easy. Unfortunately they now had to backtrack several miles through the deep rock canyon until they reached a point where they could climb the bank and begin the fabled long and difficult portage of Niagara.

On reaching the top of the river canyon on its eastern coast they made camp. The boys were exhausted from the falls but knew they were expected to do the brunt of the work so they heaved-to without complaints. They had learned early, complaints were counter-productive with Monsieur Charbonneau.

Tonight Jean-Baptiste Charbonneau gave orders in Iroquois. He had told the boys next to brute strength and total disregard of the elements, a voyageur's most important skill was communication. As the boys were already fluent in French and Algonquin, Joseph and Jean-Baptiste used Iroquois as much as possible to help them gain some understanding of important words and phrases. Like many Frenchmen, Charbonneau believed English was to become crucial to their success, so he had arranged for an English-speaking trader to join them in Détroit.

Jean-Baptiste Charbonneau was thirty-four years of age. Québec born, he was the son and grandson of prominent voyageurs. He had married Marguerite Deneau five years earlier in Montréal. She was descended from a famous line of voyageurs going back to early Québec. The advantage of a wife who was the daughter of a backwoodsman was her understanding of the unusual nature of the man and his lifestyle.

Jean-Baptiste had acquired a reputation as a bold adventurer. He had traveled as far west as any European trader. After dinner he discussed his plans. "When our fathers," addressing Jacques*, "travelled with the Vérendrye brothers, they took the Missouri River to the Yellowstone River and from there as far as the great Yellowstone Canyon. They were stopped at that point by the mountains. I have taken the Missouri past the Yellowstone River for hundreds of miles. I have gone as far as the high mountains and the great falls. The fur trade there was so good that we chose not to continue, but I believe I can find a pass near that point and find the Northwest Passage to the sea which has eluded us since the time of Cartier. You boys will see many new things, mountains beyond belief, great barren plains devoid of trees, Indians much different than ours, and wonderful new creatures."

When he had finished, Joseph spoke, "We still do not know how the English will regard our trade. Since the surrender to the British, there have been no licenses given. What if they forbid trade by the French?"

Charbonneau replied, "I hope it will not be a problem. The English are not so organized. Their people would not stand for exclusive licensing of some over others. Do not forget that the English idea of fur trade is squirrels and foxes. No Englishman could withstand the winter where we are going, and the Indians of the west are not likely to treat them kindly."

The third day they reached the summit of the portage and camped beside the falls. The boys were even more awestruck from above. Charbonneau took them exploring. "My father showed Jacques*'s father the falls when he and Toussaint went to Détroit as boys." Today the boys saw the caves and paths under the falls and Jean-Baptiste explained how the boys would tie on a rope and jump in the water, then pull the rope so they could raise standing on the water due to the strong current. "They called it 'walking the falls', but we won't try it this time. I need to have my team intact for trading."

Two days later, they reached a point in the Niagara River where the current had slowed sufficiently to allow them to launch the canoes. Charbonneau suggested that Louis* and Jacques* take their own canoe and try to keep up with Joseph and himself. The boys made a valiant effort but fell well short of the men. For the next few days they followed the southern shore of Lake Erie until the western shore appeared on the horizon. Here Charbonneau came close to the boys' canoe, "We will make Détroit tomorrow. We are going to stop near here for the night and hopefully gain some insight on what awaits us."

Coming to the entrance of a small river they turned south. After a mile or two they came to a large Indian camp. They were greeted at the bank by a few men. Soon an Indian in voyageur dress wearing a single blue feather came to the bank. Joseph whispered to the boys, "Pontiac."

In perfect French, Pontiac called out, "Charbonneau, my friend, you are most welcome. I am glad the English have not seen necessary to eat you to get through the winter." Then seeing Joseph, "And you have brought a most distinguished guest, welcome Joseph." As they entered the camp, Jacques* was taken by the fact that though they regarded Charbonneau well, they had an enormous respect for Joseph.

When they reached the center of the camp they introduced the boys. Pontiac said to Jacques*, "I knew your father as a young man, young Allard. Emulate him and you shall do well." They convened at the camp and in typical Indian fashion ate, drank and made small-talk. Not until they had finished, begun to pass pipes to smoke, and the sun had set, did Pontiac begin to speak again.

"Joseph, I have seen your son, Toussaint and your grandson at Détroit. They do well and are living and working with Saint-Aubin. They have heard the boys were coming with Charbonneau but you will be the great surprise." Then speaking to Jacques*, "I hear that your mother has re-married after the death of your good father. She has done well. This man Louis Jacques is a good man and he is wise to move to *l'Ile Dupas* where the English will trouble him little."

After Pontiac paused enough to show he had finished, Jean-Baptiste asked, "How has Détroit fared with the English?"

Pontiac replied, "Better than expected. Their leader is a man named Campbell. He seems fair and honest. He has developed ties with the Saint-Aubin and Campau brothers. He has treated the *habitants* fairly. I would dare to say little has changed. There are English traders coming at this point. They try to be unscrupulous in their trade, but this man Campbell has prohibited unfair trade to this point. I have met with him regularly and we have an understanding that my people will cooperate so long as they are treated well. I must confess however that I am still somewhat skeptical, but we shall see."

Charbonneau continued, "Do you see changes in the regulation of trade?"

Pontiac replied, "At this point I see none, in fact there seems to be little attempt to control trade at all. I hope it will remain so for your sake."

At dawn the men broke camp and began the short ride to Détroit.

Chapter 4

<u>The Milk River, Détroit - the same day:</u>

Rays of the warm June sunlight filtered through the branches of the willows as they drooped down to the water's edge. The cloudy water meandered slowly under the canopy of willows, gently and silently with only the occasional sound as it passed a rock or a fallen tree branch. The mother worked her way carefully to the river bank, keeping a close eye on the twins who followed in her footsteps. One could not be too cautious going to drink, for here they were more vulnerable than in the depth of the forest.

She slowly descended the gentle slope to the river. Before drinking she took a careful look about with her sensitive ears upright. When she felt safe, she began to drink and then instructed her twins to do the same. She did not live with the same fears as her ancestors, who were constantly harassed by wolves and large cats. These had been driven off by the men.

There had always been men, but in generations past they were quiet and often absent, sometimes for a generation or two; and when they returned there were never very many. The new men stayed in one place, made a good deal more noise and carried a stronger odor. The other men shot sticks. These shot metal from a large noisy stick that was more frightening. As the twins drank, the mother heard a human sound. She started and stood alert. It came from a long way off, so they should be safe. After the twins had drunk their fill, they bounded silently into the woods.

A mile down stream, the residents of the Milk River Settlement, as the people of Détroit had come to call it, were hard at work. Julian* Fréton stood on the bank and guided his neighbor who led a mule pulling a large log on the opposite bank. Due to its unusual course, the Milk River provided much help but also some inconvenience for the residents of the settlement. Most rivers of the area ran perpendicular to the Lake, they ran along the boundary of the long narrow 'ribbon farms' which lined the shore near the city of Détroit. The path of the Milk River started perpendicular to the lake running west but soon turned south and cut across each of the farms.

This provided everyone with a wonderful source of water distant to the lake but also created a barrier to travel from one end of the long farms to the other. Julian* Fréton came from the Brittany region of France where rivers crisscrossed the region. As a result he had some bridge building experience and was selected to lead the group project.

As the mule moved closer to the water, Fréton called to his neighbor Michel* Yax, "Have him bring the end of the log as close as possible to the stone, then stop." The men had earlier set large boulders on each bank of the proposed span. Julian had chosen a relatively narrow spot with high solid ground on each side. Now the men would pull large logs that they had cut to span the river and then cover them with planks to make the road bed.

Once the log was in place, Julian* threw a large rope across the river to Yax. Throwing lines was a great talent of Julian*'s which had served him well at the battle of Fort William Henry during the Seven Years War. Calling to the other side, "Have the Tremblays help you tie it." Brothers Louis-Michel and Pierre Tremblay, whose family ran the mills on the nearby Windmill Pointe, had come to help. Besides being expert woodcutters, they were possibly the strongest men in Détroit. Their logging experience had taught them how to tie logs so they could be pulled along their length.

After the line was secure, Julian* connected it to two mules that continued to pull the rope over a short log lying parallel to the stream to help keep the long log out of the river. When it came to the other side, it had to be lifted with a second rope to come to the level of the bank. "Now comes the hard part," Julian called. "Everyone but François* come to this side." François* Duchesne was Julian's father-in-law, first settler of the settlement, and the oldest at 61 He had a wife and five children. He would stay to control the mule on the first bank.

Along with Julian* who was 36 with a single child of one year and Yax who at 52 had seven children, there were three more residents of the settlement: Hyacinth Reaume at 57 had six children, Pierre* Champagne was 28 and had married Marie-Reine* Tremblay, cousin of the two brothers, just last year. They had one infant son. The final resident was Louis* Greffard at 22 and single.

The Tremblay brothers at 22 and 23 brought the work force to eight hardy souls. Yax guided the mule on his bank and as the log came closer, Fréton, Reaume, Champagne, and Greffard looped a third rope under it and began to lift with only some success. Then the two Tremblays placed a fourth line and with their superhuman strength the log rose magically to the level of the bank where Yax's mule brought it onto its foundation. The men cheered and after a brief rest went for the second beam. By the end of the day, the superstructure was finished. As they gathered their things Julian* remarked, "After we add the planks for the road bed tomorrow, we shall finally have our bridge."

The women had gathered the families at the Fréton farm for a dinner to celebrate the bridge. With five married couples and one bachelor the settlement boasted eleven adults. The twenty children brought the group to thirty-one. Seeing that food and drinks were involved, the Tremblay boys agreed to stay. Marie-Josephine* (Josie*) Duchesne-Fréton had married Julian* Fréton two years earlier. Still not quite 18, she was very lively and talkative and not bashful at hostessing the first such party in some time. With young Julian* II, not yet one year, papoosed to her back, she made all the arrangements and greeted everyone with only some assistance from her mother.

As was typical, the adults sat to eat with the very small children while the others played and waited to take their parents place on the next seating. Michel* Yax spoke, "I am tinking you know, how it is so long since ve are hafing such a feast." Yax had come from the Rhineland in Germany and arrived in Détroit under bizarre circumstances. He had married his German wife in Pennsylvania and decided to move to a settlement in the

36

south of the British Colonies. They became lost in Ohio and were captured by Indians and ransomed to the French Commandant at Détroit. They had converted to Catholicism and stayed to raise their family. They were now highly regarded citizens in spite of Michel*'s heavy accent and strange grammar.

He continued, "Ve are vorried from da British, but here on da Milk River, ve never see dem. And now dat der is no more var, ve can be vorking on da farms instead of all da time vorrying."

François* Duchesne added, "I could not agree more. The British have moved off most of their soldiers. Even now many of the men at the fort are French. If British traders and settlers come, so be it. Jean* Saint-Aubin always said what we need is more people. As long as we keep our Church and our farms, who cares?"

Hyacinth Reaume addressed the Tremblay boys, "How are things going at the mill?"

Working hard to chew and swallow his enormous mouthful of food, Louis-Michel responded, "Very well. Many of the young ones are now ready to work so Pierre and I are going to trade this season. Jean-Baptiste Charbonneau is due in soon from Montréal and we are going to the far west with him. We want to see it before we get married."

After dinner, Pierre* Champagne played the fiddle and everyone danced until after dark. The small settlement was starting to feel at ease after several terrible years of the worry of war.

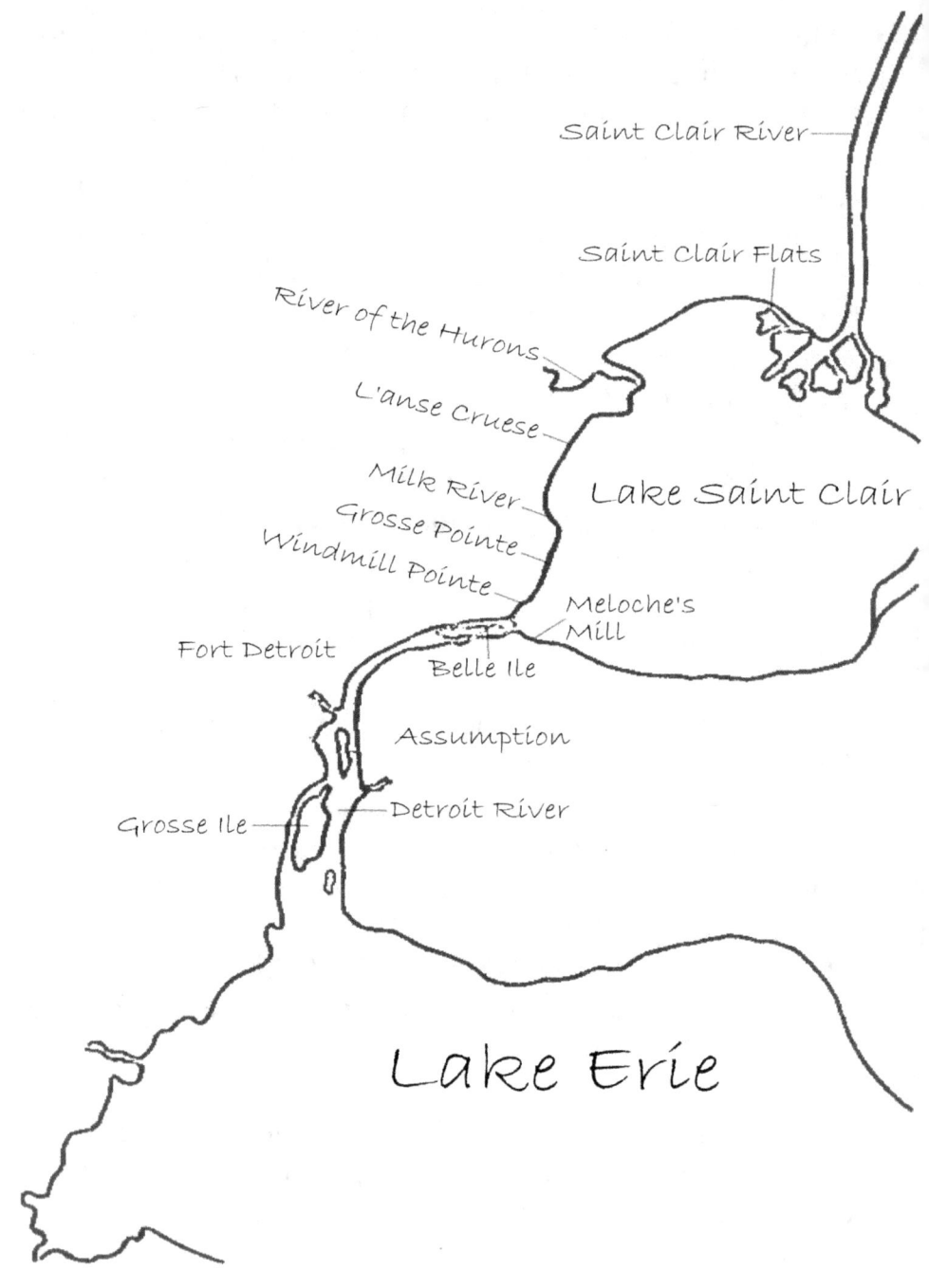

DÉTROIT RIVER REGION 1761

Chapter 5

Fort Détroit - the next day:

As Jacques* and the others approached the bend in
the Détroit River, they caught sight of the stockades of the
fort on the left bank. At this point the river turned from its
north-south course to a more east-west one. Old Joseph was
lost in memories as he thought back to the day in 1701
when he and his best friend, Jean-Baptiste* Allard,
Jacques* grandfather, had accompanied Antoine Lamothe
Sieur de Cadillac to this place. Now dotted with farms on
both sides, it was then entirely wilderness.

The enlarged fort seemed almost out of place, and the
British Union Jack which had now replaced the old Fleur-
de-Lys was a grim reminder of the new order of the
country. A greatly enlarged dock lined the shore in front of
the fort and two British sailing vessels sat along side as
three more lay at anchor in the river. The British had taken
to building these ships near old Fort Niagara as large craft
could not pass the Lachine Rapids at Montréal or the great
falls of the Niagara River. For work in the Great Lakes,
they had to be built upstream of the falls.

Joseph had been here a few times since the
beginning, each time the town was larger but it had not yet
begun to take the form conceived by Cadillac when he
announced his "city in the wilderness". They landed at a
section of the docks used by canoes. A man in British
uniform came down and in passable French asked them

their names and purpose. He was quite polite, explaining that this was the routine until they knew the locals.

As the soldier left, three familiar faces came down the dock. Jacques* wanted to run to greet them but realized that in his new adult role he should remain calm. Toussaint de Baptiste and his son Henri-Pierre were the son and grandson of Joseph. Toussaint had been the life-long friend of Jacques*'s deceased father, Pierre* Allard and Henri-Pierre was Jacques*'s best friend. They had left for Détroit after the fall of Québec one year earlier. Hugs and handshakes went around and Joseph introduced the boys to the third man, "This is Pierre* Saint-Aubin. I know you have heard many stories about him."

As Saint-Aubin shook Jacques*'s hand he said, "It was my pleasure to know both your father and grandfather well. A man from Pontiac's camp came this morning and alerted us of your arrival." Then to Charbonneau, "Jean-Baptiste, bring what you need and we will go to my farm. Tomorrow we can come to town and do business." As Charbonneau began unloading he added, "Leave what you don't need today. The guard will make certain no one touches it. As it turns out, British rule does have some good points."

Jacques* retrieved his small pack and a wooden board wrapped in a cloth. He handed it to Toussaint. "My mother told me to give this to you. She said she treasures it but believes it should now belong to you."

Toussaint unwrapped it to find a board intricately carved with the picture of an iceboat on the Saint-Laurent River. He replied, "I carved this for your late father when

40

we were boys, it should actually be yours, but I will guard it until you have your own wall on which to hang it."

As they left the dock, Saint-Aubin had a few words in English with the uniformed man who had greeted them. They walked up to the fort where Saint-Aubin had a wagon large enough for everyone, pulled by two horses. They boarded and went north on a road which followed the river as far as one could see in both directions. As they began to move, Saint-Aubin explained, "We now have a road along the shore. This way it goes past the Grosse Pointe as far as the Milk River. We still use canoes, but the British prefer roads. I believe they are genetically incapable of operating a canoe. You will see."

They travelled seven miles to the beginning of the Détroit River. The coast was lined with farms, more on the side of the fort or the north shore than on the south side which Saint-Aubin referred to as "Assumption" for the name of the church on that side. They passed the *Ile du Cochons* or *Belle Ile* as Cadillac had named it. Saint-Aubin explained that both terms were still used depending on your attitude toward the place. "There have been a few farms on it. Right now it is mainly Indian camps and the Campau families keep some livestock there."

They came to the smaller *Ile de la Pêche* and the entry to *Lac Sainte-Claire.* Here began the Saint-Aubin farms, several large well tended farms with houses worthy of the upper town in Québec City. Saint-Aubin brought the cart to the barn and the group unloaded. Saint-Aubin's farm was a wide ribbon farm going into the wilderness. The house, fields and out-buildings were clean and prosperous.

Behind the great house stood an orchard and a vineyard. Several workers tilled the fields.

As they left the cart, a worker took the horses to the barn. A plump lady in rather elegant dress came down from the house to greet them. Madame Saint-Aubin greeted each guest with a handshake and a French-style kiss on each cheek as she invited them to the house. The house was large and grand. There was a large porch which faced the spectacular view of the lake and followed maple and willow trees down to the water.

The interior of the house was more impressive. Each room had a fireplace and a glass window, and there were tables with books and figurines. The furniture made the men afraid to sit. As she explained the accommodations, it was apparent that each man would be housed indoors rather than in a camp out back. Jacques*, Louis* and Joseph were shown to a room with three small featherbeds, also a table with a large pitcher of water and a mirror. The worker who showed them the room said they could "freshen-up" before dinner.

Louis* started, "I was submerged in the river only three days ago, how fresh can I get?"

Joseph countered, "Madame Saint-Aubin is a refined lady, and this is how they live. Although her husband was a voyageur, he is now a businessman and their way of life has changed. At least throw some water in your face and slick back your hair." The boys did as Joseph said. They would never question his advice. Soon a worker appeared and summoned them to dinner.

They arrived in the large dining room that held a table set with china and glasses. Charbonneau leaned over to the boys and instructed, "Watch Madame and do as she does."

Dinner was a fine affair served by workers in stages rather than passed all at once. Jacques* watched Madame Saint-Aubin carefully and imitated her every move. At the end of dinner she came over to Jacques* and asked, "Monsieur Allard, I understand that you are the great grandson of François* Allard of Québec. May I be so bold as to ask if you wear a medallion?"

In spite of his leathered tan, Jacques* turned bright red and sputtered, "Yes'm."

She then continued, "Could I be so forward as to ask to see it?"

Jacques* untangled the medallion from the wampum he also wore around his neck and handed it to her. She held it in her hand and exclaimed, "It is true! It is alive!" She held it to her heart, then returned it. "My mother wore this for several years before I was born. She was kidnapped by Indians from her home in Massachusetts and brought with many others including her brother Samuel to Montréal. Of her fellow captives, many died, some stayed with the Indians and some, like her brother, managed to return to the English Colonies.

"An old lame Indian man cared for my mother along the way and gave her to the sisters at the Ursuline Convent. He gave her this medallion for luck. She eventually met my father who had come from France and they were married. Before I was born, she encountered your great grandfather by chance and realized that the medallion was originally his. She returned it, but I had heard all during my childhood how this medallion had magic and great luck. You are fortunate to wear it, young man."

After dinner, the men retired to the front room and began to smoke. Saint-Aubin gave them a drink, "British whiskey from Scotland, not Calvados, but enjoyable." And he began the awaited conversation, "So Jean-Baptiste, what are your plans?"

"Once I assemble my crew, we will part for the west; I hope to follow the Missouri River as far as the Great Falls or even beyond. Buffalo, bear and elk are plentiful. Even beaver still abound there. I need to see what the licensing rules of the British will be."

Responding, Saint-Aubin said, "As of now there have been no regulations. I think you will find the British quite lax on the subject. In fact I must say that I have found them altogether agreeable. They have interest in accounting for all the citizens for the purpose of tax and planning, but so far they have been much less strict than our Church has been. They plan to bring more trade and more settlers to the west, but this is exactly what we have lacked in Détroit. The Indians have been skeptical of the honesty of the traders, but that also remains to be seen. Pontiac has been tranquil, but he still makes me nervous."

For the first time Toussaint entered the conversation, "They don't seem to know how to regard the Indians and they regard us *métis* (referring to mixed blood people) oddly. I don't think they know what to expect from us."

Saint-Aubin concluded, "Tomorrow we will go to the fort and see Commandant Campbell, perhaps he can tell you more. I can tell you one thing, speaking English is a big help in business."

Charbonneau replied, "I have arranged for Jacob* Thomas Jr., Toussaint's brother-in-law to accompany us. As you know, his father was a British colonist captured many years ago who remained in Québec. Jacob* Jr. has done some trading and is perfectly bi-lingual."

Détroit - the following day:

Saint Aubin drove his cart into the great stockade. Cadillac's Fort Pontchartrain had been renamed simply Fort Détroit, still using the French spelling. The square was filled with activity. Joseph noted, "Little has changed. Most are members of the various Indian tribes, and of the Europeans, most are still French." As predicted, the British presence was not striking.

Their first stop was at the Cathedral of Sainte-Anne. Rebuilt, it was an imposing structure for the frontier with a proper spire and bell tower. It formed the traditional Christian shape with a nave and a transept making the shape of a cross. It was lit by windows and two were stained glass. The interior was otherwise rustic with the exception of two carved wooden statues, the Virgin Mary and her mother, Sainte-Anne, patron saint of the city in the wilderness. As they entered the structure they were met by a tall gangly priest.

Saint-Aubin said quickly, "Gentlemen, let me introduce Father Simple Bocquet." The curé shook hands around and welcomed everyone to his church. At six feet four inches, he was very tall for the day and at one-hundred forty pounds, scrawny for any day. He had unruly dark hair that he tried to keep down with little success and a large nose with a Gallic hook as well as side deviation due to an encounter with another boy as a young lad.

He had personally overseen the building of the grand new church and was energetic and kind to a fault, spending every waking moment dealing with the problems of his flock. He was the one man trusted by the French, English, and Indian alike. He asked Saint-Aubin, are you going to see Captain Campbell?" Then to the group, "You will find him a true gentleman. We are fortunate to have such a man in this position at this time."

Saint-Aubin answered in the affirmative and they took their leave. The interior of the stockade was quite large, about one hundred yards north and south and two hundred-fifty yards east and west. There were many small streets, some of which continued outside the fort. Other than the Church and the government buildings, there were seventy houses, several stores, two taverns and a central trading post and bank.

They stopped in front of an official appearing structure flying the Union Jack. Pierre* Saint-Aubin spoke English to the man at the door who bid them enter. Upon entry they were greeted by a middle-aged man in officer's uniform. Saint-Aubin said, "Good day, Captain Campbell."

The officer countered, *"Bonjour, Monsieur Saint-Aubin."* The conversation continued in French. Donald Campbell had been in the colonies for the past five years, and he had become relatively proficient in French over the past year. Of Scottish descent, he had worked under General Jeffrey Amherst. In contrast to the General, Campbell had a much more open attitude toward the French and the Indians and believed that an amicable association would best serve the needs of all parties. He tried to know everything that went on in the village and how it affected each of the various groups.

Saint-Aubin introduced each one of the men. When he came to Joseph, Campbell showed his local knowledge, "Welcome, Monsieur de Baptiste, I understand that you accompanied Antoine Cadillac in 1701. How do you find the city now?"

Impressed being called *Monsieur,* Joseph responded, "Certainly larger. I was then accompanied by my good friend Jean-Baptiste* Allard. Young Jacques* here is his grandson."

Campbell continued, "We now have two-thousand citizens of French descent, counting women and children. Five hundred live in the village by the fort and the rest on the other coast at Assumption or along the shore. There are several families at the Grosse Pointe north of Monsieur Saint-Aubin and farther at the Milk River Settlement. There are even a few camps on L'Anse Creuse farther north, though no farms at this time. Of course, we have many native citizens, mostly Chippewa or as some say Potawatomi. Most of the Huron camps and Chief Pontiac's Ottawa camp are south by Lake Erie. As Monsieur Saint-Aubin and his friends have informed me, we need more people to grow an adequate commerce. At this time all are welcome. I predict many English colonists, mostly farmers in the next few years, as well as some traders."

Seeing his chance, Jean-Charbonneau asked, "Are there to be restrictions on trade?"

Campbell replied, "At present there are none and I expect none. The local French traders and the Indians feel that the more trade, the better. Your reputation has preceded you, Monsieur. I understand you have been as far as the Great Falls."

"That is correct, Captain; we plan to travel there or even farther this season."

The soldier looked out the window, "I envy you sir; some day I should like to go to the great west."

With a chuckle, Charbonneau replied, "I have room for one more man especially one who knows both English and French."

Campbell returned the laugh, "Alas, duty calls here for the time being."

After a few pleasantries, the men left the fort and boarded Saint-Aubin's wagon. Charbonneau said, "Could we go to the mill at Grosse Pointe? I need to make arrangements with two men there." Saint-Aubin pulled out of the stockade gate and proceeded north. An hour later, they passed the Saint-Aubin farm on the left and soon turned up a small road to the right. The Grosse Pointe was not a sharp spit of land, rather it was a broad expansion of land into the south end of Lake Saint Clair, hence the French term *gross* meaning fat, but in the feminine to agree with *pointe,* therefore *Grosse Pointe.*

They continued onto a prominence at the south end of the Grosse Pointe which was called *Pointe du Moulin á Vent,* or now, Windmill Pointe. As they continued out, Saint-Aubin told them, "This was once called *Grand Marais,* or the great swamp, but some years ago, three brothers from Baie Saint-Paul named Tremblay came with their families and their niece and her husband, a man named Laforest. They drained the swamp to improve the mill, or now I should say mills as we have three. My brothers Jacques* and Gabriel own the mills, and the Tremblay and Laforest families run them. Guillaume* Laforest is the manager. We have one for lumber and two for grist. The Meloche family has a mill in Assumption that does both chores as well. The mills are vital if we are to see expansion."

As he approached the mills, they felt a strong north breeze. "When the wind is from the northeast, the mills work at their maximum." Saint-Aubin stopped by a man adjusting a rope turning one of the mills. They climbed down and he introduced him to his passengers, "This is the manager, Guillaume* Laforest." Most of the men knew Laforest, Jean-Baptiste Charbonneau asked, "Do you know where I can find Louis-Michel and young Pierre Tremblay?"

Laforest replied, "You will have to go to the Milk River. Today they are helping Julian* Fréton and the others complete a bridge." He called to a boy about Jacques*'s age, "Jean-Baptiste*! Come show these men to the new bridge at Milk River." The boy left his work and joined the group. "This is my oldest son, Jean-Baptiste* Laforest. Jean-Baptiste*, these men are looking for Louis-Michel and Pierre. They are at Fréton's." The men reloaded and continued north.

The road became more primitive as they proceeded north; the road side was densely forested until they came to the farms at the Milk River. The road followed the shore, large expanses of sand beach with occasional maples or willows lined the shore with a clear view of the coast at Assumption as the lake drained to the Détroit River. The farm houses were all south of the mouth of Milk River. There were six, all rustic but varying greatly in size. They were spaced over three miles. Each had a tree lined front meadow, then the house followed by a grape arbor, an orchard, and fields of varying sizes in back.

There was a crude bridge over the mouth of the river and the road became very sparse on the other side. Saint-Aubin noted, "There is little activity beyond this point other than a few traders and Indians." A small lane turned left and led along the south bank of the murky river. They followed it for a while. It turned south as did the river and cut through the developed sections of the farms in their midsections. A short while after they came to activity. A group of men were busy putting planks in a new bridge that would connect the lake side of their farms to the wooded side.

The group climbed down from the wagon and more introductions were made.
While they talked, the north sky turned black, and one of the wonderful summer storms typical of the region descended. As this group of men stood in the drenching rain, thinking of bridges and trips to the west, it is unlikely that any of them realized that this group would become some of the real fathers of Cadillac's city in the wilderness.

After the storm, the men finished the bridge and the wagon departed having added the two Tremblay boys. In the course of the morning, Jacques*, and Henri-Pierre became acquainted with Jean-Baptiste* Laforest who was exactly their age. They returned to the mill and deposited the two Tremblay men and their young cousin. Just then

Jean-Baptiste* Laforest blurted out, "Monsieur Charbonneau, can I go with you? I can work as hard as my cousins. They'll vouch for me."

Charbonneau gave a frown, "I already have one boy, but I do have room." Turning to the boy's cousins, "What do you say, lads?"

Pierre Tremblay scratched his chin, "Well, he's not as strong as Louis-Michel, but he is a lot smarter. I'll vouch for him."

Charbonneau answered, "If your father gives his permission, be at Saint-Aubin's with your cousins at dawn."

When the cart ride ended at Saint-Aubin's barn, Charbonneau said to Toussaint, "Are you and your boy up to a trip as well?"

Henri-Pierre lit up like a candle, but Toussaint frowned and said, "I'm afraid I have business with Saint-Aubin and Pontiac." Henri-Pierre's chin dropped. "But if my son wants to go, he has my permission." The boy's smile returned and he shouted, "Yes Sir!"

Then Charbonneau added, "If he is descended from Pierre Roy, he's the first man I want."

They went to the house for another wonderful dinner. Afterward, Charbonneau announced, "Madame Saint-Aubin, I must decline your hospitality for tonight. We will camp in back. I cannot let my men get soft." So Jacques* and Louis* Renaud had had their first and last night on a real featherbed.

Chapter 6

Détroit - June 10, 1761:

Rising before dawn, the men had eaten and broken their small camp in the Saint-Aubin meadow before dawn. Just before the sun, the three Tremblay-Laforest cousins arrived, all excited at the prospect of adventure. Charbonneau announced, "Saint-Aubin has offered us a ride to the fort, but I assured him we would rather walk." Each man loaded his pack and walked to the road. Charbonneau said, "It's about seven miles. We should make it easily in one hour." And he started out at a slow steady run.

The others tried not to complain, but it was more than they were used to. The only people that seemed to have no difficulty were Charbonneau and Joseph. Halfway they stopped for a brief rest. The Tremblay boys appeared near death. "I guess millwork is not as strenuous as I had been told," said Jean-Baptiste. "Soon we will be doing this for days on end, but uphill and carrying fully loaded canoes."

Their spirits having not been raised, the men proceeded. A short time later the fort came into sight. They reached the dock and checked on their canoes. Charbonneau looked them over. "Who can read?" After a pregnant pause, Jacques* timidly raised his hand. "Good, take this list to the trading post and tell them I will be by for these things in two days. Joseph and I will be making arrangements and will meet the rest of you at the tavern this evening. The *French* tavern!"

Détroit was different than Montréal and extremely different than Québec. Whereas the cities in French Canada had a slower ambience where both men and ladies travelled the streets and frequently stopped to visit and gossip, everyone in Détroit moved as though they had a mission. The Indian presence was also overwhelming. In Montréal there were many Indians, but here they were a clear majority. Even the smells were different. Québec smelled of civilization. Détroit, on the other hand, had the background scent of people and things, but it was still filled with the smell of the true frontier.

The group made their way to the trading post and entered under a sign that read, *Jean-Baptiste Rivard, Propriétaire.* They made their way to the counter where they found a familiar face, Julian* Fréton from the Milk River. He greeted the group and introduced them to Monsieur Rivard. He added, "Monsieur Rivard has recently purchased land by me, I was just telling him about our new bridge."

Détroit was the sort of place where the line between strangers and friends was sharply drawn. With this introduction, the men could feel themselves go from intruders to guests. Jacques* presented his list and explained that they were with Monsieur Charbonneau. Rivard replied, "Ah, Jean-Baptiste, how I envy you. You will go to the real frontier. Tell him to have no fear; Baptiste Rivard will have his supplies ready on time."

Having no further business, they wandered about. The Tremblay brothers said they rarely came to town and were almost as lost as the others. They left the stockade and went down to the docks where two British boats were unloading. Later they saw a group of Indians playing lacrosse on a field by the fort. They went to watch and were eventually invited to play. Only Jacques*, Henri-Pierre and Louis* Renaud were familiar with the game, so only they joined in. Later Jean-Baptiste* Laforest suggested that it was time to go to the tavern. It appeared to be true that he was smarter than his older cousins.

There were two taverns in Détroit. The French establishment was called The *Pontchartrain* and the English one simply, The *Keg*. Although the Tremblays were not skilled in lacrosse, they did understand taverns, and they ordered a round of shots and beers while they awaited Joseph and Charbonneau.

Two rounds later, Charbonneau and Joseph entered with two other men. Jean-Baptiste introduced them. First was André* Peltier. At twenty-five years, André* had come from Saint-François between Québec and Montréal a few years ago. He had worked as a voyageur until the past season when he worked at the Meloche mill in Assumption.

The second man, with a more complicated past, was Jacob* Thomas. Although he was the uncle of Henri-Pierre, the boy had never laid eyes upon him. His father was a British colonist captured by Joseph and Jean-Baptiste* Allard in a raid on Charlesbourg many years before. The elder Jacob* Thomas had remained in Québec. He married the daughter of an Indian girl and the famous voyageur,

54

Pierre Roy. He had two children, one was Monique who married Toussaint and became Henri-Pierre's mother. Young Jacob* had returned to the British colony of New York where he had worked as a trader. This year at the age of forty, he had decided to try his luck with Charbonneau who was looking for a combination experienced voyageur and English teacher.

Jean-Baptiste bade the men silent and attentive, "This will be our group. We will have four more Indians when we leave at daybreak the day after tomorrow. We will go south to Erie from where we will take the rivers to the mission at Saint-Louis. There we will find the Missouri River and head to the frontier. We have several neophytes. Among them are three boys. I count on you more mature and experienced men to help them learn as well and a quickly as possible. For you boys, you will be expected to work without complaint or excuse. No one will ask you to do the impossible, although it may seem so at the time. I must warn you all that I have made the group large enough that I can cut any one of you loose at any time or place if you do not fulfill my expectations. I am hopeful that this will be a safe and extremely profitable trip. However, I can not guarantee any of that. What I can guarantee you is the most fantastic adventure of your life. Now Joseph and I have further work to do." Rising from his chair, "Jacob* you are in charge tonight. See that all of them are still alive and at least marginally sober in two days."

As Joseph and Charbonneau made their way to the door, Louis* Renaud was counting on his fingers. He finally calculated that he had been suddenly promoted from boy to man. Jacques* watched carefully as Charbonneau departed. He was reserved and unimpulsive, unlike any other voyageur he had encountered. He reminded him of his late father and that made him feel secure.

Sensing the end of the lecture, Pierre Tremblay ordered another round. Sensing the end of all discipline, Jacob* Thomas shifted abruptly in his seat. Given the difference in age and experience between him and the others at the table, he felt this a good time to assert himself. "Let me tell you lads a few things about our boss, just in case you don't know. Jean-Baptiste or *Monsieur Charbonneau,* who he shall be to you until you earn otherwise, is the most skilled voyageur today. I left good jobs in New York to come work with him. His father and his grandfather, as well as his wife's family, have always been fine traders. Jean-Baptiste has collected all their skill without their wild ways. Do not take his counsel lightly and obey him instantly. Do this and you will not go wrong, and will be less likely to tangle with me. That being said, you may proceed to work on your hangovers."

As the evening progressed, several men, local or from Québec, stopped to visit and share stories of the great voyageurs of the past. Countless glasses were drained in the name of men like Pierre Roy, Grosse Pierre, Joseph Parent, and Robert* Reaume. In the morning, Jacques* and Henri-Pierre knew why their fathers had always limited them to two drinks.

Chapter 7

The Docks of Détroit - June 12, 1761:

The dark horizon of Lake Saint Clair was giving way to a small crescent of sunlight as the men made their way down the docks, each hauling a load of supplies from Rivard. As the ten men stacked their cargo on the dock, they were briefly introduced to the remainder of their team: four Indians of indeterminate age, two Algonquin, one Huron and one Iroquois.

Charbonneau barked orders; each object went into a very special place. In addition to the two canoes the men had brought from Montréal were three much larger canoes, possible to handle with two men but much better with three or four. Once the cargo was loaded, he assigned seating, having obviously given it some thought. "Henri-Pierre take the center of the first large canoe. Jean-Baptiste* Laforest will go in the center of the second, and Louis* Renaud, center of the third." Once everyone else had a position, "Jacques* take the front in my canoe." Not being certain if this was a vote of confidence or the opposite, the boy did as instructed.

As the men boarded the canoes, Charbonneau ordered, "Watch your stroke and cadence. The older men help the younger. Follow me, I have the youngest member in my canoe so keeping pace should not be difficult. *Allons y!*" As soon as they had established a rhythm, Jean-Baptiste called out the familiar song of the voyageur…

Chante, rossignol, chante,
Toi qui a le Cœur gai.
Lui y a longtemps que je t'aime,
Jamais je ne t'oblierai.

Jacques* used all his effort to keep up with Charbonneau's pace. He was happy not to have been called to sing as it would be difficult to sing and keep this pace at the same time.

Á la Claire fontaine
M'en allant promener
J'ai trouvé l'eau si belle
Que je m'y suis baigné

With the downstream current, it took little time to reach Lake Erie and then the Maumee River in the southwest corner of the lake. Reaching the mouth of the river, they turned down without as much as a break in rhythm. As they neared Pontiac's camp, a hopeful Jacques* Allard managed to get enough breath to ask, "Will we stop at Pontiac's camp?"

To his disappointment, "Not today, there is someone further down who will have more information important to our plans, and we should wait until we are tired."

The day passed with no change in the program, only occasional correction commands from the various canoe captains. Joseph sat in the back of the second small canoe and three of the Indians took the back seat in the three large canoes. The banks of the river were beautiful, sloping meadows, occasional small cliffs, trees dipping to the water's edge. The river was wide and deep enough so no portaging was necessary. They passed two farm houses nestled close to one another and a third isolated and burned. The sun rose high above and hot at noon but the group moved on. Finally in late afternoon, more than twelve hours from their departure Charbonneau headed for shore at a small Indian camp. He sprang from his canoe as though he had only been in it for a few minutes, "I apologize for stopping so early in the day, but I would like to talk with these people."

He and Joseph proceeded to the camp while Jacob* Thomas gave orders, "Bring the canoes up far enough to avoid losing them. Take what you need for tonight and set it out here. We will wait for instructions before we make arrangements for fire or food."

After they completed their task, Pierre Tremblay fell to the ground, "My God, I think I'm going to die. What happened to easing into things?" Before anyone else could speak, Thomas picked up Tremblay who clearly outweighed him by fifty pounds. Without difficulty he took him to the bank and flung him into the river effortlessly.

"Ease into this!" Then turning to the others, "If you are fatigued, I suggest you refresh with Monsieur Tremblay. Monsieur Charbonneau is easing in. However he must harden you ladies before we meet the difficult tasks ahead. I warned you. No complaints."

The other men went to the edge to wash and rest when Charbonneau and Joseph reappeared. "As I had hoped, the chief has invited us to eat. Hopefully after dinner we will see what the attitude of the locals is."

Dinner was roasted pheasant and fish along with cornbread and a sweet fruit drink. Afterward there was dancing by some of the women. The men in Charbonneau's party were all too exhausted to be very interested. Later the pipe was smoked. The chief began, "We welcome Charbonneau because we know he is honorable as were his father and grandfather. However I must warn you as you are my friend. Some weeks ago we met with Englishmen who came to trade. We did so as is the custom, but in the morning, they had left taking many of the items they had given us the night before. In addition they took two of our women who were forced to find their way back some days later when the English had lost interest in them. I have not gone to Chief Pontiac with this story. We will wait to see if it is an isolated incident. If, however, it is not, I fear there will be great trouble that may influence our good relations."

Then Jean-Baptiste rose, "I am distressed to hear this news. As you know, the French now have no control over the English. I am told that the man Campbell at Détroit is honorable. We will have to see."

As they walked back to the camp he told the men, "I feared this would happen. We will have to be careful with all Indian groups from now on and try to keep our distance from the English." When they returned to the camp, Charbonneau, Joseph and Jacob* Thomas sat by a small fire to talk. The rest were asleep in minutes. The next thing Jacques* heard was Charbonneau telling them it was time to go.

The group arose slowly. Jacques* could not believe the stiffness in his joints. Even Henri-Pierre who was never tired or sore was moving slower than his eighty-five year old grandfather. In fact Joseph rose quicker than anyone other than perhaps Charbonneau and Jacob* Thomas. Before breakfast, Charbonneau said a short prayer asking God to protect them on their journey. This would become a daily ritual revealing the gentle and civilized side of the man.

"Today we will get in a full day's travel and not stop early. I will try to pick up the pace some. At camp tonight we will began to speak English for practice. Monsieur Thomas will aid us."

Trying to straighten up, Louis-Michel Tremblay asked, "How can we talk it when we don't know none."

"I would suggest that you talk less and listen more. It may even improve your French." Louis-Michel was beginning to wonder if this was a good idea after all.

As the canoes started southwest, Charbonneau again broke into the song that had filled the Canadian frontier for one hundred and fifty years.

Chante, rossignol, chante,
Toi qui a le Cœur gai.
Lui y a longtemps que je t'aime,
Jamais je ne t'oblierai.

The river remained unchanged. The current was weak and the water high so the paddling was simple and there was no portage. The deciduous forest continued, interrupted only rarely by a small group of farm houses. Charbonneau told Jacques*, "These are small French communities; they have kept the houses together to protect from the occasional Iroquois raid just as we did in Québec. The solitary houses are usually English settlers. You will notice that they are frequently burned or simply abandoned."

Early in the day, Jacques*'s muscles loosened but as the afternoon wore on, he began to fatigue and feared that he would not be able to finish the day. By the time Charbonneau called for the camp, he could scarcely think. They had paddled without interruption of the cadence for over sixteen hours. They pulled the canoes onto a sandy bank by a clearing and Thomas started to bark orders in English. Some were obvious and others required a little translation, but the men all pitched in and soon the camp was made and a small fire was burning.

Charbonneau demonstrated his broken English, "Tomorrow night we make two groups, one for to make the camp and one for to hunt the food." The men ate and most were soon fast asleep as Charbonneau, Joseph, André* Peltier, and Jacob* Thomas smoked by the fire, and Charbonneau played the harmonica.

The following morning was much the same. Charbonneau said his prayer and gave orders in his broken English. They were not difficult to understand as they were the same instructions he had given in French the day before. That evening in camp, Charbonneau presented each one of the three boys and Louis* Renaud a package. When they opened them, they found deerskin jackets much like those worn by the voyageurs. When they tried them on, they were surprised they were too large. Charbonneau indicated they should put them away and save them until later in the voyage.

The Source of the Maumee River - June 26, 1761:

Two weeks into the voyage the men were beginning to endure the routine. They were surprised when Charbonneau called a halt early in the day, "This is where we leave the Maumee. We have a portage of several miles. It will take the rest of today and tomorrow."

They were surprised the portage was not as difficult as they had feared. The trail was worn by other voyageurs, the terrain flat, and the canoes not too heavy. The Tremblay boys did well as lifting was what they did best. The optimism of the new men was soon dampened by Charbonneau, "Don't get too confident. Once we reach Saint-Louis, we will get our real supplies, and the terrain in the west is not like this." Two days later they reached the Wabash River.

"Today we will change positions. Jacques*, Louis*, Jean-Baptiste, and Henri-Pierre will take the back of their canoes. The Tremblays will take turns at the back of theirs." This promotion to the most important role in the voyage thrilled the young men. It was clearly a sign of the confidence Charbonneau now had in them.

The day was a disaster. They had made less than one-third their usual distance and the Tremblay canoe had capsized. Fortunately, nothing had been lost. At dinner Charbonneau chose to speak French, "As you can see, you men still have some to learn. A canoe is like a musical instrument. You must know how to summon its talents. We shall begin to mix positions and partners. Study the method of the man in the back. Everyone has his own technique. Learn from them. I promise you that when we reach the Missouri, you will all be able to take total control of the canoe." After a short pause, "Or have died trying."

That night after dinner Jacques* and Henri-Pierre finally had enough reserved strength to sit up and talk for a while. The two boys had been life-long best friends in Québec but had little time to talk since Jacques*'s arrival at Détroit. "Jacques*, when we were boys in Québec, we always did well in the canoe race. Each of us could easily control the back, but this is different, the weight, current and the speed. I am humbled."

Jacques* replied to his friend, "I had no idea it would be so difficult, but we can do it and I think this may indeed be my destiny."

Four days into the Wabash River, Jacques* was finally getting beyond the sheer agony of the work. Paddling was becoming easier and he could concentrate on currents, the shapes of banks, the nature of the water, and learn from the more skilled men. The past three days found him at the front of a large canoe with Pierre Tremblay in the center and the Iroquois Guide, Thundercloud, at the rear. Having worked with voyageurs for twenty years, Thundercloud was a skilled canoeist. He spoke only a little French, but as the men were trying to learn Iroquois, it was a good opportunity for Jacques* to improve his language as well as his canoeing skills.

Jacques* had come believing he was a good canoeist, but there was much to learn. He was beginning to understand the subtleties of gaining the most speed and most direct route with the smallest expenditure of energy. Each bend in each river was different and would be different still tomorrow. Jacques* had formed an attachment to the Iroquois brave who obviously took pride in teaching the boy his craft. While the other three Indian guides spoke reasonable French, Thundercloud's French was poor. He spoke in a combination of his native tongue with some French and some Algonquin words scattered in.

"Beaver house ahead. Beaver put house there for reason. Need deep water to leave without notice and away from current to protect house. You go upstream, stay close to beaver. Downstream stay away, more fast."

Each day was filled with new knowledge in "reading the stream", how the ripples formed, how a leaf behaved in the stream, why trees fell where they did, which channel was the main - all things that Jacques* had lived with all his life without realizing how important each could be. A week into the Wabash, Jacques* and Thundercloud were selected at camp to go forage for game. A short while into the woods, they came to a clearing and saw a deer at the edge. Thundercloud carefully lowered his rifle and took aim. He dropped the buck with one shot. They fell upon cutting the animal when there was a rustle in the brush. Thundercloud picked up his rifle and waited. A large wolf appeared and uttered an evil growl.

Thundercloud took aim, but Jacques* stood up, "Don't!" As the Indian carefully lowered his weapon, Jacques* stooped and cut a piece of meat from the deer's flank. He walked slowly over to the wolf and laid the meat down two feet from the beast. The wolf carefully advanced, took the meat and turned slowly into the brush.

Thundercloud laughed, "Henri-Pierre say you charm animals. He right." With that they finished the chore and carried the deer back to camp.

After dinner, Thundercloud who was generally quiet felt the need to talk, "Young Allard charm wolf in woods tonight."

Louis-Michel Tremblay asked, "What's charming? What happened?"

"Wolf come to take deer. Jacques* give him piece of meat and wolf leave. No trouble."

Tremblay looked puzzled, "Damn, boy, I don't think I'd stick my hand out with a piece of meat. Charm or no, how does he know when the meat ends and you begin?"

Jacques* merely shrugged, "I knew he wouldn't hurt me."

Jacob* Thomas spoke up, "I've heard of this. Don't let your rifle fall too far behind you."

Thundercloud added, "Brother of my mother is charmer. Very special in world of Iroquois. He say, 'special gift. Must be careful. If man charm to harm animals, the gift will be taken away.'"

Charbonneau stood, "I agree with Jacob*. Be careful. Well, I think I'll turn in."

Upon landing for camp a few days later, Charbonneau announced, "We should reach the Ohio River tomorrow. There is a Miami camp near here. I'm going to hike over and see what they have to say." He and Joseph left through an Indian trail. Two hours later they returned.

"Bad news. English traders have been through and treated them unscrupulously. The Indians are more than a little angry. They did not invite us to stay. I think we should move camp. We will backtrack two miles. If anyone wants to find us, they will think we went ahead rather than back. We should also start to post a serious guard each night."

The Ohio River - July 20, 1761:

The downstream current of the Wabash had made for fast runs. Now the even more rapid speed of the wide Ohio would make them even faster. Although downstream was easier than upstream travel, the boys learned that that was no reason to be lazy. Charbonneau instructed, "Our goal each day is to gain distance. Downstream is no less work, it is merely different, and the distance gained is much greater."

Encountering more rapids and small falls, they began to master the art of knowing when to portage and when to ride. Portage was difficult and lost much time, but a hole in a canoe would lose a day or more of the trip. More significant damage could spell catastrophe. As the boys would always want to try the thrill of the rapids with their new skills and strength, Charbonneau always had the last word. The third day of the Ohio Jacques* discovered the reason for the gift of the new shirts, "My arms won't go in my sleeves."

Charbonneau laughed, "I guess you are becoming a real voyageur." Two days later he again placed the neophytes in the back of the canoes. This time the results were different. Their distance was still below standard, but only a little. At camp he announced, "Maybe we will make

Saint-Louis before winter." Two days later they saw the Mississippi River.

"Well, lads, the vacation is over, you have seen your last downstream cruise." For men raised on the Saint-Laurent, it is difficult to be impressed by a river. This one was very different, but it was impressive. Very murky and very wide and not usually as fast as the Saint-Laurent, it was a medley of shapes and currents and variations. The boys had learned to read the river downstream, but reading it upstream was not exactly the opposite. It seemed that just as they had become masters, they were again beginners.

The banks of the Mississippi were wilderness. Some places the river was so wide one could scarcely see across it if the day was dreary. The experienced men knew exactly where to place the canoe. Occasionally they could even make the canoe float upstream against the current. Joseph explained, "Every time there is a change in the current, there is a sweet-spot, a counter current where the paddling is easiest and sometimes it is even a reverse current. Learn to look for it; soon you will see it instinctively." Soon they saw the small mission buildings.

Great Falls •   North Dakota
                South
                Dakota
          Nebraska   Iowa
          Kansas   • St. Louis
            Missouri

CHARBONNEAU'S ROUTE 1761-1762

Chapter 8

Saint-Louis - August 1, 1761:

The men landed near the buildings. Stepping from his canoe to the land, Charbonneau exclaimed, "Gentlemen, welcome back to French Canada." In 1761 this place was more a crossroads at a small Indian mission than a town. It actually did not have an official name although the voyageurs called it Saint-Louis in reference to a term used by some of the missionaries.

Charbonneau had explained that officially the French still held most of the land west of the Mississippi including this mission which sat in the large territory called Louisiana. Because of the mission's position to the Mississippi, Missouri, and Ohio Rivers, certain supplies could be obtained. Charbonneau told the men, "Joseph and I will go see who has what we need. The small building there is a sort of tavern. After you get the canoes stowed, meet us there."

The "tavern" was deserted except for a scrawny old man behind a small counter. The men sat at one of the three tables and asked for beer. The old man replied, "All we got now is corn whiskey, won't have beer till the fall." As he brought a jug and a few rough glasses he continued, "Been lots of traffic this year. Lots of thirsty people going south to *la Nouvelle Orléans* to get away from the British. We been out'a beer for a month." As he wandered back to the counter, Charbonneau and Joseph entered.

"We will have our supplies in the morning, this was easier than I had expected. It seems many people are traveling south and west away from the British. There has been a big market for supplies, and some merchants from Canada have come down to fill the need. It looks as though this place is going to become a major trading post soon."

Morning found the men hauling their supplies to the river. Charbonneau was doing an inventory as they loaded, "We have a large number of useful goods such as knives, pots, pans, bottles, candles, and traps. Many of the desperate people fleeing Acadia traded these for food so there is a good supply on hand. We also have maple syrup and tobacco which are rare in the northwest. All of these things are coveted by the Indians who have seen French trade for a few seasons. As we proceed west, trinkets and woven cloth are more prized by the Indians who have yet to learn of the function of other European goods. It will be our job to change all of these things into valuable furs."

Once they were fully packed, the men understood why Charbonneau had said portage would be more difficult after Saint-Louis. A short while after leaving the small mission and post, they came to a great fork. As they headed up the western fork Charbonneau announced, "The Missouri River will be our home through the fall." During the next two weeks Jacques* realized that as Charbonneau had predicted, he had become a truly skilled canoeist. More amazing than this was his strength. Objects that he would have struggled to lift at the start of the voyage could now be lifted easily with one hand. Jacques* had always been amazed by the strength of the voyageurs. Now with no small amount of pride, he realized he was becoming one.

The Missouri River - July 14, 1761:

Days were becoming routine, and the men were handling the voyage to Charbonneau's satisfaction. English and Iroquois lessons continued until camp was set, then they generally lapsed back into French. They even had enough energy at night to sit around the fire and smoke. This was a particularly beautiful night, clear with a warm breeze from the north. Now that the crew was not totally exhausted at night, they took to the age-old voyageur custom of stories at the fire. The younger boys, Jacques*, Henri-Pierre, and Jean-Baptiste* Laforest had taken to asking Joseph to tell stories, usually about the many adventures he had with his best friend and grandfather of Jacques*, Jean-Baptiste* Allard.

As with many old Indians, Joseph was a wonderful teller of tales, and the truth be known, he had wonderful stories to tell. As time went on the three older "boys", Louis* Renaud, and the Tremblay brothers came to listen as well while Charbonneau, Andre* Peltier and Jacob* Thomas planned the trip. A careful observer would notice these men also listened from a distance.

"When Jean-Baptiste* and I were eleven, our fathers took the older boys to the *rendez-vous* near *Trois-Rivières*. Our mothers gave us permission to go on a two-day hunt. We happened upon a band of young Iroquois headed toward Charlesbourg. They were drinking and acting odd. In those days the Iroquois made periodic raids on the villages and burned farms. We followed them from behind. When it became apparent they were up to no good, we began to take them out one at a time. They were many, perhaps forty. I would make myself seen to the last man in their single file. He would try to shoot me but Jean-Baptiste*, who was better than most Indians with a bow, would shoot them first. We continued this for a day until they realized what we were up to, and a few turned to stand against us while the rest proceeded. We eventually prevailed." Looking at Jacques*, "Mainly due to your grandfather's skill with the bow, but the rest of the band had a head start and beat us to Charlesbourg." Then yawning, "I fear that is enough for tonight. Monsieur Charbonneau has use for us in the morning and we need our rest."

Jacques* and Henri-Pierre had heard this story many times before and never tired of it, or any of Joseph's tales; but the others were held in suspense. Louis-Michel Tremblay said, "Can't we hear a little more? At least tell us how it ends."

"This is truly enough for tonight, but if you think, I am still here and so is Charlesbourg."

As the journey progressed, they became more impressed with the oddities of the Missouri. Charbonneau had told them, "It is alive like no other river. It moves, not merely flowing but moves from side to side and place to place. Each year it alters its course, sometimes to a place out of sight of its previous location."

It was true the river bed in places was as much as two miles wide, but the stream less than one hundred feet with the bed representing many previous courses of the river. Snags of fallen trees were everywhere as were sandbars, frequently taking the depth from many feet to a few inches suddenly and without obvious cause. The water was muddier than the Mississippi. Sometimes fish were plentiful yet oftentimes there were none, again without obvious reason. There were cliffs on the bank, sometimes over one-hundred feet high, sometimes a mile or two from the river.

Trees grew along the river banks in places but were frequently uprooted either by storms, floods, or sudden changes in the river course. The trees away from the bank became more and more sparse as the journey progressed. That afternoon camp was being set with Thundercloud and Jacob* Thomas giving orders in English and Iroquois. Jacques* and Henri-Pierre had been sent to forage for game. As they returned to camp a group of men in canoes was approaching.

In the frontier it was prudent to expect anything so the boys held back with their rifles ready as the first canoe landed. Charbonneau went to the bank and was soon shaking hands with one of the men so the boys proceeded. Charbonneau brought the man to the camp and introduced him, "Pierre Deneau is my wife's cousin. I've asked them to stay." As they brought the canoes ashore, Jacques* noticed with suspicion they were relatively empty.

That night at dinner Deneau announced, "We are headed up the Missouri to the Cheyenne that we will follow to the *Belle Fourche*. We heard in Saint-Louis last week that you boys were headed up."

Charbonneau used this to ask the obvious, "You have made excellent time. I notice you travel light."

Laughing, Deneau replied, "We are not trading this year but hunting. Buffalo. The English will pay dear for their hides. We shoot and skin them so we can travel upstream fast with empty canoes."

Joseph asked, "What do you do with the meat?"

"Eat what we need and leave the rest for the coyote. Seems a waste, but the money is in the hide. If we get some Indians to help, they keep the rest."

As Deneau and his men left in the morning, Joseph said to the boys, "For 150 years the Indian has trapped or hunted the animal, traded the furs to the voyageurs and used the rest. Ways are changing." That night the boys persuaded him to finish his story.

"As it happened, it was Sunday and a great festival was on in Québec city. Everyone had gone, or should I say, almost everyone. Our mothers had stayed because one of the small children was ill." To Jacques*, "Your great grandmother was an educated woman. Her brother was a Bishop in France. She was teaching my mother how to read and write. They heard the commotion and saw a fire in the Pageot barn next door. Your great grandmother went without caution to free the animals. When she arrived she realized the fire had been set. She returned quickly to her house. My mother had left with the children but had left a message written in flour spilled on the table, *caveau,* referring to a hidden cave where they would hide. Knowing the children were hidden, your great grandmother left with your grandfather's bow and led the Iroquois away from the house. She killed three with the bow and her knife. They were about to take her when your grandfather and I arrived. We shot some but there were too many. Just then a man appeared from the woods and killed the rest of the Iroquois. It was my grandfather, the great Henri. He had been away for many years but had heard of the planned raid and returned. Both your grandfather and I were gravely injured, but we recovered and were treated as heroes. In truth we were lucky little boys."

Pierre Tremblay exclaimed, "I bet you were proud."

The old man thought for a moment, "At first, yes, but as time has passed I see there is little glory in the killing of any man for any purpose. We were all protecting our homes against influences none of us could control. I hope now our country is free of European wars, and the white men regardless of nationality and the Indian regardless of tribe can live more peacefully. But we shall see, perhaps I am just too old." Then adding, "And it is certainly too late, we have more work tomorrow."

Late the following day they spotted a burned canoe on the shore and went to investigate. As they landed they saw several scalped bodies on the ground. It was quickly apparent that it was the Deneau group. A man came cautiously out of a small stand of trees accompanied by a boy Jacques*'s age. He and Charbonneau apparently recognized each other. The man spoke quickly and quietly, "Jean-Baptiste, thank goodness it's you. We saw the canoe and landed a short while ago. This man," referring to a body, "was still alive and told us they had stopped to talk to some Indians about aiding them in their buffalo hunt. The Indians became enraged and killed them."

Charbonneau looked about, "Must have differed on the subject of the buffalo hunt."

The man said, "We must bury them."

Charbonneau stopped him, "No. Touch nothing. We must leave immediately and get as far away as possible. If they know we are here, they will think we are for the same purpose and we may meet the same fate. Quickly." They boarded their canoes and headed north, traveling as long as the light would allow. They then camped, hid the canoes, ate cold pemmican and slept without a fire with three guards posted at all times. As soon as the sun hit the horizon, they departed and paddled hard all day.

That evening they were able to make a proper camp and talk. Charbonneau started with an introduction, "This is Jean Drouillard. Jean lives on the south shore of Détroit at Assumption. What brings you to the Missouri, Jean?"

"We thought that we would try our hand at trading this winter as no license was required. This is my son, Pierre, he is sixteen yesterday. We should have stayed closer to home."

Charbonneau continued, "We are headed to the Great Falls. You are welcome to travel with us for a while, but I think it would behoove us all to get out of this region as quickly as possible." The men agreed and the boys invited young Pierre Drouillard to listen to a story of Joseph while the older men planned.

When the older men were alone, Jean Drouillard continued, "The boy's mother sent him to be educated at the Jesuit mission school in Assumption. Lad's very intelligent, but now he just wants to read books. I thought it would be good to get him into the wild. Frankly it may have been a bad idea to come alone. Could we impose on you to allow us to accompany you to the frontier?"

Charbonneau thought for a while, "As long as you pull your weight, why not?"

The two groups talked on, and the still of night descended with only the call of birds and sound of water occasionally interrupted by the howl of a wolf. No one could have known how the decision of this night would influence the lives of some of the men and alter the future of North America.

Chapter 9

<u>Mouth of the Cheyenne River - August 29, 1761:</u>

The group made camp near the first major fork they had seen in some time. The terrain had become boring. The eastern bank was flat grass-covered plains as far as one could see. The west side was somewhat hillier but equally as boring, only the occasional tree, and the weather had become intensely hot.

Jean Drouillard had some experience but was older, not as strong or capable as the other men. His son adapted well, and as Drouillard had indicated he was intelligent. He took to the language lessons immediately and was already fluent in Iroquois and English. They had some contact with the Dakota Indians, part of the larger tribe called Sioux. He had already begun to master this language and soon was better at interpretation than any of the Indians in the party.

The group of boys had now grown to four, each sixteen years of age. Joseph treated his enlarged group of boys to another tale. "During one of the senseless wars between England and France, the English and Iroquois tried a raid on Beauport. Jean-Baptiste* Allard and I were in the Militia and sent to head off a raiding party. We scouted ahead, found them, and were able to send a group behind them. Their leader was a stupid man named Johnson. We ambushed them easily and they retreated with hardly a shot. We managed to capture the leader, Colonel Johnson who died the next day. We also captured a colonial militia man named Jacob* Thomas. As you know, he stayed in Québec as a valued citizen. His daughter married my son Toussaint and his son, Jacob* Jr., is traveling with us today. We also captured Johnson's African slave, a fine man named Tom who travelled with us on other adventures. He and I married *métis* sisters named de Baptiste. We both took this as our own family name. This man's family now lives in Détroit and helps other slaves as they are able. Jean-Baptiste* had the wisdom to keep the colonel's uniform. The best part of the story occurred many years later after the death of Jean-Baptiste* Allard. The British were burning the north coast of Québec before the fall." Again looking to Jacques*, "Your father remembered the uniform and had old Jacob* Thomas wear it and convince the British soldiers that they were to leave the area. His ruse worked and Charlesbourg was saved."

The next day they encountered enormous debris floating downstream, and they soon saw the cause. An unbelievable number of animals were crossing the river at a shallow sandbar. Everyone had heard of buffalo but only Charbonneau, Peltier, and Thomas had seen them. Even old Joseph had not seen them before. The herd stretched as far as could be seen on either side of the river. Joseph exclaimed, "Perhaps this is why I was to come on this journey."

Charbonneau interrupted, "Thundercloud, go shoot two. The rest of you stay in your canoes in the deep water in case a stampede starts." Thundercloud carefully killed two of the beasts on the periphery and other than some noise, nothing else happened. The Indian was then able to float them downstream to the canoes where he brought them to shore and he and the other guides began to process them, first removing the hides. "These will be good this winter." And then the meat which would feed them for a few weeks. He explained that the Indians used all of the buffalo, the bones for tools and the intestines for water sacks.

Three days later they saw a cloud of black birds on the horizon. Buzzard were a familiar sight on the prairie, but usually only a few birds over some dead animal. Here there were hundreds. As they progressed the stench of carrion became overwhelming. Eventually they saw the cause. The prairie was littered with rotting carcasses intact other than for their hides. Charbonneau said quietly, "This is what Deneau was after. This is the future." The Indians were silent for the rest of the day.

As they followed the Missouri north, the plains became more barren and trees were only seen by the river bank; the rest was thick brown grass. At the end of August they came to a large Indian camp. Joseph and Charbonneau went into the camp and quickly returned. "This is a tribe of Yankton Sioux. They are friendly and wish us to stay." They landed the canoes and walked into the camp which was more like a village. Jacques* was impressed by its size. Much larger than eastern camps, it was two miles across and contained hundreds of people.

As they proceeded among the tents Charbonneau explained, "These are teepees made from long poles and buffalo hide, easy to erect and take down, and excellent for travel. Obviously there is not enough wood for huts like our Indians have. Each family has its own tent. They are very secure and can withstand any blizzard with a fire inside the tent, and in the summer they can open to be cool."

There was a large gathering at the fire with an obvious order as to who sat closest to the fire. The men were invited to sit and woman brought around food, various meats, bread, and some unusual vegetables and roots. After eating, Charbonneau and Joseph met off to the side with the chiefs. They asked young Pierre Drouillard to join them as he was already becoming familiar with the local Indian dialect. The rest of the men sat around the fire and watched dancing by both the men and the women.

Eventually the chiefs returned to the group and the head chief asked Charbonneau something motioning to the voyageurs. Charbonneau came over and said, "He wants to know who our strongest man is."

Jacob* Thomas replied, "Louis-Michel."

Tremblay stood up obviously pleased to be singled out when a large Sioux brave came forward. Thomas told him, "They want you to fight him."

Louis-Michel Tremblay looked at the man easily a head taller than he, "Fight him?"

Thomas laughed, "It's a custom, real friendly though."

Tremblay carefully approached the man who caught him with a punch that took his feet off the ground and laid him on his back. He rose slowly and charged. The Indian sidestepped and he went flying past to the delight of the audience. Tremblay regrouped and charged again. He managed to land a punch as the Indian grabbed him around the waist and lifted him over his head and flung him down. Tremblay did not get up.

The Indian came over and offered a hand and brought him to his feet. He held his hand up with Tremblay's and the audience hollered and applauded. He then brought Tremblay over to a young lady and led them to a tent. Tremblay looked at Jacob* Thomas who said softly, "Your prize." The Indian then opened the teepee and closed the skin door after they had entered. A while later the celebration died down and the men returned to their camp without Louis-Michel.

In the morning Louis-Michel Tremblay staggered back into the voyageur camp. "Damn! What a night. What would they have done if I won the fight?"
Jacob* Thomas looked up casually, "Cooked and eaten you."
Tremblay sat down not knowing what to think.

Charbonneau reported, "Last night the chief said that he would have furs to trade when we return in the spring. He has also given us a guide who should be very useful." As they prepared to leave, the guide, a man named Falling Rock, came by. He had learned some French from missionaries. Introductions were made and the group departed. One week later, the Missouri turned west.

Chapter 10

The Missouri River - September, 1761:

As the Missouri adopted a westward course, the water became wide as a lake with slowing of the current. Eventually it returned to its narrower contour with a more difficult current. They came upon an Indian village larger than the last. Falling Rock told Charbonneau, "These are western Sioux, they should welcome us." The group landed and the guide and Charbonneau went to find the leaders. They returned a short while later. "They have invited us to stay. They expect a buffalo herd by tomorrow and have invited us to take part in the hunt. I think it would be of interest and considered amicable if we would accept."

That evening Charbonneau was surprised that a few of the Indians had rifles. He had not seen them this far west. "From traders," said Falling Rock, "Still not popular as the Indians find them too slow to reload compared to the arrow, but they will use them in the buffalo hunt as you will see tomorrow." After the subdued festivities at the Indian camp, the men returned to their small camp in the periphery. Falling Rock explained, "We leave tomorrow before dawn. We will be split into three groups, each to go with a different group of hunters. We should leave two men here to watch the camp and canoes."

Before dawn they were ready. The Drouillards had volunteered to stay with the camp. As the men began to leave, Falling Rock announced, "Leave your rifles. You will not need them and they will only slow you down."

Perplexed, the men left their weapons. They joined the Sioux just as they were to leave. Each of the three groups was assigned to a native group. Falling Rock gave a brief explanation, "We will come around the herd and make noise with these sticks." He passed out hollow sticks that made a loud noise when struck together. "We will chase the buffalo to a 'drop' west of here." Not totally clear on the concept the men proceeded with the tribe.

As the sun reached the horizon, they heard a noise not unlike a large herd of cattle. When they came into view, the men were amazed. The animals reached at least two miles across. There were several hundred. Louis-Michel Tremblay whispered, "Damn!"

Falling Rock countered, "Small herd." The Indians brought their groups slowly to flank the herd. When the chief gave a sign, the noise began and the buffalo started to move away from it, slowly at first but soon the speed rose to a full gallop. Jacques* could see that his group had managed to start the herd in one direction and that the other two groups flanked them so as to control their direction.

A Sioux brave had gone ahead and started enough of a fire at their destination to cause smoke. They now drove the beasts toward the smoke. As the stampede continued, its force and speed became unbelievable. Certainly nothing could survive being in front of it. Eventually there was a large noise from the front and confusion began to overtake the animals. A large cloud of dust began to form in front and the herd slowed a little. Soon it was apparent that the men were driving the herd over a small cliff to their death. The Indians on the left had fallen back and all three groups convened on the right side by the cliff. Jacques* could see the carnage up close as the animals fell or trampled each other to their end.

The Indians with rifles then brought out their weapons and began to shoot into the air. It had its desired effect of turning the herd to the left and away from the cliff preventing the annihilation of them all. As the chaos ended, many of the woman and older children from the village appeared. Everyone descended on the task at hand with studied precision and efficiency. The animals were retrieved, skinned, gutted and otherwise dissected. The parts were then carried back to the camp.

By mid-afternoon they were back at the camp with about fifty buffalo. Skins were being prepared, meat was being cooked or preserved, bones and intestines were being processed into tools and sacks and the best buffalo heads were being fashioned into headdresses. The activities of the evening were considerably less subdued than those of the previous night. The dinner could only be described as gluttonous and the dancing and singing wild. Young women made advances on some of the traders and some were accepted enthusiastically. A particularly lovely young lady approached Jacques* who turned red, quickly excused himself, and ran back to the voyageur camp.

In the morning, Charbonneau woke the men and began to bark orders in broken English. As the sun rose, the same attractive young Indian girl came into the camp and ran to Jacques* speaking rapidly in her language. Falling Rock came over, "She says you are the man with magic eyes and that she must go with you." As the young girl continued to speak, she took Jacques*'s arm, "She says that she will be your slave and do all your bidding day and night."

Jacques*'s face turned redder than Falling Rock's and he could only sputter. Then as the young girl fell to the ground and held him around the leg, two young Sioux braves came and grabbed both the young girl and Jacques* and began to speak rapidly. Falling Rock continued to translate. "They are her brothers. They say you have spoiled her and they want to cut off your manhood." Desperately planning his next move, Jacques* noticed a smile on Charbonneau's face and knew with intense relief that he was the butt of a joke.

All the men began to laugh and Jacob* Thomas said, "Young Allard, if you are going to be a voyageur, you will have to loosen up some." Then the young girl pulled Jacques* behind a bush. When they were alone, she gave him a small peck on the cheek and ran off. When he emerged, redder than ever the men were having gales of laughter and Charbonneau declared, "Enough fun for today, *Allons y!*" Today Jacques* rode with Jean-Baptiste Charbonneau, who asked his opinion of the buffalo hunt. The boy replied, "The most amazing thing is using the rifle to save the animals."

The next several weeks consisted of constant movement, encountering Indian tribes as they proceeded west: Mandan, Crow, Blackfoot and Flathead, each more dark and primitive than the last. Charbonneau met with the leaders and discussed trade. As Jacques* had learned, the best furs were caught in the late autumn and early winter. When they made their way back home they would encounter the finest furs and Indians ready to trade. Charbonneau enjoyed a reputation among these people and they valued his trade. As the season wore on at the end of October, the few deciduous trees shed their leaves and snow was in the air. Then they caught their first glimpse of the fabled mountains, massive compared to the Laurentians, covered on the bottom with fir trees, becoming barren and snow-covered on top, often extending into the clouds themselves.

Chapter 11

Great Falls (now Montana) - Winter 1761:

By the middle of November, they reached the great falls of the Missouri River. As falls go, it was formidable but not seemingly impassable. Charbonneau explained, "This is a series of falls and rapids which stretches for many miles. The Indians have told me that it takes a month to portage in good weather. We will make our winter camp here and hunt the large deer called elk. They come to the valley in the winter and their furs are valuable and their meat delicious. If the weather stays good, we may be able to make the portage during this time."

Fortunately, the plains had given way to forest, and wood was plentiful and cover from trees available. The men cut and constructed two strong shelters and laid considerable wood for burning. Upon completion they began to scout for hunting and for Indian trappers. During the first week they had no contact with local tribes until one morning Charbonneau awoke with a start to a surprising sight, two Indian braves on horseback! To his knowledge, there were no horses anywhere this far west. Charbonneau and Falling Rock spoke with them and invited them to stay.

The two men had learned some French earlier from military explorers and missionaries, so communication was facilitated. The Frenchmen were surprised that the horses had not come from the east but from the south and west. "Men in the south called Spanish bring the horse many years ago. Now many wild horses, and they come north to us."

Charbonneau inquired into the fur trade. "Beaver very good here, many pelts. We have heard name Charbonneau. It is said you are good man, we trade with you."

Charbonneau asked, "I am interested in portaging the great falls, can you guide me before the snow?"

"Can guide but not before snow, too hard. We go after, more easy." Charbonneau pondered this but thought it best to let the subject lay.

Then he asked, "Is it possible for two of these boys to go with you for a short while to trap beaver?"

"If they good workers. We are best. I am called Big Beaver, and my young brother here Little Beaver. We start in three days. We come back for them."

The next day they encountered their first elk. They managed to shoot two of the beasts almost as large as caribou and moose. The furs were excellent and the meat wonderful. If the men did not run out of elk recipes, they would eat well this winter. Charbonneau had decided that Jacques* and Henri-Pierre had the greatest potential and sent them to go with the Beaver brothers. He felt that a first hand exposure to beaver trapping with true experts would be of great value.

That evening there were more questions to Falling Rock about the Flathead tribe. "They are a peaceful people. They war sometimes with the Blackfoot but usually in defense. They do not travel as much as other tribes and have been in this region beyond any memory. In ways they are like the French. They value fun to work." Two days later, the Beaver brothers returned without their horses but ready to trap.

<u>Foothills of the Rocky Mountains - December 1761:</u>

West of the Great Falls the terrain rapidly became mountainous and heavily forested with conifer trees. The hills were embroidered with small rivers, streams and small lakes, many formed by the abundant beaver. Jacques* and Henri-Pierre had spent two winters with Joseph in the Québec wild. They trapped what they could, but the valuable beaver were now sparse in the east. Joseph had told them tales of the days when men could trap as many as they could carry each day. Now they saw such a phenomenon first hand. Each small lake had many beaver houses, and the inhabitants weighed as much as seventy pounds compared to twenty or thirty pounds in Québec of 1760.

The boys had learned with European-style metal traps that were now popular in the east. The Beaver brothers made their traps from materials available. They were simple but clever wooden devices that acted as a basic snare. In spite of their primitive nature, Jacques* and Henri-Pierre found that in the hands of these experts, there was rarely an empty trap in the morning.

In Québec the boys had often used food, usually fish, to attract the beaver. The Beaver brothers used exclusively castoreum which the boys had rarely seen. "Best bait for the beaver," explained Little Beaver while demonstrating on a recently trapped animal. "Cut out this small gland from base of tail. Strong smell." Waving it in front of the boys. Jacques* found it the foulest smell he had ever encountered. "This make mama and papa beaver want to mate. Works better if mixed with very secret Beaver brother ointment. Put small piece on wood trigger and when beaver comes to smell, he is ours."

The special ointment was not nearly as strong as the raw material, but did seem to work better and did allow for much more bait from each gland. Each morning they would work in pairs, one boy and one Beaver brother. They would visit the trap circuit, remove the beavers and move the traps. "Beaver too smart to come back to where he lost his friend." They would then repair and reset each trap in the new location with a small dab of Beaver brother castoreum ointment. They would return to camp by noon and carefully skin the beaver and sew the pelt to wooden circles to cure it with the right amount of tension. "Good fur from beaver is easy part. Hard part to make perfect pelt for best trade."

At night they would dine on beaver. Although the brothers had an endless number of ways to prepare beaver and make it edible, it was evident that the value in beaver would never be as food. They processed what they did not eat into dried pemmican which could be kept indefinitely and easily transported as food when fresh game was not available.

After dinner the brothers talked and the boys listened. Although the brothers spoke enough French to communicate easily, the boys did manage to gain a reasonable understanding of the Algonquin dialect spoken by the Flathead. As Falling Rock had indicated, the Flathead were gregarious people. The brothers were filled with tales of the region, of the great mountains and rivers to the west and the magnificent creatures that inhabited them as well as the buffalo hunts of the plains.

The hunting camp consisted of two teepees by a rock ledge covered with forest. The brothers shared a tent as did Jacques* and Henri-Pierre. One morning two weeks into the adventure the boys arose and realized the neighboring tent had company. Two women had joined the brothers. Big Beaver announced, "Today your big chance. Little Beaver and I have work in camp. You two run traps today."

The boys were thrilled at the vote of confidence and left filled with enthusiasm. The enthusiasm faded as they realized not only did they have twice as many traps as usual, but without the expertise of the Beaver brothers, things proceeded rather slowly. However, they did manage to make camp loaded with furs by mid afternoon. Little Beaver emerged from the tent looking rather tired. He took a quick look at the furs and grunted, "Good, now make pelts." And he disappeared to a muffled series of giggles from the tent. By nightfall, the boys had processed the pelts. The brothers and their two guests emerged and joined the boys for dinner.
"This Sunflower and this Quiet Stream. They are from our village." After eating, Big Beaver stood, "Tomorrow, we do the work." And the two girls rose, giggling and took the boys into their tent.

Jacques* remembered that Jacob* Thomas had told him, "If you want to be a voyageur, you will have to loosen up some." So he decided to loosen up some. By the next afternoon the boys were more exhausted than they had been from the previous day of trapping and had experienced a different form of education. After dinner the two women disappeared into the woods.

One week later Big Beaver announced, "Have all the pelts we can carry, time to return to village." He had secured the pelts into eight packs that could be carried on one's back. Each weighed about one-hundred pounds. They each loaded two packs and began to follow the brothers through a series of mountainous Indian roads. The brothers moved apparently unaffected by the weight. The boys did not appear so unimpaired but did their best to keep up. Two days later they came to the Flathead village.

The community was considerably smaller than Falling Rock's Sioux village. The dwellings were similar buffalo hide teepees but interspersed in the trees in a relative clearing up against a massive granite cliff. They were welcomed and sat by the chief at dinner. Big Beaver had told them that they could keep one of the eight packs of pelts for Charbonneau and the Flathead would keep the other seven for trade. The Flathead were at least as friendly and social as the Québecois Algonquin.

After dinner there was dancing around the fire and the two young ladies from the wilderness camp appeared and sat with the boys. Jacques* was surprised to find they spoke French fairly well. There had not been much conversation at their first meeting. They invited the boys back to their tent for the night. Some conversation did ensue and Jacques* and Henri-Pierre learned that a missionary had accompanied a military party a few years before. "This man spent the winter teaching the children

94

French and French religion. We were not so impressed with the religion but we did learn French language."

In the morning the women prepared breakfast then provided Indian slippers or the native form of snowshoe and took the boys hiking into the mountains. Afternoon found them at a summit with a panorama of the great snow-covered mountain range to the west. Quiet Stream had become Jacques*'s companion. Untrue to her name she was the most talkative, "The great mountains ahead divide the land as far as the land can be seen. On this side live the Flathead and the Blackfoot. On the other side is the land of the Nez Perce."

Jacques* seized the moment to ask the question, "Why are your people called 'Flathead'? Your heads are not flat."

Quiet Stream giggled, "The other tribes of the region have a peculiar tradition of trying to make their heads long and pointed. We do not follow this custom so the others call us 'Flathead'". The boys had been regarding these two as women but were a bit surprised to find they were each one year younger than Jacques* and Henri-Pierre. In the Indian culture, as in the French-Canadian, this was the age of womanhood. The foursome made their way further and stopped at a cave where the Indians made a camp. They built a fire and produced food. After they ate, they talked into the night.

A confused Jacques* Allard awoke at sunrise lying comfortably in a buffalo skin, naked in the arms of this amazing French-speaking woman he had found in the wilderness. The two young women arose, stoked the fire and began to prepare breakfast. They insisted that the two young men remain in bed until it was ready. After breakfast they took their packs and proceeded to the west. At midday they arrived at an overlook on a lake ringed with fir trees and mountains that reflected in the amazing turquoise water as perfectly as a mirror from Paris. As they descended they could see steam on the near shore.

As they approached the beach Sunflower said, "Hot springs." When they reached the steaming pool, the young women undressed and dove in, the men followed suit. The remainder of the day was something the men had never anticipated in their wildest dreams of the frontier. The women made a camp at the pool which held the temperature of a summer day. The women remained naked and the men, not knowing what to do, complied. After dinner they passed a pipe of an unusual tobacco that had the same effect as alcohol. As Jacques* relaxed he had the nerve to ask, "Why are you doing this?"

Sunflower followed, "Doing what?"

At sixteen and a child of war, Jacques* was inexperienced, but his mother had taught him the facts of life regarding sex. "We have made love many times in the past two days, what is this about?"

Quiet Steam smiled, "We like you. We find this pleasant. The man who came and taught us French was also perplexed by this, but it is the Indian way. Most Flathead eventually take a long term mate, but before this we do as we wish. We do not see it as bad."

Jacques* continued, "What about babies?"

She replied, "It is about babies. We are a small village. In small villages, if there is no outside contact, the babies become weak. The best babies come from the traders such as you. If we make love with the Beaver brothers, we use herb that does not make babies. With you we do not use the herb"

Henri-Pierre spoke up, "My mother and my grandmother were from Frenchmen and Indian women."

Sunflower jumped in, "You see, this is how the strong are made. My father was Flathead, but from a different village."

The conversation turned to more mundane matters. When they arrived the next day back at the Flathead camp, Jacques* Allard was more confused. In simple terms, he was in love. The Beaver brothers indicated that they would leave in the morning for Charbonneau's camp. Jacques* asked Quiet Stream if she wanted to come with him.

Her reply, "I will stay with my people. We shall meet again."

Chapter 12

<u>The Great Falls - January 1762</u>:

Hauling their pack of furs to the edge of the Indian camp and not looking forward to the two day march on the Indian roads now with two feet of new snow, the boys were met with a pleasant surprise. The Beaver brothers awaited them on horseback! They broke the pelts in two parcels and each horse carried one brother, one boy and one-half a beaver pack. They arrived at Charbonneau's camp in half a day.

The camp was unchanged but for the snow and a growing mound of elk furs. That night the boys told the story of the adventure. Big Beaver added at the end. "Boys each got woman now too." Jacques* and Henri-Pierre blushed and they were forced to confess amid no small amount of ribbing from the older men.

Jacob* Thomas said, "I took an 'Indian wife' some years ago. She ran off eventually, but to tell the truth, she was too bossy."

André* Peltier added, "I had one for a short time two years ago. She worked me to death in the day and wore me out each night." After gales of laughter and other stories of dubious accuracy, the men went to bed for the night. In the morning the brothers departed and Little Beaver told Charbonneau, "We return in three days to portage the falls." Still unsure how this would work in the deepening snow, Charbonneau agreed tentatively. Three days later they were awakened by a large commotion.

Quickly exiting the shelters, they were met with a familiar sight. Charbonneau smiled, "Now I understand. I just never thought about it out here." The brothers stood grinning with three sleds and three teams of dogs.

Henri-Pierre immediately went to check the dogs. His family had raised sled dogs in Québec. Big Beaver explained, "These dogs came many years ago with tribe to the far north where they live in teepees of ice. Part wolf." Henri-Pierre indicated that his great grandmother had bred Algonquin dogs with wolves and produced a similar breed. He asked if he could try the sled and the Flatheads were amazed with his skill. Big Beaver said, "You come to drive third sled."

They departed in the morning. Charbonneau chose Henri-Pierre for his dogsled skill, young Pierre Drouillard for his interpretive skills, and Jacques* who he believed would become the great voyageur of the group. "Jacob*, Joseph, and André* must stay to watch the camp and keep the others busy with the elk." The sleds were remarkably similar to those used in the east. Each brother and Henri-Pierre stood on the back of the sleds to drive and Drouillard, Jacques* and Charbonneau each sat in a sled. They took off with a jolt and sped out of sight in minutes.

The dogs followed the Indian roads with ease and at break-neck speed. By afternoon they were well into the foothills. They had followed the course of the Missouri River which was reminiscent of the Sault Sainte-Marie as it flows from Gitcheegumee or Lake Superior as the British had renamed it. It was an unbroken series of falls and rapids. By the end of the day Charbonneau realized why they had waited for the snow. Little Beaver suggested, "Beaver here like crazy. We should set few traps each evening and empty in morning. Short time each day, when we return, we full of beaver." Charbonneau agreed and even he became impressed by the number of beaver they could have for the investment of very few hours a day.

The Missouri continued south and in two weeks it became navigable again. They soon came to a three-pronged fork and Big Beaver said, "Take last fork and go west to the great portage." They followed this fork which turned west into the high country. Soon they were on the top of the world. Even Jean-Baptiste Charbonneau, who never showed great emotion, was overwhelmed by the view as they stood on a clear sunny day on the great continental divide, looking over endless mountains in all direction. In spite of a stiff westerly breeze pushing occasional clouds of biting snow, the view was spectacular, "Dear God almighty, this is the true frontier of the world!"

After a short while Little Beaver interrupted, "Better go and get down some, we turn to ice up here at night." They loaded and began their western descent. Two days later they saw civilization. Big Beaver told them, "Nez Perce, name from French missionary because many have ring in nose. Very big tribe, whole area of this side of mountains. Friendly too" Then looking up and grinning, "Sometimes."

The Nez Perce village was very similar to the Flathead camp; the people resembled the Flathead as well.

The primary difference was the number of horses. At least forty stood in a small area on the western border of the camp. They seemed to know the Beaver brothers and were welcomed to stay. That evening they talked with the chief and a few others, the Nez Perce language was similar to the Flathead, and by the end of the evening young Pierre Drouillard was beginning to use it effectively.

The chief was very talkative, "We do not see the French but for one or two missionaries, and the Blackfoot killed and ate them. Many years ago the White man of Spain came with the horses, but they have been gone for many years. They came from the sea through the great river and sometimes as far as the Snake."

Charbonneau jumped at this and asked Drouillard to ask more about the sea. The old man continued, "Some days from here," pointing west, "is the river we call Snake. It runs to the Great River which has no other name but runs to the sea."

Charbonneau said quickly, "Ask how many days to the sea."

Drouillard did and the chief responded, "Many days on horse to Snake, faster with dogs in winter. Two weeks on snake, three or four on big river."

Then Charbonneau asked, "Can you show us the way to the Snake?"

"You seem an honorable man; I will send a brave with you."

At this point dancing began and the chief offered women to the men. The Beaver brothers were gone in a flash, but Charbonneau thanked the chief and declined. The boys knew that Charbonneau never went with the Indian women and later he told them, "I think you two have had education enough for now." They went to their tent. The usually calm Charbonneau could scarcely sleep with excitement. Perhaps his goal was in sight.

The next morning they left with a new man, Wild Turkey, an affable sort, younger than the Beaver brothers. They made their descent rapidly through many passes. Charbonneau was constantly checking his compass and making notes and maps. Two weeks later, they arrived at a river. Wild Turkey told him, "This Snake, from here north and west to Great River, some portage, not too bad. Great River very big. Then out to sea." Charbonneau worked on his maps by the fire light throughout the night. In the morning he announced, "If we are to make our return on time, I fear we must turn back today."

He continued to check his maps on the return trip; soon they were back at the Nez Perce village. He profusely thanked the chief and presented him with some items he brought for trade. In turn the chief gave him a few pieces of local jewelry. They departed in the morning. They crossed the divide and continued down. When they reached the Missouri Charbonneau said, "We should restart our beaver trapping, and we will be fully loaded when we reach camp." A week later, they were indeed full. Charbonneau declared, "Jacques* and I will stay and organize the pelts. You four can go and forage for something good to eat this week."

Jacques* and Charbonneau started the tedious job of organizing and packing the pelts for transport. Suddenly there was a commotion in the woods. A blood-covered man stumbled into the clearing. Speaking French with a British accent he said weakly, "Please…"

Jacques* rushed to him and in an instant the man had Jacques* with a knife to his throat and a second man held a rifle on Charbonneau. "Everyone be calm, all we want is these here pelts. Make a move and the boy is dead."

Jacques* was petrified. They told Charbonneau to drop his knife which he did. But he went straight to the man with the gun and started to protest. The man hit him with the rifle butt and threw him to the ground. Charbonneau began to stand, apparently dazed. Then in an instant that Jacques* could not comprehend even after the fact, the man with the gun fell to the ground. Jacques* felt the grip on his arm loosen, and the man behind him fell as well.

When he could look about, Jacques* realized that while on the ground, Charbonneau had drawn a knife from his boot and thrown it into the chest of the man with the rifle. In the same motion, he had taken a knife from around his back and slit the throat of Jacques*'s captor. All of this had occurred before anyone could react in the slightest. This calm man who said a prayer each morning had killed these two men in less than a second.

Jacques* was suddenly taken with nausea and vomited on the ground. Charbonneau came over and said. "Get over it; we need to dispose of these two. First see what they are carrying." Jacques* hesitated and Charbonneau said, "The law of the frontier: If you betray the honor of voyageurs, you forfeit all you have." He searched the men and removed everything of value and then threw the bodies into the nearby ravine. Without hesitation he went back to the task of sorting the pelts.

That evening Jacques* asked him, "Can you show me how to do that?" Charbonneau laughed, "The task is simple, it is the determination that is difficult." Each subsequent evening for many nights, Charbonneau instructed the boys in frontier combat.

A week later they came to the Flathead camp. Henri-Pierre and Jacques* were greeted enthusiastically by Quiet Stream and Sunflower. They even had a friend for Drouillard, Quiet Stream's sister, called Assounderchris, which meant Sleeping Star in Flathead. That night they spent as much time talking as loving. When they returned two days later to the voyageur camp Jacques* asked the men about Indian women.

Thundercloud had the most opinion, "Indian women are more independent than French. They have a great say in the decisions of the tribe. They may stay or leave at their will and have any man they wish. If the chief dies without a son, the chiefdom passes through the line of the mother. Indian women are a force to contend with. Your problem is you have been trapped by Indian castoreum" Two days later they returned to the Flathead camp. The three young women were not there. Little Beaver told them, "They had to go take care of some business for the tribe."

They broke camp in the morning and began to backtrack through the tribes they had visited on the approach. Each had many furs to trade for the items Charbonneau had brought. When they reached the lower Missouri, they had as many furs as they could carry. Portage would be very difficult due to the enormous weight particularly the large canoes which held enormous quantities. Charbonneau pointed out that they could have never trapped this quantity of fur themselves. "Trade is always superior to trapping." As Charbonneau had hoped, this had been a very profitable voyage.

As they made ready to leave the frontier, Charbonneau carefully stored his notes and maps which would bring him back to his ultimate goal. He did not realize that events far away and outside of his control would prevent him from ever seeing the sea.

Chapter 13

Détroit - June 1762:

Almost one year from their first arrival, the men reached Cadillac's docks. Charbonneau was first to step ashore, "I am going to speak with Rivard. The rest of you stay with the furs." He returned an hour later with Pierre* Saint-Aubin. "Monsieur Saint-Aubin has invited us to his home. In spite of the English guard at the dock, I want one man to guard the furs, Jacob*, I fear it must be you." True to his form, Jacob* Thomas agreed without complaint. The rest of the group disembarked and loaded into Saint-Aubin's wagon. Saint-Aubin asked Charbonneau, "Do you have any French coins?"

"Yes, several."

"Give one to the guard." Charbonneau complied and they joined the others and departed. Saint-Aubin explained, "Another British custom, but worth the price. French money is still used in Détroit, but I hear it is being replaced with English coin in the east. It is best to spend it now while we still can"

The city in the wilderness had not changed during the winter. Pierre* Saint-Aubin's farm was as picturesque as ever. Madame Saint-Aubin welcomed the men and Charbonneau indicated they would camp in back. Soon Henri-Pierre's father, Toussaint who was also the son of Joseph, appeared. He warmly welcomed his family members and Jacques* Allard who realized that this was now his family as well. Toussaint told them, "I have been helping with the planting as well as 'other things'."

Dinner was extraordinary, especially for men who had been almost a year in the wild. After dinner the men retired to smoke, drink and talk. Saint-Aubin began, "There will be some small fur market in Détroit this year, but the main market will be Montréal as it is accessible to both the French and British colonists. I suspect that is where you will find the best price. The English are in charge, but the bankers have always been Scotsmen so I would expect little change."

Charbonneau replied, "Baptiste Rivard told me the same. Who wants to continue with me?"

Jean Drouillard said, "Pierre and I will want to remain home."

Joseph spoke privately with the boys and announced, "We are in. The boys want to see the fur market."

The downstream ride was quick and easy with the exception of the portage at Niagara. The weight of the furs and the steep long grades were arduous even with their newly acquired strength. Charbonneau said, "I have always taken comfort in the fact that we don't often bring furs uphill." They had made a brief stop at Pontiac's camp but the chief was up north maintaining his allegiances with other tribes. After the portage at Lachine, they reached Montréal.

Montréal - June 30, 1762:

As Détroit had changed little, Montréal had grown. The British presence was marked and English traders filled the streets. The British government had made this, rather than Québec, their primary post in Canada due to its access to the Hudson River Valley and the ports of New England. The fur market had been in progress since May when the traders returned from the more proximate frontiers, but now that the traders were arriving from great distances interest was greater.

The French system had required licenses which included a relationship with a banker and fur merchant. Things were simple but not competitive. Now the English had less control and the merchants, bankers and traders were free to do as they wished. Charbonneau was well known and he was approached by several merchants and all three bankers during his first hour on land. His collection of furs was the best of the year so competition was fierce. He made an agreement with a banker named Macintosh who had dealt with the French traders in the past. Macintosh would in turn sell the furs to the merchants at auction.

They moved the furs to the town square for inspection and sale. Jacques* and Henri-Pierre had seen the fur market in Québec, but in those war years it was small and reserved, and most deals had been sealed ahead of time. This was entirely different; pandemonium reigned. Men were everywhere, some in frontier dress and others in elegant city clothes. Everyone was shouting: some in English, some in French. When word arrived of Charbonneau all attention came to them.

There was great interest in the quality and variability of his wares. Men who had spent their entire life in the fur industry had never seen beaver pelts as large and luxurious as those trapped by Jacques* and Henri-Pierre beyond the great falls. At the end of the day, all sales had been completed. Charbonneau settled with Macintosh and took his men to *Les Coureurs de Bois*. The old tavern had not changed. Even with some English presence, it remained a true shelter for voyageurs or more accurately, the outside world remained a true shelter *from* voyageurs. The place reeked of smoke, sweat and beer. The floor was covered with blood and tobacco spit. To the casual observer, this would seem to be the last place to display money, but for a man like Charbonneau, nowhere was safer.

He brought out the treasure and gave each man his share. "This is English money; I am told it has more value now than French." Jacques* and Henri-Pierre had never seen so much money. After paying for a few rounds, Charbonneau arose, "I am off to see my family. I plan to be in Détroit by September; if any of you wish to join me, leave word with Rivard." And he was gone.

As the boys and Joseph left, Joseph said, "Give me your money." Both boys handed it over, "I may not be a Scotsman, but I think I will be a better steward of this than you will." He gave them each a few coins and they walked toward the river. Jacques* stopped and began to stare downstream. Joseph broke his concentration. "We will go with you."

They made their way back to the canoes, took theirs and headed northeast. Two days later they saw the church steeple of the small village of Sorel, then the three narrow islands known as *l'Ile Dupas*. They landed on the western bank of the center island where a small farm was being energetically worked by a family. They beached the canoe and walked up to the house. A lady on the porch saw them and came down. She suddenly called, "Joseph!" and came running. When she came closer, she stopped and stared at Jacques*. Jacques* Allard had grown four inches over the past year. He had a full beard and long black hair tied in back. His waist was thinner and his shoulders greatly larger. The lady threw her arms around his neck. "My God! Had it not been for your eyes, I might not have recognized you. And Henri-Pierre, how wonderful you look as well. Joseph, you took my boy and brought back these two men."

By now the rest of the family was arriving at the scene of the commotion. Jacques*'s youngest sister Marie-Anne, age eight, began to giggle uncontrollably at his beard. His brothers all shook his hand and his oldest sister, Marie-Angélique, came carrying a small child. His mother, also Marie-Angélique*, said, "And this is your new half-sister, Charlotte Jacques." His stepfather finally came up to the crowd and exclaimed, "Dear God, boy! Had I known you would grow like, this I would have insisted you stay on the farm!" He declared work over for the day and they retreated to the large front porch for refreshments.

After the death of Jacques*'s father, Pierre* Allard, his mother had married Louis Jacques, who had been a close friend of Pierre*. After the fall of Québec the family moved to this remote island. At that time Jacques* had chosen to go with Charbonneau. At dinner, the boys gave a detailed description of their adventure with the exception of Sunflower and Quiet Stream.

Louis Jacques reported, "We have had no trouble with the British and the farm is going nicely. There is abundant land here, and you are all welcome to stay for as long as you wish, forever if you like."

Jacques* said pleasantly, "Thank you sir, but we must return to Détroit tomorrow."

Marie-Angélique added, "You can stay in the boys' room; it's quite large."

Jacques* returned, "No ma'am, we will camp in back."

That night by a fire in the back of the farm, Joseph said, "We can stay longer, you know."

Jacques* replied, "No, I can see I no longer belong here. The frontier is now my home." In the morning after a tearful farewell, the canoe headed upstream.

Chapter 14

<u>The Missouri River Valley - November 1762:</u>

Jacques* sat baking in the sun on a rock ledge 200 feet above the river. Quiet Stream stood looking over the edge; the sun glistened on her bronze naked body still wet with sweat from love making. As Jacques* went to stand, Quiet Stream dove over the edge. He screamed and rushed to see her disappear into the river far below. Just then he heard Henri-Pierre, "Jacques*!" He opened his eyes to see his friend looking over him. "Charbonneau is already up and almost ready to go. You had better get going now!"

As he stood and shook his head, Jacques* said, "I had the strangest dream. I think it's the tobacco from the Sioux."

"Well, dream or no, Charbonneau is ready to go."

This year's voyage to the frontier had started late, and progress had been slow. The group was smaller this year and they had not met with enthusiasm from the Indians. Most of the Indians east of the Mississippi had met with English traders the year before and not been treated fairly. They had been civil with Charbonneau due to his past performance, but it was clear that they were changing their attitude toward white man in general. Even the Yankton Sioux were reserved although Falling Rock had again agreed to guide them.

Joseph had elected to stay with Toussaint in Détroit. Pierre Drouillard had come without his father. Jacob* Thomas was along with Pierre Tremblay and Jean-Baptiste* Laforest. Thundercloud and another Indian made

112

a total of ten counting Falling Rock. Both André* Peltier and Louis-Michel Tremblay had stayed in Détroit as well. Charbonneau had told them he hoped to make it as far as the great falls, but to his disappointment they would not have time to go further. The second night after the westward bend of the Missouri, they had company.

A group of six traders and two Indians landed shortly after they had made camp. They were English and knew little French. Fortunately the men had begun to master the new language so communication was no problem. It also gave the French the advantage of making comments only understood by their group. Charbonneau subtly told Thundercloud to gather all the Indians at a second fire so he could get more information from the English.

Charbonneau generally discouraged alcohol at camp, but he made an exception and offered his guests a drink. After dinner and a few drinks they began to talk. The leader, Ben Johnson, was the most talkative, "My people are from New York. We couldn't afford enough land to live on so we moved to the Ohio. We got run out first by the French, then the Indians and now that we won the war, the government says we can't stay. So two years ago we took to trading. Did pretty good the first year in the Ohio, but now the Indians there are as mad as the colonists are at the government. So last year we went up by Lake Erie, but there's lots of competition there. So we hear that there's good trade up here. Good furs and the Indians aren't so crafty. We got some real junk to trade, but they say they don't know no better."

Trying to learn more, Charbonneau said casually, "I find the Indians know value and have long memories."

"I'll tell you where the value is, Frenchy, the land. The sooner we move them out the better. We can all go back to farmin' like the Lord intended."

Unable to control himself, Henri-Pierre said, "Maybe the Lord wanted them to have the land." Charbonneau gave him a look to remind him he had been told not to speak.

Unaware of Henri-Pierre's lineage, Johnson replied, "Hell sonny, these savages don't know what land is for. Anyway, if we give 'em something of value, we try to have it kinda disappear when we leave in the morning." Then standing, "Thanks for the drink, Captain, I think I'm goin' to bed."

In the morning Charbonneau's crew was up and ready to leave while the English slept off the night before. Charbonneau instructed everyone to make certain nothing was "missing" and they left the camp to the English. That night they compared notes with the Indians. Thundercloud reported, "One guide is Iroquois and the other Sioux. They are treated badly. I believe this will be a bad trip for all of them. If men like this continue to trade, I fear for the future. Trade is based on trust and these men quench trust as a driving rain quenches fire."

Great Falls - January 1763:

Winter camp was set near the camp of the previous year, but this time in immense depths of snow. The men began to hunt the elk when one morning the Beaver brothers appeared on dog sleds. "We think we find Charbonneau here. Want to know if boys want to come get

114

beaver." Charbonneau had thought they might do as well with the elk, but the pelts of last year were excellent, and he could see that his three boys were anxious to say the least.

Charbonneau proposed, "Meet back here in one month." The three boys were off in a flash. As they had hoped the first stop was the Flathead village. To their immense joy they found their three lost loves. The following morning, the brothers awoke the couples and proposed, "Each boy take squaw and work traps. We manage."

The group left that day and set a camp with four teepees. One for each couple and one for the brothers. Initially the brothers gave advice and help, particularly to Pierre Drouillard who had little trapping experience. As the weeks wore on, the couples became more independent and the brothers got more rest. By the end of the third week Jacques* realized that he was experiencing why Champlain's original plan for the colony had failed. In the wilderness, it was easier to be Indian than French.

As promised they returned to Charbonneau's camp at the end of February accompanied by the brothers and the three young women and a large cache of the finest beaver pelts. Seeing them approach, Pierre Tremblay exclaimed, "Looks like we got eight Flatheads now."

The boys had taken to Indian dress and with their dark tans were only distinguishable by their beards. They presented Charbonneau with their pelts. He was obviously impressed. "If you can produce merchandise such as this, you can dress as British soldiers." Dinner was full of tales of the wilderness. At the end of the evening Charbonneau announced, "I hope to make an early return this year. We will break camp tomorrow."

At dawn, the three young men said farewell to their Flathead friends and lovers and disappeared toward civilization. At the next camp Charbonneau met with the three young men. "All young men crave the Indian way when they begin in the frontier. I was no different. However we were visited by a small Sioux party in your absence and received news of further difficulties between the tribes and the English. Apparently things are deteriorating back home. I want to return as soon as possible and would like you all to return to your French dress for now. Henri-Pierre, I know you are *métis*, but for now, this is what I ask."

The Mission of Saint-Louis - March 1763:

The post had doubled in size since the men passed it in the autumn. They met some friends of Charbonneau at the tavern, "Old Louis XV has settled with the English. He signed the Treaty of Paris this winter. All land east of the Mississippi is now officially British. This side called Louisiana remains French, but there is some talk of Spain taking it. For now people are free to travel to the Cajun country at *la Nouvelle Orléans*. People are passing through going south every day. A man named Pierre Laclède has come with a group of men and is starting a proper post here and plans to have a village. At this rate it will soon be as large as Détroit."

Charbonneau interrupted, "How are things in Détroit?"

"Not good. A new commander named Gladwin has arrived and Campbell is now second in command. The new man has let the traders have their way with the Indians and has limited the amount of gun powder the Indians can have. Pontiac and his boys are real angry. Doesn't look good to me, so we're off south to be Cajun, at least for now. You might want to think about it yourself, Jean-Baptiste." The rest of the evening was filled with tales of British indiscretions and Indian unrest. They left at dawn.

Western Lake Erie - April 1763:

Just before entering the lake, the men came to Pontiac's camp. Where it usually held one or two hundred Indians, tonight there were at least two thousand. The usual subdued fires blazed wildly. Charbonneau and Jacob* Thomas went with their Chippewa guide to see what was happening. When they returned, "We have been told there is a big meeting tonight, but because we are trusted we can stay. Try to keep a low profile and stay back from the center of the meeting."

Food was served and as the sun set, the chief appeared. Tonight Pontiac was not dressed in French clothing. He was naked to the waist and painted. He stood on a large rock to be seen and heard by all. He spoke in his usual orator's voice but tonight in Algonquin. "Last night I was visited by the Great Spirit who spoke to me":

"I am the maker of the heaven and the earth, the trees, lakes, rivers and all things else. I am the maker of mankind; and because I love you, you must do my will. The land on which you live I have made for you and not for others. Why

do you suffer the white men to dwell among you? My children, you have forgotten the customs and traditions of your forefathers. Why do you not clothe yourselves in skins, as they did, and use the bows and arrows, and the stone pointed lances which they used? You have bought guns, knives, kettles and blankets from the white men, until you can no longer do without them; and, what is worse, you have drunk the poison fire-water, which turns you into fools. Fling all these things away; live as your wise forefathers lived before you. And as for these English - these dogs dressed in red, who have come to rob you and your hunting-grounds, and drive away the game - you must lift the hatchet against them. Wipe them from the face of the earth, and you will win my favor back again, and once more be happy and prosperous. The children of your great father, the King of France, are not like the English. Never forget that they are your brethren. They are very dear to me, for they love the red men, and understand the true mode of worshiping me. "

Author's note. This is taken from <u>The Conspiracy of Pontiac</u> by Frances Parkman and meant to represent the actual speech by Pontiac to his people.

Pontiac then broke into an eloquent tirade against the evils of the English and plans to vanquish them. Charbonneau carefully passed the word to his men to make a slow move to the canoes. Fortunately, the moon was full and visibility was adequate to launch the canoes and proceed toward Détroit. The sight of the flames and the sound of the meeting were apparent all the way to the mouth of the Détroit River.

<u>Détroit - the next morning:</u>

The men landed at Cadillac's docks at dawn. Leaving the rest of the men to watch the canoes, Charbonneau took Jacques* and went directly into the stockade, then straight to Rivard's post. "We are likely to get the best information there."

Jean-Baptiste Rivard was just opening his door when they arrived. He bid them enter. The shop had doubled in size, the shelves were heavy with trade merchandise: pewter plates, burning (magnifying) glasses, knives, blankets, candles, traps and Dutch ovens as well as rifles, powder, and lead. "It's been a busy season. British traders are all wanting this to trade in the north and west. Some of the local Indians are buying it outright. They think they get better treatment that way."

Checking to make sure they were alone, Charbonneau launched into an abbreviated description of the meeting at Pontiac's camp. Rivard whistled low, "Doesn't surprise me. The new commander, Major Henry Gladwin, came to supersede Campbell in the fall. Not fair like Campbell, Treats the Indians poorly and lets the traders cheat 'em. Campbell's the only soldier doesn't treat 'em like dirt. Something is bound to happen."

The door swung open and Pierre* Saint-Aubin entered with his brother Charles*. They joined the conversation and after a brief report, Saint-Aubin said, "Sounds bad, we better pass the word."

Charbonneau replied, "I would like to leave and make for Montréal as quickly as possible."

As they went to leave, Rivard called to Charbonneau, "There will be a fur market here this month. If you want, I can take some of your common furs and sell them for you here. Make your trip faster." Charbonneau indicated that may be a possibility and they were gone just as two English traders entered.

The taller of the two asked Rivard, "What's up with the Indians lately? Actin' right weird."

Rivard shrugged polishing his counter, "You know, Indians get funny in the spring."

At the docks Charbonneau announced, "Jacob* and I will take the Indians to Montréal. Jacques*, Henri-Pierre, and Drouillard, you boys can take half of what you and your women caught and sell it at the market for your share. It will be good learning. Maybe Monsieur Saint-Aubin will give you some advice. The rest of you take what's in these two canoes to Rivard and he'll move them for you for your share. We're off for Montréal. Anyone interested in next September, leave word with Rivard." By noon, all the furs had been transferred to Rivard's post and Pierre* Saint-Aubin suggested they go south in his cart.

They came to Windmill Pointe first, and Saint-Aubin told Jean-Baptiste* Laforest and Pierre Tremblay. "Tell your families to have a representative at Meloche's mill at dusk." As they continued north he told Jacques* and Henri-Pierre, "Rivard has bought land on the north side of the Milk River, Joseph and Toussaint's family are working it and living there." They crossed the old bridge where the road crossed the stream and they saw a small house on a piece of newly cleared land that followed the north shore of the Milk River. "Tell them about the meeting at Meloche's and have them spread the word to the other Milk River *habitants*." Then to Pierre Drouillard, "You go with them and find your father when you cross to Assumption tonight."

They were enthusiastically greeted by Henri-Pierre's mother and younger sister. Soon Toussaint and Joseph appeared from the fields. The boys related the story of Pontiac, and the foursome plus Drouillard crossed the river to the farm of Julian* Fréton. They informed him of the meeting and told him to spread the word to the settlement. They then returned home.

Jean-Baptiste Rivard had recently purchased this land but continued to live on his farm closer to town. He had an arrangement with Joseph and Toussaint to farm the land and split the profits. The two men had built a small house and started a respectable farm. They broke early for supper so the family could hear about the voyage before they left to cross the Détroit River. As Joseph had been on the trip the preceding year they even included a brief mention of the three Indian women. Since both Toussaint and his wife Monique were products of *métis* mothers, they had more understanding of the phenomenon, although the boys did portray it in a more platonic manner than the facts would have it.

When they discussed the encounter with Pontiac, Joseph responded thoughtfully, "My grandfather Henri said this day would come. I fear equally for both our people, Indian and French. I hope there is someone at the meeting as wise as old Henri."

After dinner the four men launched a canoe and proceeded south and east around the upstream tip of *Belle Ile*. Across from the tip of the island on the south shore called Assumption sat the mill of old Pierre* Meloche. After the recent death of old Pierre*, his son, another Jean-Baptiste, had taken charge. Always referred to as simply "Baptiste" he had a good relationship with Pontiac. Although the mill was in Assumption, Baptiste Meloche lived on the north shore directly across from *Belle Ile*.

There was a considerable crowd. Beside the men from the north end, Jacques* saw a number of others he had seen before, men with names like Dequindre, Beaubien, Lesperance, Campau, and Marsac as well as several he had never seen. Baptiste Rivard brought the group to order, "As you have heard, last evening Chief Pontiac had a large gathering at the Indian Camp on Lake Erie. Jean-Baptiste Charbonneau and his men attended. Unfortunately, Charbonneau and Jacob* Thomas have left for Montréal so we should hear from one of the others who were there."

Suddenly Jacques* realized that only the four 'boys' were present at both the Indian meeting and the meeting tonight. To Jacques*'s horror Rivard continued, "Young Allard, perhaps you could tell us what you saw." As Jacques* rose, terrified, to his feet, Henri-Pierre whispered to him, "Pretend they're a wolf."

Jacques* laughed and gained a small amount of confidence. "It was a large gathering, Pontiac appeared in war dress. The fires burned brighter than is common as Pontiac told of a vision from God. He was told to take back the Indian ways and destroy the English." After a wave of comments Jacques* continued, "He also said he was told he was not to hurt his French brothers." Then contemplating some, "What concerned me the most is it was the first time I have seen fear in the eyes of Monsieur Charbonneau."

There was much commotion and many men had opinions to give. Rivard tried to maintain control, "Please speak in turn. I recognize Jacques Campau." Jacques held a large farm south of the Saint-Aubin farms. He also controlled much of the Campau business and wealth. "I fear we must face the fact that the British are firmly in control, and our only hope is with them, not against them. I fear Pontiac is on a suicide mission."

Rivard shouted above the commotion, "It seems Baptiste Meloche is not in agreement. Baptiste."

Meloche was a rough and impulsive man, but a man of great influence especially on the Assumption side of the River, "Look about you in the streets. The Indians are the dominant presence in our community. Pontiac has forged allegiances from the Atlantic to the Mississippi. There is word of a Cherokee revolt in the Carolinas. I believe if we support the Indian, we may have our country back."

Rivard again shouted, "Please, some order. Perhaps Pierre* Saint-Aubin has a different thought."

Saint-Aubin stepped forward, "My father felt that cooperation was the key to our success. It is clear that alliance with either side on the part of the French has its problems. I believe we should keep a low profile and try to remain as neutral as possible. I too see the plight of the Indian, but I believe they will fail."

The next hour consisted of differing opinions and disagreements with a few fist fights for good measure.

Rivard stood on a counter and shouted, "Messieurs, Please! I believe we have someone who may share some wisdom. Joseph, would you give us your thoughts?"

The old Indian stood. At eighty-seven, he was still strong and alert. Although he was the last full-blooded Algonquin of his line, he had lived his entire life among the French. Although recognizable as native, his dress, speech and demeanor gave him a European air. The room fell silent for the first time.

He gazed silently over the crowd, then spoke, "I have been to the far north and the far south. My son, Toussaint, has been to the far east and far west. I came with Cadillac the day he founded this city in the wilderness. I see the way of my ancestors cannot survive in this modern world, but I fear Chief Pontiac will be more successful than you think. However he will not prevail. I further fear if the French stand firmly with Pontiac they too will be destroyed. If they stand firmly with the British, they will no longer be trusted. The best course of the French is to be visibly neutral. As my old friend Jean* Saint-Aubin said, 'Europe cannot forever rule this land'. After this affair with Pontiac, the colonists French and English will make it their own." That evening Pierre Drouillard left for his father's farm in Assumption, and Jacques* and Henri-Pierre went home with Joseph and Toussaint. Joseph had taken to sleeping at a small camp in the back rather than the house. In the morning he was gone.

During the next two weeks the city was abuzz with rumors and whispering. Rivard noted that the Indians had purchased every metal file in his store and the two blacksmiths had been busy filing down rifle barrels for many of their Indian customers. Clearly something was about to happen.

PONTIAC'S WAR 1763

Chapter 15

<u>Fort Détroit - May 7, 1763:</u>

Major Henry Gladwin looked out his window at troops training in the square, "The young Indian whore that has been visiting my bed confides in me that Indians are cutting down their rifle barrels to hide under their robes and ambush the fort. Pontiac has moved his camp to Assumption. I believe today is the day." Sneering he continued, "Now I know Indians are good for at least two things, sexual favors and betrayal of their people."

Captain Donald Campbell winced, he had spent the past two years making peace with the natives and the *habitants*, now Gladwin in his arrogance had destroyed it all and he feared it would end badly. He had already debated this point at length with his commanding officer to no avail. He merely replied, "Yes sir."

A soldier entered and saluted the officers, "Major Gladwin, sir, Chief Pontiac is outside the walls with many braves. He is requesting a meeting with you."

Gladwin replied, "Very well, this is it."

The three men exited and Gladwin ordered the Lieutenant to call his troops to order in the yard. Then he asked the soldiers to let the Indians enter. Pontiac and nearly three hundred of his men entered. When they assembled, it was clear to Pontiac he had been expected. He asked Gladwin why the square was filled with armed soldiers. Gladwin sneered and said, "Just training." Pontiac surveyed the group and realized that his ruse had failed and turned and ordered his men to exit.

He said to Gladwin, "I will return."

The next day Pontiac moved his camp to the land by the farm of Baptiste Meloche on the north side of the river across from *Belle Ile* and close to the fort. The next day he and his braves assembled outside the fort. Donald Campbell was sent to speak with them, "Captain Campbell, we demand entry to the fort."

Campbell replied as politely as possible, "I regret I have been ordered to prohibit your entry."

Pontiac glared at Campbell, "Monsieur, you have been an honorable man; it is unfortunate that it is only you. This will end badly." He threw a spear into the ground and his men left quickly with cries that were heard through the village.

In the morning Campbell appeared at Gladwin's office, "Major, I regret to report that during the night, Pontiac's men raided the Turnbull farm next to the fort, killed the family and burned the buildings. They then went to *Belle Ile* where they killed and scalped three members of the James Fisher family."

Gladwin sneered, "If it's a fight he wants, it is a fight he shall get."

Campbell interrupted, "I'm afraid there is more, Major. We are surrounded by at least 1000 Indians who are denying entry or exit from the fort. I fear we are besieged."

Gladwin threw a glass he was holding against the wall, "I'll show him a siege. What do the *habitants* make of this foolishness?"

"They seem to be quite silent on the subject, Major, going about business as usual."

"We'll see about this. Get me one of their leaders."

Campbell soon returned with Jean-Baptiste Rivard. Gladwin stood, "Monsieur, these savages seem to think they can hold the British Empire hostage. I want you to go out and set up a meeting with this Pontiac for us. I know you are all tacitly friends and he will not harm you." Rivard merely nodded and left with Campbell. Gladwin went to the rampart and watched as Rivard walked out and engaged one of the Indians, after a great deal of hand waving; they mounted a horse and rode off.

A few hours later, Rivard returned to Campbell's office, "Chief Pontiac says he will meet with Captain Campbell and another man at the farm of Antoine Cuillerier tomorrow morning to discuss a truce."

Gladwin grunted, "Captain, take Lieutenant McDougall and Monsieur Rivard tomorrow and see what the savage wants."

That afternoon Rivard returned alone on horseback. Reporting to Gladwin, "Pontiac says that his terms are for the British to leave Indian land forever."

Gladwin sputtered, "Why the impertinence. Where are the two others, Campbell and McDougall?"

"Pontiac said they will be returned when his terms are met."

"His terms? His terms! I'll show that dishonorable savage terms. Tell me, Rivard, what do you think these savages want?"

Rivard hesitated, "If I may be so bold, sir, they want what the Indian has always wanted, to be left alone. If not, then treated as everyone else."

Gladwin threw another glass. "That will be all, Monsieur Rivard."

The siege of Détroit set in, no one was allowed in or out of the fort without permission of Pontiac. The French went about the business of farming and did without the materials generally available through the fort and trading post, but their level of self-sufficiency was adequate and food was no problem. Inside the fort was another matter. The British soldiers, their families and British traders and farmers had all taken refuge inside the walls after the massacre of two of the most prominent families of British soldiers, Fisher and Turnbull. The food stores ran low and only small amounts made it in from outside. Two parties of soldiers had made it out but neither returned.

Pontiac had settled behind the farm of Baptiste Meloche, and the officers Campbell and McDougall had been moved to the Chippewa camp. News occasionally came from the outside, and from the British position it was all bad. Fort Sandusky on Lake Erie had fallen to Indians the third week in May. Fort St. Joseph near Lake Michigan fell May 25, Fort Miami on May 27, and Fort Ouiatenon near Saint-Louis on June 1. But the worst was yet to come.

Fort Michilimackinac - June 4, 1763:

Cadillac's old northern outpost was now located on the southern side of the straits at the tip of the Michigauma Peninsula. The village had grown to the size of Détroit. The

130

British soldiers at the fort had heard of uprisings to the south, but their relations with the Indian remained good. The garrison at the fort held 35 British soldiers and a few family members under Captain Etherington. There were also several English traders who had come up through Détroit the year before to trade this area.

The local Indians consisted of an Ojibway tribe of over one hundred and a second camp of Ottawa. There was a trading post run by Alexander Henry. The old Jesuit Mission of Saint-Ignace remained on the north side of the strait. Today was the birthday of King George III so Etherington had deemed it a holiday and the fort was quite relaxed. The Ojibway Chief, Wawatam, had come with many of his braves. They went to Henry's post and bought knives and other items and returned to the meadow outside the fort and began a game of lacrosse.

It was a wonderful warm June day. Soldiers and civilians alike sat and picnicked on the grounds while watching the game. One of the Indians made a wild shot which went over the walls into the fort. As the crowd laughed the teams went to retrieve their ball. What happened next was too fast to comprehend. The Indians appeared from all quarters armed with guns, knives and hatchets. Before mid afternoon they had killed and scalped every British soul, soldier, civilian or trader except Alexander Henry who they kept captive in his post. They harmed none of the French, but insisted that they leave the fort as the gates closed with the Indians well in control.

General Jeffery Amherst was having a bad day. In fact he was having a bad year. The conqueror of Canada, he had assured the British Government that the Indians posed no threat to the colonies. With the dreadful massacre at Michilimackinac and the recent fall of forts at Venango in the Ohio Valley and Presque Isle as well as the abandoning of all British outposts in the area, the besieged fort at Détroit held the only remaining British soldiers in the western great lakes region.

As he paced the floor, Colonel Henry Bouquet awaited orders. The general stopped and turned, "There is a small outbreak of smallpox at a small village near here. Send someone to obtain drainage. We shall plant it in the woolen blankets the savages so prize and give them as peace offerings." Bouquet was no saint, but he stared incredulously at the General. "This is not a suggestion, Bouquet. Do it!" The Colonel saluted and left.

As the door shut it again reopened with one of the General's aides. "Word from the Ohio Valley sir, Fort Pitt is attacked and under siege." General Jeffery Amherst sank into his chair wondering if there was a place for him to hide in this vast country.

Fort Détroit - July 4, 1763:

Besides food and other necessities, the fort was low on ammunition. Gladwin had learned that Jacques Baby had a small armament shop and a large supply of lead. He called a small party and instructed them. "You are to leave before dawn and get material for musket balls from this man. His farm is just to the south and if you are careful, you can do this undetected."

Soon after they were clear of the fort, they saw a lone Indian brave. The Lieutenant in charge told the men to stay down, but one of the men whose wife had recently died due to lack of supplies became enraged and grabbed the Indian and slit his throat. Before the others could stop him, he scalped the Indian. "Just what he deserves." he muttered. The others restrained him and made their way to the Baby farm and back to the fort having accomplished their mission.

The following night a man came calling at the gates. To their surprise it was the long-captive Lieutenant George McDougall. He was allowed entry and the men came rejoicing at his return. Their joy was ended by his story, "We have been held in the Chippewa camp since our capture. Apparently yesterday a group of soldiers killed and scalped a young Indian. Unfortunately he was the son of the Chippewa chief. The chief was enraged and came to get Campbell and myself. In the confusion, I was able to escape. I don't know what became of the Captain."

The answer came the next morning when the Chippewa dropped Campbell's body at the gates. When they retrieved him, they could see that they had cut out his heart. Gladwin only sneered, "It looks as though making nice with the savage was not helpful."

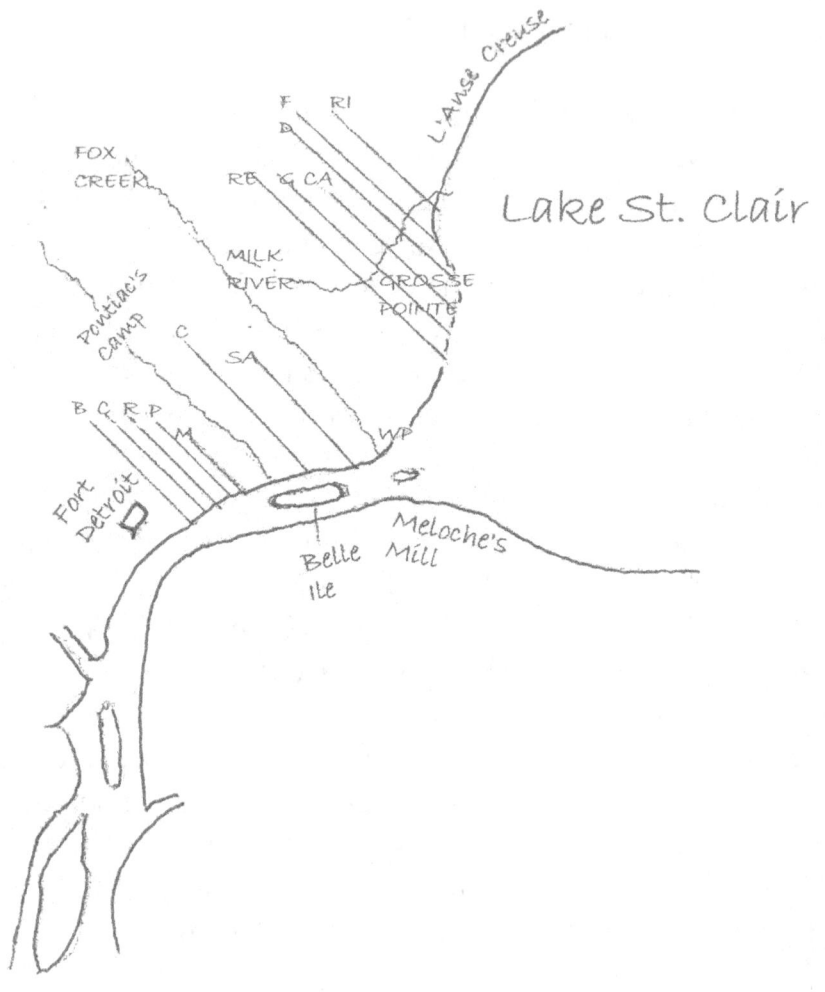

FARMS OF THE DÉTROIT RIVER REGION 1763

FARMS OF THE DÉTROIT RIVER REGION AT THE TIME OF PONTIAC'S SIEGE.
(Left to right)

B: Beaubien Farm.
Ch: Chene Farm.
R: Rivard Farm.
P: Parent Farm.
M: Meloche Farm.
C: Campau Farm.
SA: Saint-Aubin Farm.

WP: Windmill Pointe and farms of Laforest and Tremblay.
Re: Reaume Farm.
G: Greffard Farm.
C: Champagne Farm.
Y: Yax farm between D and C (not shown).
D: Duchesne Farm.
F: Fréton Farm.
Ri: Rivard farm worked by Jacques* Allard and Toussaint's Family.

Pontiac's camp shown on Parent Creek

Chapter 16

<u>Fort Détroit - July 28, 1763:</u>

The siege continued, but some Indians were growing weary. The Chippewa and Wyandotte camps had agreed upon a fragile truce with the British which allowed some travel in and out of the fort. Relations with Pontiac's Ottawa camp remained hostile. On the morning of the 28th a great cry came up from the sentry on the southeast turret. "Boats approaching!" Soon fourteen boats with almost three hundred British soldiers landed.

Gladwin met the officers at the gates. "Captain Dalyell and Major Robert Rogers reporting." The officers quickly adjourned to Gladwin's office. Dalyell was most talkative. "We have come from Niagara where there are frequent attacks, but the fort stands. Along Lake Erie, all forts, Sandusky, Presque Ile and others are abandoned and burned to the ground. We have been sent to help you defeat Pontiac."

Gladwin replied, "I welcome the support, but we have made recent truce with some tribes, perhaps the time is not right."

Dalyell objected, "Our orders are to take Pontiac and now. He is said to be camped above this Parent's Creek. We will stage a full assault in four days."

As they continued their discussion, a young French woman who was cleaning in the next room took her supplies and left quietly. Soon Jean-Baptiste Rivard saddled his horse and rode to the farm of Pierre* Saint Aubin and soon one of the Saint-Aubin sons arrived at the farm of Toussaint with the message, "Tonight at Meloche's mill."

The *habitants* had met periodically during the siege. The old mill in Assumption was convenient and out of sight of the British. Once the group was assembled, Rivard took the floor. "Troops have arrived from Niagara and plan an attack at Pontiac's camp in four days on the first of August. We should move all families in the area of Parent's Creek to other farms. This will include Campau, Saint-Aubin, Beaubien, Chene, Meloche and Parent. I suggest using the Milk River Settlement as a shelter as it will not involve crossing by the fort. The farms of Julian* Fréton and Toussaint de Baptiste will be most distant and safest. If asked we will say it is for a celebration of a French holiday, no one from the fort will know the difference."

The move involved twelve families and more than one hundred men, women and children. They met on the banks of the Milk River on July 31 and true to their story and in true French fashion had a grand picnic which lasted late into the night. In the morning, everyone remained except Jacques Campau who took his rifle and left saying, "I'll be at my farm. I'm not letting any of these damn rascals burn it."

Fort Détroit - August 3, 1763:

Before dawn the gates of the fort opened and two-hundred and eighty British soldiers made their way quietly north. When they arrived at the small bridge over Parent's Creek, Dalyell said, "The camp is across the bridge and up above the Meloche farm house." As the first men came across the bridge they were met with a sudden Indian whoop and waves of gun and hatchet-wielding Ottawa braves. More than twenty men were chopped and sent into the stream. As the Indians retreated, they chased them to the camp above the farmhouse.

There was no one at the camp and soon the British were again surrounded. The Ottawa had taken refuge in the house of Meloche and began picking off redcoats one by one. Major Rogers and his men made it to the farmhouse to the north. They believed all the farms were empty but when they entered this one, they were staring into the musket of Jacques Campau. "You boys can take shelter, but my family is under this trap door and if you make a move against them or me, you're dead." The battle raged with Campau holding his gun and never flinching even when an Indian musket ball slightly grazed his forehead.

Eventually Rogers realized the futility of the fight and called for a retreat to the fort. Fifty-nine British had been killed. The next day they emptied the bodies from the creek which ran red for an entire day. The creek once named for Joseph Parent, the first man in Détroit, would henceforth be known as "Bloody Run".

The siege continued with diminished fervor. Later in August, General Amherst was called back to England in disgrace and replaced by Major General Thomas Gage. On October 7, in an attempt to quell the uprisings, King George III signed the Royal Proclamation of 1763. This prohibited colonists from buying or selling land west of the Appalachian Mountains. On October 31 Pontiac appeared at the fort under a flag of truce, where he discussed terms of peace with Gladwin before he and many of his men headed back to Lake Erie with plans to head west. The city in the wilderness would return to normal, at least for a while.

The Milk River Settlement - November 1, 1763:

The harvest at Toussaint's farm was coming to an end. In spite of the siege, the French farms prospered under their tacit neutrality. Jacques* and Henri-Pierre had received news that due to the hostilities, Jean-Baptiste Charbonneau would not be passing through Détroit that year. The news had caused the young men to consider their options and an interesting one presented itself in the form of an unusual animal. Found along the rivers near Lake Saint-Clair, it was smaller than the beaver, without the flat tail, but its fur every bit as fine. Jean-Baptiste Rivard had told them that there would be a good market for their pelts in the spring.

Because Jacques* and Henri-Pierre had made a good profit from their furs the previous year, they decided to buy supplies and trap this creature with an unusual Chippewa name, and due to its smell was called "muskrat" by the English. They had further learned that an enormous colony of these creatures lived in the marshy waters at the north end of the lake. Jacques* contacted Jean-Baptiste* Laforest, Pierre Drouillard, and Jean* Renaud and put together his group. At the ripe old age of eighteen, Jacques* Allard had gone from boy to head trader.

Chapter 17

<u>Boston, Massachusetts - November 1763:</u>

Samuel Adams stood in front of thirty men, who met in the back of his tavern regularly. Many were members of the colonial legislature but all had one purpose in mind. "Gentlemen, it seems our majesty and his government continue their voyage to disaster. After letting that fool Amherst stir up the natives for no good reason, especially with the hideous tainted blanket idea, they are giving them back the very land we fought the French for. In spite of this, Pontiac has gone to the Illinois country to continue his mischief, and raids along the east coast seem to also continue. When the crown irritates the natives, they become irritated at the colonists as well. Our plans will be better served if the natives are with us rather than against us. I have just returned from Virginia where I met with our friend George Washington. As you know he has considerable military experience, most of it losing battles with the French and Indians."

After some laughter, he continued, "He believes we will need some Indian allies and certainly some Indian methods of war if we are to eventually make this country our own. I have asked Samuel Price here to meet with us. As some of you may know, he has worked many years as a trader in the frontier. He has contacts with French and Indian. I am asking him to take a small band as traders to the Détroit country and attempt to forge some alliances to help our cause." Then lifting his mug of beer, "To us gentlemen, may we live free or die."

SAINT CLAIR FLATS 1763

Chapter 18

The Saint Clair Flats - November 1763:

The four young men were in heaven. The trip to the flats had taken three days as they had stopped to explore along the way. In a hurry they could probably do it in one long day. They had moved their camp twice since arriving, trying to find the ideal location. The current camp was on an island with dry land and good tree cover. The Saint Clair River formed three channels emptying into Lake Saint Clair. The island was formed by the north and middle channels and the camp stood on the middle channel before it entered the lake.

Instead of the traditional wood voyageur shelter, they had used deer skins to build Indian style teepees. They had started with the metal traps purchased from Rivard and fish for bait, but after they caught several muskrat, they made a version of Beaver Brother's castoreum ointment that worked beyond their wildest dreams. Some mornings they had no empty traps. They decided to expand and made wooden traps such as they had seen in the Flathead country.

Not only did the new traps work, they even caught the occasional beaver that had escaped the early voyageurs who came around the time of Cadillac and had removed almost all of the flat-tailed beasts. Firewood was plentiful; dinner was always available from the lake. A hole in the ice right off the camp provided as many perch and pickerel in a matter of minutes as they could eat.

Studying their enlarging supply of pelts, Henri-Pierre remarked, "If the lake had remained open, we could take this home to store. As it is, it will only take us two days to return in the spring, a great improvement over the trip from Great Falls." They would finish their rounds including skinning by mid afternoon, so they built an *ah-key* rink to fill their spare time.

One afternoon in December as they had an intense game going, they were encountered by four Ojibway men of about the same age. They stopped the game and realized this was a friendly encounter. The Frenchmen invited the Indians to join them. All eight were skilled at the game and it continued into the twilight. When it became too dark to play, they invited the Indians to stay. They dined on fish from the camp and quail carried by the Ojibway. Then as they had done countless times in the frontier, they smoked and talked. The natives comprehended French but as the four French were very comfortable in Algonquin, it became the tongue of the evening.

The Indians were members of a small nomadic tribe wintering two islands to the south. "In the past we have traded with Détroit. This year it is uncertain due to the hostilities with Chief Pontiac. What is the thinking of the French in Détroit?"

Jacques* realized this was a tricky issue, "The French remain friendly with both the English and the Indian. However, the English now have a poor attitude toward the natives. In the past we have travelled to the frontier with a larger group, but this was not done this year because of concerns of further hostilities. It is why we have come to this place to trap by ourselves and in turn trade at the post in Détroit."

The most talkative of the Indians, a man named Broken Oak, replied, "Perhaps you can come and speak with our chief and you could trade with us and in turn with the English." Seeing no disadvantage, Jacques* agreed to go with them in the morning.

In the morning the men quickly serviced their traps and headed for the Indian camp. They crossed the southern channel of the river which was now frozen and headed east through a frozen marsh to a small frozen channel which bordered a large, heavily forested island. They proceeded inland to a small lake in the center of the island where they found the Indian camp. "Lake of Goose," Broken Oak explained.

The camp was small, no more than fifty people. The chief, Broken Oak's father, greeted the men and invited them to eat. Two Indians were cleaning an enormous fish that hung from a tree branch. It had the appearance of a fat pike but more yellow and extremely large. At over five feet in length it was larger than anything the men had seen outside of the sturgeon on the Saint-Laurent. "Muskellunge," explained Broken Oak, "Sweet fish, one feeds whole village."

At dinner the men tasted the great fish which was indeed sweet and delicious. After the chief spoke, "We are of the Ojibway tribe. We are brothers with the Ottawa to the north and Pottawatomi to the west. Our band has been called *Sauteuse* by the French due to a contest we have which you shall see tonight.

"From time beyond memory we have hunted and trapped this land. We have traded for many generations with the French who we believe are our brothers. Now the English have come and cannot be trusted. We followed Chief Pontiac, but now are alone. We will trade with you if you wish."

Jacques* stood, feeling uneasy in his new role as spokesman, "We did not anticipate the honor of trading this year, however, when the ice clears we will go to Détroit for trade goods and return for furs." He was pleased to see that this arrangement seemed acceptable and the festivities began. The fire was enlarged and dancing and chanting began. Two men placed long poles in the ground and tied a third pole between them and parallel to the ground. The pole was set at about three feet. The young Indians in turn ran to the pole and jumped over it. Suddenly the men realized why they were called *Sauteuse* in French or "Jumper" in English.

The Frenchmen were invited to jump and knowing that they could not decline without insult, they took their turns. To their amazement, everyone but Pierre Drouillard was able to clear the bar. The pole was then raised and the event repeated. This time only Jacques* succeeded. On the third height, he too failed. The Indians continued until the bar was higher than any of the men were tall. At this point, only Broken Oak cleared the bar. After the contest, they sat and smoked and watched the women dance. In the morning they returned to their camp and traps.

As the winter progressed, the pile of pelts mounted. Jacques* realized that if Rivard had been correct in his estimation of their value, and with the additional trade from the *Sauteuse,* this would be a profitable season indeed. They encountered their new friends frequently and visited each other's camps regularly. The Frenchmen even became tolerable jumpers.

Saint Clair Flats, Middle Channel - April 1764:

The ice had cleared and the men were making ready for their voyage to Détroit. The day was as hot as the winter had been cold, and the men had even shed their shirts. Their large collection of furs would require two trips. They would make the first leaving one man with their *Sauteuse* friends and the remaining furs. The others would deliver the first load to Rivard and return with trade items. The Indian furs meant that they would probably need a total of three trips to return with all their goods. The trade was simplified as they already knew what items the *Sauteuse* favored.

As Jacques* stretched he noticed something upstream, "Canoe. And not Indian." As it approached he said low, "Damn! English. I will go to the bank; you three stay back and keep your rifles close." As the canoe approached, one of the Englishmen hailed in French and in a friendly fashion. Jacques* proceeded slowly to the bank remembering his encounter of English voyageurs two years ago with Charbonneau.

As the canoe landed the first man jumped off and offered his hand, saying in good French, "*Bonjour monsieur*, may we be permitted to land?" Jacques* gave a noncommittal nod. Suddenly the man stared at him strangely, "Allard?"

146

Not knowing what to think but not forgetting the lesson of the day with Charbonneau, Jacques* replied cautiously, "Why yes."

The Englishman continued, "Why you must be the son, the son of Pierre*."

Again noncommittal, "Yes."

Then the Englishman turned to his comrade and said, "Jacob, please put down your weapon. This man is the son of my old friend, Pierre* Allard."

Jacques* did not lower his guard. This was an enormous coincidence or a clever trap. The man continued, "Your medallion, I recognize it. My name is Samuel Price." Offering his hand which Jacques* took cautiously, "My Aunt Elizabeth was given that by an Indian many years ago. She wore it herself. I met your father many years ago in Détroit at the camp of Pontiac. Some years later I had the opportunity to aid him at the battle of Fort William Henry."

Knowing this was too good to be a ruse, Jacques* lowered his guard. Price continued, "This is my partner, Jacob Andrews. I believe we may be of mutual assistance in some business we have. May we spend the night?"

Jacques* realized this was one of the first important judgments he had been asked to make as leader of the voyage. He felt an odd sensation from his medallion telling him these men were to be trusted. He agreed. They landed their canoe and prepared dinner. Later they passed a pipe and talked. Jacques* indicated simply they had come from Détroit to trap and were preparing to return to sell their furs at the fur market.

Taking this in, Price began, "We are here on quite a different journey. If you are truly your father's son, you are to be trusted. What I am going to tell you could easily be used against us by the right people." Price was about fifty and much older than Andrews who was not much older than the Frenchmen. "Although we are traveling as British traders, we are on a much different mission. We represent a collection of men in New England who believe it will be our destiny to free this country from English rule. We were sent to Détroit to see if we could form some alliances with the French and the Indian as we believe they can aid us in what we see as a mission for the common good."

Henri-Pierre could not help himself, "Why would we above all people trust any British, colonial or not?"

Price replied, "A worthy question. I hope you know something of my assistance to Pierre* Allard at Fort William Henry." Henri-Pierre nodded. Price continued, "We have some finance and I am prepared to offer security." He handed a small sack to Jacques* who looked inside. Price continued, "As you can see, these gold coins represent considerably more wealth than all your furs. At the end of our business, you may return all, some, or none to me as you see fit."

Jacques* turned to his friends and spoke in Algonquin. Price quickly interrupted, "I should be honest and tell you that I too speak this language."

Jacques* was favorably impressed, but continued his discussion this time in the Flathead dialect. After some discussion, he returned to Price, this time in English, "I accept your offer. However, let me warn you, not all the French will be easily convinced of the value of your scheme, and I fear few, if any, Indians, will be."

For the first time Jacob Andrews entered the discussion, "Are there any Indians in the area with whom we could meet?"

The Frenchmen regarded each other and after some private discussion, Jacques* replied, "There are some in the vicinity but I am unsure how they would regard this. Perhaps if Henri-Pierre and I went to see them we could let you know." They agreed and went to their beds.

When morning came they rose early and Jacques* and Henri-Pierre made their way to the *Sauteuse* camp where they met with Broken Oak and his father. After considering the story the chief replied, "I have not found many honorable English. That this man helped your father carries weight. If you men believe they are to be trusted, I am willing to hear them. Come tonight."

That evening the six men returned to the Indian camp. After dinner the chief spoke for a while, and then invited the English to speak. That night Jacob Andrews was the spokesman. In spite of his youth, he had lived some time among the eastern natives and spoke Algonquin fluently. "When I was a boy, my family died in a fire. I was recued by a man of the Delaware tribe who gave me shelter for three years. After this I returned to the home of my father's brother. I understand the thinking of the Indian, and I cannot blame them for regarding the British with contempt. I can only tell you that I see the British fathers from Europe as our common enemy. We see a land where all, colonist and Indian alike, can be free."

The chief regarded him carefully, "And do all British colonists share your opinion?"

149

Andrews returned, "Do all Indians share yours?"

The chief actually laughed, and he stood and came to Andrews, "For now we will be your allies, but I cannot trust all of your kind and will continue to keep my own counsel."

In the morning Price came to Jacques*, "Would you consider letting us take some of your furs to market? You have my money and I will pay you later in coin what we receive for them at Détroit. We will arrive at a later time so as not to be suspicious. This will save you one trip and we will be able to pass ourselves off as simple traders. We will establish ourselves in the city and later you can privately put us in touch with French who may be sympathetic to our cause."

The two groups agreed and Jacques*'s party left the next day with half of their furs. They would return to the *Sauteuse* camp with trade goods as planned while Price and Andrews would arrive in Détroit independently. Jacques* told them to contact him at Toussaint's farm when they were ready. As the men pushed off, Price said, "Remember, we are counting on your absolute discretion. There are those in Détroit who would see us hang if they know of our true intentions."

They crossed the large bay at the north of the lake, arriving at a large river that emptied into the lake at the point forming the northern border of *L'Anse Creuse* or "deep cove" in English. Henri-Pierre told Jacques*, "This is the River of the Huron, as a Huron band camps near here. My father and I traded with them the winter before you came to Détroit." They decided to stop and feeling some confidence as a trader, Jacques* suggested that they meet with the Huron.

River of the Huron (today the Clinton River) - May 1, 1764:

A short distance upstream the men found the Huron camp. Being from the Iroquois culture, the Huron established permanent villages with log houses and did some farming. The village was larger than that of the *Sauteuse* with at least 200 inhabitants. The chief recognized Henri-Pierre and they were cordially greeted. "We welcome the son of Toussaint and his friends, come and dine with us, and tell us the news of our friends in Détroit."

After the chief had spoken, Jacques* broached the topic of trade. The chief replied, "We have not seen English traders this season possibly because of Pontiac. But there have been a few French. If you have trade items, we are interested."

Jacques* told him they could return in several days with the necessary items. Then, feeling some comfort with the chief, he added, "Have you heard of English colonists wanting allegiance with French and Indian to fight the British government?"

The chief regarded this man with different colored eyes for some time trying to read between his words. Then cautiously, "I find alliance between Indian and any English unlikely. Their race has not been honest in trade or treaties. They treat the Indian poorly. If another sort of English exists, I would have to see them first to believe it and even then my heart would be suspicious." Jacques* decided wisely to let the topic drop and returned to the more immediate questions of their mutual trade.

The next day the men made the south end of the lake, stopping at the Milk River and landing on the bank of Toussaint's farm where they were enthusiastically greeted. They went to the house where Henri-Pierre's mother and sister made dinner and heard about the adventures of the season. They included the stories of the *Sauteuse* and the Huron but did not mention the English.

The night was warm, and the men went to smoke on the porch after dinner. When the four young men were alone with Toussaint, they broached the subject. After hearing the story, Toussaint thought for a long while. "I know the man Price; he has always been a rebellious sort where the British government is involved. It is likely they are to be trusted. The larger question is first, are we interested, and secondly, if so, with whom would we dare discuss this. Tomorrow take your goods to Rivard and proceed directly back for your trade with the tribes. I will think on this and perhaps obtain counsel from someone I know I can trust. It would bode poorly for all if this fell to the wrong hands."

Landing at Cadillac's old docks the next morning, Jacques* and Jean-Baptiste* Laforest went to Rivard's store. They soon returned with Baptiste Rivard who examined their furs. "There has been no traffic from the Montréal traders due to Pontiac. There have only been some furs from the locals and the few English traders who were brave enough to travel. Bring these up and I will store them for the market. These muskrat are superior to my expectations; you will do well this year."

In the post Jacques* asked, "Can you give me an advance for trade items? We have two tribes waiting with more furs."

Rivard laughed, "Even better. Don't you have anything left from last season?"

Jacques* only shrugged. Actually he had not touched the money from the last two years, but Toussaint had counseled him not to say anything and pretend that like most French voyageurs, he spent it immediately. They selected what they needed from Rivard's stores and loaded their canoes and headed north.

The weather was warm with occasional rain. As the water of Lake Saint Clair warmed very quickly compared to the waters around Québec, they were able to shoot ducks returning north, and fowl replaced the diet of fish and muskrat that had sustained them all winter. The *Sauteuse* greeted them warmly. Broken Oak reported that Andrews and Price had departed the day before with the remainder of the Frenchmen's muskrat pelts. They completed their trade and headed south where they finished their business with the Huron. Neither tribe mentioned the topic of the English revolt.

The night before returning to Détroit, they camped on the shore of L'Anse Creuse. Jacques* addressed the group after dinner, "This matter with Price and Andrews is concerning me. It is imperative all four of us maintain strict confidence and mention it to no one until a plan has been made at home. A leak could spell disaster for all of us. We are not even to mention it to any family members aside from Toussaint who already knows." And in the Algonquin fashion, he took his knife and made a small cut on his forearm. The others did the same and they all made their oath with blood.

Chapter 19

<u>Détroit - May 15, 1764:</u>

Rivard was ecstatic at the sight of the Indian furs. Along with muskrat and beaver they included bear, wolf, fox, deer and mink. "These will represent a sizable portion of this year's market."

Indeed they did. At the end of the market Rivard presented Jacques* with a sum more than the entire Charbonneau take of last year. It was in English coin and all belonged to the four young men. As previously agreed, Jacques* took half and the others split the rest. Jacques* felt a little sheepish about this, but both Charbonneau and Rivard had firmly instructed not to vary from this traditional method, "Don't forget, you will get one hundred percent of the bad when it comes your way." With their new-found wealth the men headed for the Pontchartrain Tavern but had only two drinks before each left for their homes, still carrying most of their new wealth.

The next morning Jacques* and Henri-Pierre jumped into the planting with Toussaint. Before midday they took a short break, and for the first time Toussaint broached the subject, "I have advice from someone I trust. I am counseled to seek out Pierre* Saint-Aubin. He is trustworthy and has ready contact with all the concerned groups. In addition, do not forget that Madame Saint-Aubin is the daughter of Price's aunt, Elizabeth* Price." Jacques* felt a shock from his medallion.

After dinner they took Toussaint's cart and headed south to the Saint-Aubin farm. Old Pierre* Saint-Aubin sat smoking on the porch when they approached. He welcomed them, congratulating the boys on their successful season, the news of which had already spread through the town. After small talk, Toussaint suggested they walk to the river.

The full moon illuminated the water as it flowed from the lake into the Détroit River. One small campfire burned across the river on *Belle Ile*. As they approached the beach, almost entirely eroded by the high spring water, Saint-Aubin queried, "Why the secrecy?" Before anyone could respond he said in a low voice, "Of course, Price. I thought I recognized one of the two English traders that came a few days ago. Samuel Price. I haven't seen him since we were young men years ago at Pontiac's camp. It's him, and he's up to something. Am I correct?"

Toussaint shook his head realizing that just like his father, Saint-Aubin knew what was happening in the city in the wilderness before it even happened. "You are correct, Pierre*, they contacted the boys while they were trapping on the marsh this spring. Jacques* should tell you the story first hand." Jacques* marshaled his courage and gave a concise summary of the meeting and the events to the present time.

Saint-Aubin whistled, "This is certainly more than I expected. This will take some thought." Turning to Henri-Pierre, "Run to the house and ask Madame Saint-Aubin for a bottle of that Scotch whiskey and four glasses."

When Henri-Pierre returned, Saint-Aubin arose from the rock he had seated himself on to watch the river for a while. "The scheme has merit. He is correct that the English colonist cannot prevail without help from the Indian and French. Their way of fighting is just what the British colonists need.

"Any breach of secrecy will spell disaster for many. First, we must consider if the chance of success is good enough to warrant the risk." He poured a round, and the men downed the drinks. "We should contact one or two more men we can trust and hear Price out; then decide. I will take care of that and you can contact me when you hear from Price. Remember, if you see him in town, no one must know that you have ever spoken." And after two more rounds, they left Saint-Aubin and departed for the Milk River.

A few days later Jacques* and Henri-Pierre went to town for supplies. They entered Rivard's with their list. As Baptiste Rivard took the list, Price and Andrews entered. They went directly to the counter, "We need salt!"

Rivard looked up calmly, "Yes sir. As soon as I complete this order."

Price stood his ground and said, "I need salt and you can take care of Frenchy here when I go." He pushed Jacques* aside violently. Wondering how to react as there were several other people in the store, Jacques* arose and hit Price directly on the jaw. Price got up and started toward Jacques* when Henri-Pierre came between them and said to Jacques*, "It's alright, we can wait."

As Henri-Pierre restrained him, Price said, "That's right, have your half-breed buddy take you out before you get hurt." Jacques* and Henri-Pierre went to the porch as Price said to Andrews, "That will be the day when I wait for an Indian and his lumberjack friend."

After they took the salt and left, Jacques* and Henri-Pierre reentered and completed their business. As they picked up their order, Rivard said softly, "Nice act." Surprised, the young men exited quickly. When they left the porch, they saw Price and Andrews. Price was rubbing his jaw and glared at Jacques* who barely noticed the subtle wink.

When the men returned to the farm, they did not mention the encounter. That evening, Jacques* went to his coat pocket and found a piece of paper.

Come to the Pontchartrain tomorrow night. Pass me the time and place just as I passed this to you.

Jacques* showed it to Toussaint with a brief explanation. Toussaint left immediately for Saint-Aubin's.

The Pontchartrain Tavern - May 25, 1764:

The house was half full of local French businessmen and *habitants*. Young Paul Marsac was behind the bar. His father, Francois, owned the establishment but Jacob who was in his early twenties and single, without any clear direction in life, generally worked the late shift. The tavern was a low log structure with a dirt floor. Although the windows were all open on this warm night, the smell of beer, smoke and sweat prevailed in spite of the fresh breeze. Jacques* and Henri-Pierre entered, going to the bar, "Two beers, Jacob."

The bartender obliged, "I hear you boys did right well trapping this season."

"Not bad."

"Keep me in mind for next year; I have to get out of here. When I'm not working, my mother is bringing women over for me to marry."

"We'll keep you in mind."

At this point the door burst open and two unexpected guests entered. Andrews and Price came to the bar, "You have any good drink or just that French swill?"

Marsac replied, "Good drink must be over at the Keg," referring to the English tavern."

Jacques* turned and got up to Price's face, "We don't usually get the carriage trade here."

Price pushed him back and Jacques* wrestled him to the floor. Paul Marsac came over the bar and grabbed Price and ushered him out the door. As he stood threatening Andrews, the Englishman left under his own steam. As they stumbled down the street toward the Keg, Price retrieved a paper from his pocket.

Meloche's mill. Tomorrow, dusk.

Meloche's Mill - May 28, 1764:

Old Pierre* Meloche had come as one of the first settlers to Détroit. He built and ran the old mill which still stood on the south side of the river at Assumption. Pierre had died a few years ago and his son Baptiste ran the mill. Pierre*s daughter Marie-Catherine* Meloche, at the age of twenty-seven, had just taken her third husband, Jacques*'s friend André* Peltier who worked the mill with Baptiste. There was no question that both Meloche and Peltier felt closely allied to the Indians.

The old mill was a stone tower with its wind vanes facing upstream. The men met in the adjacent warehouse that contained wood, grain and supplies. Because of its location upstream, any view of it was blocked from the fort including most of the north coast by the long *Belle Ile.* When Toussaint, Jacques* and Henri-Pierre arrived, only Baptiste Meloche was in the mill. Soon Pierre* Saint-Aubin arrived. He explained to Toussaint, "We have also told Peltier and Rivard. We thought the fewer people tonight the better. I can speak for Rivard and Meloche can speak for Peltier."

A few minutes later there was a knock and Samuel Price entered with Jacob Andrews. Price's jaw was still swollen. He went to Jacques*, "Remind me never to pick a real fight with you." As Jacques* started to apologize, he was stopped. "Forget it. It was a convincing performance and that is what counts." Price introduced himself to Meloche and introduced Andrews to the others before getting down to business.
"We represent a group of colonists who realize a permanent rupture with England is certain. Although it may not come for a while, it is now time to forge alliances of interested parties. Today the eastern Indian is happy with the Proclamation of 1763 prohibiting settlement in the Ohio. The colonists are soon to break this and the government will not stop it. With that, the fragile Indian alliance will end.

"We have fought beside the British soldiers against the French and Indian and realize their style of battle is the only way to defeat the British Empire. The advantage to the French colonist is the same as that of the English colonist. Our real problem is the Indian. When the revolt does come, the British will stage a western front from Détroit. If they have cooperation of the Indian, we will be doomed. If nothing else, we require training in Indian methods."

Meloche replied, "At the present time, the Indian of our area have had enough of the British. The problem for them is to separate the government from the colonists. To my mind a difficult task. In addition, I don't think we have heard the last of Pontiac."

Saint-Aubin added, "At this point in time, I don't think you will convince many Indians. If hostilities occur in the east, it would be wise of the government to enlist the Indian to fight with them. Toussaint, you have as much insight here as anyone, what do you say?"

Toussaint thought for a moment, "In any war in this country, the side that properly uses Indian methods will win. Not just raids such as the Iroquois did in the old days for the English, but true Indian battle as we used against Braddock at Fort Duquesne. The Indians do not take well to long term war plans. Until something is imminent, it is foolish to foster anything but trust. We can do that at this side and keep our communications open. Other than this I don't think we should do anything at this time."

After further discussion, Samuel Price brought things to a close, "We will take our report home and be in touch by next year unless something happens sooner."

The two Englishmen left and the Frenchmen were left to themselves. Saint-Aubin broke the silence, "We should pay more attention as to who may be open to this cause. We also need to reforge our friendship with the tribes. Young Allard has started with his trade in the region. We need more men to go next season to trade with the area tribes and remind them that the French are fair and trustworthy, especially when compared to the British."

Toussaint added, "The most difficult task will be to show a difference between the British government and its politics to those of the English colonists. Even I have trouble with this." The men left for the evening to go home and plant the best growing season in Détroit history.

Chapter 20

<u>Saint Clair Shores - November 2007:</u>

Jim Trombley turned left out of Ben Champine's drive and headed south on Jefferson Avenue. He, Becky and Ben were finally on their way to meet Angela's great-grandmother. As always, when Jim drove he gave a lecture on early history, "In the nineteenth century this area was lined with long narrow "ribbon farms". They went as far back as the owners wanted to clear. The only road was the one we are now on. The mile roads and drains or creeks that follow each one were added later. Now the drains are covered.

"Some of the streets have the old French names like Allor, Forton, even Champine, Gauthier, and Trombley." As they crossed Nine Mile Road, "This small river is called the Milk River and still extends back into the neighborhoods until it is also covered. The Milk River Settlement was an early collection of farms, and the river cut through the middle. There's an historical marker here across from the old Edsel Ford estate. Old Henry Ford bought the land from the farmers and gave it to his son as a wedding present.

"As we enter Grosse Pointe there are more names like Renaud, Allard, and 'Robert-John' which has now been Anglicized. Gaukler Point at the level of the Milk River and the Ford estate marks the end of L'Anse Creuse where you live and the beginning of the wide point called Grosse Pointe." The road began to follow the lake overlooking the breakwall with all the large homes on the right side of the road. Soon homes appeared again on the left and Jim made a left hand turn onto a road called Trombley. They followed rows of stately homes to the lake where they turned right and saw some of the grandest residences in the region. "This is Windmill Pointe. My Trombley ancestors ran a group of mills here along with their Laforest cousins. It was then a swamp. As you can see it has had improvements."

They came to and crossed a small bridge. "This is Fox Creek, site of the Fox Indian uprising in 1712. There's another historical marker." The creek was lined with small hoists and boat houses. The transition to the other side was jarring to say the least. "We have now crossed Alter Road into Detroit as you can see the neighborhoods have not been so well maintained." They turned right and passed rows of burned-out shells and boarded-up buildings until they again reached Jefferson and continued their ride south. "Streets here have many of the very old names: Chene, Rivard, Saint-Aubin, Beaubien, Campau and even Cadillac."

They passed a stone bridge crossing the river, "Belle Isle has been vacant land, Indian camps, farms and other things. It is now a park. Across from here was Parent's Creek, the site of Pontiac's camp during the siege of Détroit." Approaching downtown, he turned left at a sign indicating the Detroit to Windsor Tunnel. Waiting to pay the toll, he explained, "The tunnel was built many years ago and was a marvel in its day. It was once easy to cross before we turned our customs officers into storm troopers."

They exited the tunnel and turned left heading back north, retracing their original route but now on the other side of the river and lake. "Windsor was just part of Détroit until after the American Revolution. It has always been a smaller town. Originally it was simply called the south coast, then Assumption for the early church, then Sandwich as British Canada and, finally, Windsor. Many of the French families remained after the revolution but they never subscribed to the separatist fervor of the British Loyalists who flocked to this side."

As they followed the lakeshore to the east, the countryside rapidly became rural. Unlike the Detroit side, the towns were small villages separated by farmland. Soon they came to a sign WELCOME TO BELLE RIVER. Driving through what seemed a time warp to the early twentieth century, they saw a large modern structure with the sign, FIRST-NATIONS RETIREMENT VILLAGE. Trombley turned in, "Well, I guess this is it." They parked and entered the lobby.

The building appeared to be like most retirement homes but decorated in native art and decidedly up-scale. "Casino business must be good," remarked Becky. They came to a young lady at a welcome desk.

Ben Champine approached her, "We are here to visit Lucille Lecaine."

The young lady looked up, "Yes, Lucy told me to expect you. She is not back yet but she asked me to take you to her apartment and tell you to make yourself at home." As they walked to the apartment, they could not help notice all signs were in English and French as in much of Canada, but unlike the rest of Ontario, the French was first. "Here we are." She opened the door and let them into a surprisingly large apartment. The back wall was all windows with a spectacular view of the lake. "As I said, make yourselves comfortable. She should be back any minute."

Like most retirement apartments, it was filled with pictures. The threesome's focus was instantly drawn to a wall filled with wood panel carvings. Trombley perused them, "These are all similar to ours, some even by the same artist." The next wall was floor to ceiling books. Becky inspected them, "Voltaire, Rousseau, Aristotle, Franklin, Mark Twain. These make Jim's library look like dime novels."

Ben looked at a book sitting on a table next to an easy chair. It was open with reading glasses sitting on the pages, "René Descartes, in French."

The door opened and their hostess entered. Lucy Lecaine was all of four feet ten inches and seventy pounds. She had dark skin that though very old could still be described as lovely. Her white hair in a long braid, she was dressed in jeans and a flannel shirt that looked as though they had been fitted at Bloomingdale's. She had a marvelous Indian amulet hanging from her neck. Most impressive was a late model lady's Remington rifle which she carefully hung on a rack by the door.

"*Bonjour*, I'm glad you found your way. Sorry I wasn't here to greet you. I shoot skeet on Wednesday mornings and we ran late today. I love these cold clear days when the clay pigeons just float in the air. Well, Angela tells me you're interested in my carvings."

166

Jim Trombley finally got his mouth closed far enough to speak. "Yes, ma'am, we are very interested. Do you know who the artist was?"

"Of course I do, can I get you something to drink?"

Not wanting to appear too anxious, Becky answered, "Only if you were going to, we don't want to be a nuisance."

"Don't be ridiculous. What do you say to coffee?" They all nodded. Lucy went to the kitchen where she ground beans and filled a French press. While they waited she said, "Mind if I smoke?" Even though they secretly did, they said no. She pulled out a paper and a small canvas sack and rolled a cigarette. "I hate this modern tobacco and those little filters that people throw all over the ground. I say if you have to filter it, why smoke?" When the coffee was ready, she poured four cups on a tray and brought it with real cream, sugar in cubes, and a bottle of Calvados. Picking up the bottle, she said, "I take it black but use a little of this in the winter." The threesome followed suit. "What can I tell you?"

Becky made introductions and began. "Ben has a carving such as yours of an iceboat in front of French Québec." She pulled the board from a bag she carried. "It seems to be by the same artist."

Lucy inspected it, "Toussaint de Baptiste, my third great grandfather."

Trombley jumped in, "Do you know anything about the man?"

"Of course, he's my ancestor."

"What can you tell us?"

"What would you like to know?"

Becky said softly, "Everything."

Lucy chuckled, "Can't say that I'll live that long but if you want to listen, I'll try."

"We are all ears."

"Well, he was born in the area of Québec; his father was Québecois Algonquin and his mother French *métis*. Her name was de Baptiste so they took that name. She had a sister who married an African slave who had been captured by Toussaint and his friend; I'll remember his name in a minute. That de Baptiste family came to Détroit early and was prominent around the Civil War, but that's another story.

"Well, Toussaint and his friend, Pierre*, that was it. Well, they were inventors and they made iceboats and that's what your picture is about. But they were adventurers and that's the best part."

Trombley interrupted, "About when was he born?"

"I think…" she went to the shelf and pulled out an old bound book. "Here it is - about 1716 in Charlesbourg, that's just north of Québec. Anyway they went to the west…"

The story went on and the three friends never left the edge of their seats. At 6:00 chimes rang. "Oh that's the dinner bell. I could invite you but one old fool at a time is probably enough for you folks. Tell you what, if you want, we can walk across the street to a little place where we can get a bite and talk easier. Or have you had enough?"

Trombley answered, "Not nearly enough."

They walked into the chilly November evening to a small building across the street called "Frenchy's" with a red neon sign that unfortunately had lost the 'F'. The interior was typical rural Southern Ontario. Tile floors, wood paneled walls and wooden tables with paper placemats showing a map of Lake Saint Clair and pictures of local fish. The walls were hung with the occasional pike and walleye trophy. They sat down and learned that in typical Ontario fashion, the specialty of Frenchy's was English-style fish and chips.

After they ordered, Trombley asked, "Where did you get all your information?"

"Well, the tribe has records, and my grandmother always told stories, I guess hers did too and so on. You see, we didn't have television. I still don't. Angela and Lucien had one but I just couldn't get interested. Rather do some light reading."

Ben couldn't resist, "Like Descartes?"

"Exactly, *Je pense, donc je suis* is a lot better than watching someone perform and then have people ridicule him." Ben was beginning to wonder if this was really happening. Then she continued, "Where was I, oh yes, after the fall of Québec, Toussaint moved to Détroit. His friend, Pierre*... I remember, Pierre* Allard. Well, he died and his son came to Détroit as a boy with voyageurs. At that time Toussaint had been close to Pontiac and..."

By the time Pontiac raised the siege of Détroit, Frenchy was turning off the light. They returned to the residence and said good night. Becky said, "We can't thank you enough for the story,"

Lucy looked up, "Story, that's just the beginning. We didn't even get to the American War for Independence."

Trombley returned, "Sounds as though we'll be back."

Lucy produced a card. "This has the number of the residence. They make us carry them so we can give them out if we forget who we are. Call when you can come and I'll tell you how it fits with my schedule."

As they approached the tunnel, Becky broke the long silence, "This was amazing on so many levels, I don't know where to begin."

Trombley replied, "I feel like I just struck gold."

Ben added, "I'm going to need a beer. Let's go park at our house and we can walk to the Blue Goose."

Chapter 21

The Mississippi River - August 1771:

It had been ten years since Jacques* Allard first saw the Mississippi. Then it had been true wilderness. Now they passed boats and canoes almost every day. Jacques* and his friends had spent four seasons trapping in the marshy flats of northern *Lac Sainte-Claire*. They had gained wonderful experience and honed their skills at trading as well as wilderness survival. They had built good relationships with the tribes of the area, but the call of the real frontier was too compelling, and when Jean-Baptiste Charbonneau returned to Détroit, the men agreed to follow him again and had done so for the past three years.

Détroit had changed little in this time. Settlers both French and English arrived from time to time, but the population had changed by only a few hundred. There had been six commandants since the ill-fated Gladwin; the current commander was James Stevenson who seemed a rather likable fellow. The biggest controversy was that Lieutenant McDougall, who had escaped Pontiac's captivity, had been allowed to purchase *Belle Ile*. The *habitants* had been in the habit of allowing their stock to graze there, and he objected. The French responded to this as they did to most British orders. They ignored him.

Pontiac had caused trouble in the Ohio and Illinois regions for some time but eventually he signed a treaty in July of 1765. He was killed near Kaskaskia in 1769 very close to the spot where Jacques* now steered his canoe. As expected, the British ignored the Proclamation of 1763 and settled the Ohio Territory. The local Indians were unhappy but remained at peace.

Samuel Price and Jacob Andrews continued to trade the Détroit region regularly and continued to tacitly expand their relations with the French and some of the Indians. England had levied a number of tax acts without the representation of the colonists and the unrest in the east continued to grow. As the British administration of the Northwest Territory including Détroit was so haphazard, taxes were only occasionally levied and virtually never collected. In fact the government had little idea of who owned what in Détroit, and Lieutenant McDougall was possibly the only Détroit resident ever to pay his tax.

In the Milk River Settlement, Toussaint continued to farm Rivard's land. Louis* Greffard was no longer a bachelor having married Marguerite* Saint-Aubin, Pierre*'s daughter, in 1765. She was also the granddaughter of Elizabeth* Price. Louis* Renaud no longer traveled with the group as he was due to marry Marie-Anne* Saint-Aubin, daughter of Jacques* Saint-Aubin that month. Louis* had used his trapping money to purchase a farm in the settlement.

On a sadder note, Julian* Fréton had died in a farming accident in 1767. With four young children to raise, Josie* Fréton married Alexander Bloudin dit Ellair who had recently arrived from Québec. They continued to till Julian*'s farm.

Jacques*'s day dreams were interrupted when Charbonneau called, "Town-ho," indicating their approach to Saint-Louis. Though Détroit had changed little, Saint-Louis had exploded. The migration to the south continued and the post became the major stop on the frontier. In addition, numerous people, mostly French but some British, had settled for farming or for business.

They landed at the canoe livery. This year the group numbered seven voyageurs and two Indians. They planned to pick up Falling Rock at the Sioux village along the way as well. The voyageurs included Charbonneau and Jacques*, who at twenty-five was now considered second in command, as well as Henri-Pierre, Jean-Baptiste* Laforest, Pierre Tremblay, Paul Marsac, bartender from the Pontchartrain, and Pierre Drouillard. Drouillard had come in deference to Jacques* and Charbonneau. He had turned down many offers made due to his excellence in Indian languages.

Saint-Louis as a village was as large as Détroit. It boasted one small English tavern and three booming French taverns. They headed for *Roi Louis Neuf* named for the canonized King of France himself. They met Charbonneau's friend, Boucher, "This year I'm off for the frontier. The last three I traded in the Adirondacks. Last year nothing but trouble. The English are pouring into the Ohio to settle in spite of the King's proclamation. The English traders are stealing the Indians blind. Old Pontiac may be dead, but his spirit is alive and well in the east. Worst of all, the tribes no longer know who to trust, so they trust no one. Tribes with whom I've traded my entire life would not let me enter their camp last year, so I'm going

west where the British have yet to piss off all the natives."
Jacques* and Henri-Pierre listened intently but remained silent.

In the morning they loaded their supplies and headed up the Missouri River. Several days later they arrived at the Sioux village of Falling Rock. After dinner the group spoke around the fire. Then Jacques* asked the chief about the English. "Some English traders last few years. Not honorable men. Last year they came and stole from us; however we found them and added to our scalp collection." Then laughing, "Not come back this year."

That night Henri-Pierre said quietly to Jacques*, "Too bad the Sioux don't have a tribe in the east."

One week later in the center of the great plains of what is now Montana, they saw a large cloud of black birds. As they passed the area they saw what they had expected, a field of naked, rotting buffalo carcasses. Falling Rock said, "English skinners. They come with canoe and trade guns and liquor to the Shoshone for horses. With horse they can kill many buffalo with gun. Then they return east by canoe. Guns and liquor bad stuff for Shoshone."

At camp one day short of the Great Falls, they heard a commotion a short distance down the river bank. Jacques*, Henri-Pierre, and Pierre Tremblay went to investigate. They came upon a small camp where three men had two Indian girls tied to the ground. One of the three turned and saw the voyageurs. In English, "You Frenchies will have to wait your turn."

Henri-Pierre became enraged and jumped the largest of the men, Pierre Tremblay and Jacques* followed suit with the other two. The Englishmen had been drinking and were easily overpowered. As Henri-Pierre was releasing the girls, a fourth man appeared from the woods. There was a gunshot and Jacques* felt a searing pain in his side. The last thing he saw was the man throwing a knife at Pierre Tremblay. Henri-Pierre was quickly on the man. This man was stronger than the others and not drunk.

He wrestled Henri-Pierre to the ground with a knife poised at his throat. Fortunately, Henri-Pierre had the man's wrist. After what seemed an eternity, the man fell limp. As Henri-Pierre arose, he saw the girl he had released standing with a frying pan in her hand. Henri-Pierre ran to his friends. Jacques* was breathing but in a bad way. The man's knife was in the heart of Pierre Tremblay. Henri-Pierre ran quickly to their camp and returned with help. They moved the two others to the camp.

After attending to Jacques*'s wound, Charbonneau said, "It is very grave. We must quickly bury Pierre and make our way immediately to the Great Falls. It will be young Allard's only hope." They quickly laid Pierre Tremblay in a shallow grave on the bank and packed the canoes.

Charbonneau noticed Falling Rock had disappeared, but he suddenly reappeared from the forest holding four bloody scalps. "Business now finished, girls run back to their village."

Fortunately there was moonlight and they were able to make the falls by daybreak. Jacques* was unconscious and breathing weakly. Charbonneau sent Henri-Pierre and Falling Rock to the Flathead village. They returned a short while later with Big Beaver and two horses. Big Beaver secured Jacques* in front of him on the horse and they made their way back to the village.

Jacques* awoke in a fog. The pain in his flank was immense. He was looking into the eyes of his old love, Quiet Stream. He thought he was dreaming, and he knew he was dying. Quiet Stream that softly, "You must be brave and strong. I am going to help you. Chew this." She gave him a wad of wet leaves. He obeyed and soon was overwhelmed by a strange sensation and relief of his pain.

The relief was fleeting as the Indian woman put her knife in the flame of the fire next to them, then probed the wound and expertly extracted the musket ball. The pain was terrible. She then heated the knife and stuck it deep into the wound searing the edges. This pain was unbelievable. She then packed the wound with more leaves and seared it shut with the flat edge of her red hot knife. Jacques* lost all consciousness.

An old lady, who had overseen the project, came to Charbonneau. "Your friend is very grave. I fear he shall die, but the girl wants to tend him. We will see. Come back in a few days." And as Charbonneau turned, "For his body."

A voyage to the frontier cannot halt for niceties, and the men returned to their work. They were all visibly shaken but none so much as Henri-Pierre. "It was my fault. I was impulsive. I saw what they were doing to those girls

176

and lost all reason. Now due to my imprudent action, two of my friends are dead".

Charbonneau sat next to him, "This is the life in the wilderness which we have chosen. It is never safe and it is never certain."

Chapter 22

<u>Flathead Indian Camp, Great Falls - October, 1771:</u>

Snow was falling softly from a cloudless sky. He heard a voice and turned. It was his father, "My father gave it to me for good luck, now I am giving it to you," and he hung the medallion around the boy's neck. He felt the familiar tingle but it was farther down, in his side.

He opened his eyes, a blur, then they focused on wonderful dark brown eyes, "I knew I would save you, and I have."

He was encased in something and could not move. His side hurt but otherwise he felt fine, hungry, "What happened?"

"You were shot." Suddenly he remembered. "But I have saved you. You must rest."

The boys were playing ah-key on the old pond in Charlesbourg. His brother Pierre shot the ball. Henri-Pierre caught it, but he was now on the frozen Saint-Clair Flats, and the ball was a small furry animal. "If you can't get bigger muskrat than this we will never make any money."

He again opened his eyes to the lovely brown-eyed gaze, "You were dreaming again. Drink this." She held a cup of a warm bitter liquid. It burned all the way down.

It was his father again, "Run with me to Uncle Franny's." They ran to the porch and found a chest, his father took out a red coat, "Put this on."

He donned the coat and turned, it was Samuel Price, "We need Indians, not redcoats."

He was very small. The screams were terrifying. He saw the great bear throw the woman into the trees. The bear came for him. They stood and stared at one another. Finally the great bear spoke, "I will not hurt you. You have much to do."

This time he really woke up. The same lovely brown eyes, but he could scarcely move. "Where am I?"

"You are safe. Your friends brought you and I saved you. Tomorrow we will remove the poultice and sit you up, drink this."

The next day Quiet Stream and the old woman removed him from the poultice. He had been encased in a cocoon of wet leaves. Sunflower came in and she and the old woman helped him stand while Quiet Stream bathed him with hot water. It was glorious. She wrapped him in a blanket and fed him soup, real food for once. Then he fell asleep but this time did not dream.

Each day he became stronger. He could stand alone and was starting to walk. He went outside the tent, but the snow was now deep and he could not get far. The next night Quiet Stream crawled under his deer skin with him. "Now we shall see how well you really are."

Two days latter, Charbonneau entered the tent, "Well it looks as though it will take more than an English musket ball to get you."

"So it would seem."

"It is now late November, next month I plan to try to get closer to the sea. If you are fit you are invited."

"I'll be fit." The next week Jacques* left for the voyageur camp.

The Beaver brothers arrived with three sleds. The voyageurs had collected enough elk and other large furs to satisfy Charbonneau; and he, Jacques*, Pierre* Drouillard and Henri-Pierre left for the Northwest Passage. They followed the Missouri to its source, then over the mountains and down. This time they had enough time to make it to the river that led to the sea. Charbonneau told them, "This summer I met an English sailor in Montréal. He has sailed around to the Pacific coast and believes he has seen this river from the other side. He said the Spanish called it the Columbia River. The real question is how to do this in the summer when there is no snow. Once the canoes get to the source of the Missouri, portage would be virtually impossible."

Realizing they had run out of time he ordered them to turn back. As they began the descent down the eastern slope, they encountered a band of Shoshone on horseback. The Beaver brothers knew them and they camped together for the night. Charbonneau learned that the Shoshone had been collecting horses for many years and were now a race of horse riders. Two days later he had a brain-storm. "Of course! Arrange for the Shoshone to meet us at the end of the Missouri and ride to the Columbia. The only problem would be making or bringing canoes to continue to the sea. That's how it is to be done!"

By the beginning of March, they were back at the Flathead village. Something was clearly amiss as there was little activity. They were met by Pierre Drouillard's woman,

Assounderchris or Sleeping Star. She was obviously distressed, "It was terrible. English traders came, they were civil. However one of the men became ill and eventually died. Soon much of the village was taken with a pox. Many have died." Jacques* opened his mouth and she anticipated his question, "Yes, Quiet Stream, and Sunflower also, and all of my family. I am sorry."

They made their way sadly back to the voyageur camp and began preparations for the trip home. The day before departure, Pierre Drouillard came to Charbonneau. "Jean-Baptiste, would you allow Assounderchris to return to Détroit with us? There is little now to keep her here."

Charbonneau gave some thought, "If this is what you want. She is not as strong as Pierre Tremblay but probably smarter. Realize, however, an Indian wife in the wild is quite different from an Indian wife in civilization, even in Détroit."

Chapter 23

Détroit - May 1772:

    Jacques* and Henri-Pierre walked slowly down Rue Saint-Anne. The widest of the roads inside the fortification of Détroit, it was relatively busy on this Saturday night. With nothing to do, these two young adventurers with lost loves were contemplating their future. "My father says that Baptiste Rivard is going to want to move to his farm next season." The shopkeeper had married a daughter of Michel* Yax after the siege and now with five children was ready to take to farming. This meant that Toussaint would have to leave or stay as a worker.

    Jacques* replied, "We could go live with the *Sauteuse*. It would be fun and they have many single women."

    Henri-Pierre stood and started down the Rue Sainte Honorine, "It's a thought." They came to the Pontchartrain Tavern which was always their eventual destination and entered. They were surprised to see Pierre Drouillard sitting with Jacob Andrews and Samuel Price. Andrews and Price had become local fixtures as they had traded, or seemed to have traded, the area now for a few years. They were less circumspect than in the past. The English were oblivious and the French were either sympathetic to them or did not care. They also spoke rapidly in French which prevented even the bilingual British authorities from understanding them.

"Drouillard, what brings you over from Assumption with these two rascals?"

Samuel Price spoke up in French, "Things are rapidly taking form in the east. The British have aggravated virtually all the colonists, and Samuel Adams has formed groups to oppose them and demand representation. A conflict is imminent; it's merely a question of when. We need someone with Drouillard's language skills and French background. Now that he has an Indian wife, it's perfect."

Drouillard added, "Assounderchris and I are leaving with them for the east in a few days." After describing more about British indiscretions and Samuel Adams's plans, the threesome left for the south shore of Détroit.

As they left, Louis* Renaud entered with an unfamiliar man about the age of Jacques* and Henri-Pierre. "Gentlemen, let me introduce, Etienne-Godfroy* Balard. Monsieur Balard has recently come from Baie Saint-Paul and is settling a farm by me."

As the men shook hands Balard said, "My father's farm is at Les Eboulements. My mother is a member of your famous Tremblay clan." One good thing about French-Canadian society, there was always a common acquaintance to break the ice.

Renaud continued, "What about you two? You can't chase Indian women forever. No offense, Henri-Pierre. The Saint-Aubins still have a number of marriageable daughters. There are still several areas available by us for farming. I know you two still have all your trade money. What do you say?"

The men gave pleasant non-commitments and lapsed into local gossip. After a few shots and beers and a description of every young girl in the town, Jacques* and Henri-Pierre returned to Toussaint's cart and headed home. When they reached the Milk River, Toussaint sat smoking on the porch watching the moonlight over the lake. After some small talk, Jacques* broached the topic of the farm. His own father had died in Québec when Jacques* was just fourteen. For the past eleven years he had regarded Toussaint like a father.

Toussaint thought a while and replied, "When I was young, your father and I always yearned for adventure. More often than not we found it. Eventually we settled down and I have no regrets. I believe it is worth considering, and although it would not seem so now, I actually believe some day this land could be worth something."

The next morning, the family took the cart to town for mass at Sainte-Anne. Afterward Father Simple Bocquet took the opportunity to welcome the voyageurs home and ask when they were going to marry and settle down. On the way home, Henri-Pierre's mother, Monique, suggested they pay a visit on the newlywed Renauds. Toussaint pulled the cart into the yard set in the middle of the Milk River Settlement. It was a bright brisk spring day with a strong northeast wind bringing wonderful whitecaps onto the blue water of *Lac Sainte-Claire.*

Marie-Anne* Saint-Aubin-Renaud ran to the cart and embraced Jacques* and Henri-Pierre. At eighteen she was full of life and also great with child. Louis* came down from the house being followed by a black and white border collie. "Welcome, have you come to be our new neighbors?" Marie-Anne* invited them to stay for lunch.

They attempted to decline but she insisted. She and Monique went to the house and Marie-Anne* ordered Louis* to run next-door and invite the Balards.

Soon the neighbors appeared with a papoosed infant in tow. As the women brought out a table and began to prepare, Monique remarked, "This reminds me of the old days in Charlesbourg. Each Sunday we would have a picnic after mass in the square or on someone's lawn."

Marie-Anne* replied, "We could begin again if more new families moved nearby."
As they gathered to eat the men were introduced to Marie-Françoise* Souchereau-Balard and her infant son, Etienne-Godfroy* Balard, Jr.

During dinner Madame Balard remarked, "Monsieur Allard, I believe your grandfather travelled to *la Nouvelle Orléans* with my grandparents. In fact I believe that Henri-Pierre's grandfather as well as Marie-Anne*'s were along. My grandfather was a voyageur. His name was Jean* Gauthier. He traded out of Kaskaskia near what is now Saint-Louis. My grandmother was a Kaskaskian *métis* woman named Capieioufseize* who was baptized Marie-Suzanne-Jeanne*. Their daughter, my mother, did not live the Indian ways and returned at the age of sixteen to Montréal with her uncle. There she met and married my father."

After eating, the men walked south along the lakeshore where there were a few miles of frontage of prime vacant farmland. Three weeks later, Jacques*, Henri-Pierre, and Toussaint were at the notary's making a deal. Their land contained half a mile of frontage on the lake and extended forever. The Milk River crossed it about half a mile inland and contained an old beaver pond at the level of the river. The summer was spent with time split between farming Rivard's place and developing the new one, building a house, and clearing enough land to plant. Fortunately, Jacques* and Henri-Pierre had saved a good deal of money and were able to hire help with some of the work, as Henri-Pierre's sister had married and moved to the south shore over the winter. They would only need to house the four of them for now.

Chapter 24

Détroit - September 1774:

Growth of the city remained slow as did growth of the Grosse Pointe and Milk River settlements. Jacques*, Henri-Pierre and Toussaint continued their farming although they only farmed enough for their family's needs. Each fall, they would close the house and Monique would go live with her daughter's family in Assumption while the three men would trap and trade the Saint-Clair Flats and upper *Lac Sainte-Claire.*

Toussaint continued to believe in the value of the land, and they had saved their money to obtain more parcels in the Grosse Pointe area. Some they let out to tenant farmers who would split their crop profits with them. Paul Marsac had taken a Sauteuse woman and rented one of these farms. Technically Jacques* was the owner as the British were cool on the concept of a *métis* landlord. Their English colonist friend, Jacob Andrews, had remained to trap with the group, while Samuel Price continued back and forth to Boston. As before, the British in the city in the wilderness remained oblivious to their clandestine scheme. Andrews had similarly taken a Sauteuse woman and the farm next to Marsac, also leased from Jacques*.

The Québec Act of 1774 tied up the loose ends of the fall of Québec. The Archbishop of Québec managed to make a favorable arrangement with the British government. The British Province of Québec would include all of old Québec. In addition it would include the Ohio and Illinois country from the Appalachian Mountains to the Mississippi River. The southern border would be the Ohio River and the northern border, the ill-defined Canadian Tundra. This new Québec, of course, included Détroit. As part of the agreement, the French-Canadians were allowed to keep their French civil law and the Catholic Church.

The Allard Farm - September 10, 1774:

As usual, Samuel Price and Pierre Drouillard had arrived at night. Word had gone out and now Paul Marsac, Jacob Andrews, André* Peltier, and Baptiste Rivard had gathered. Price lost no time, "Things are heating up nicely in the east. Unjust taxes continue to mount, and this winter, colonists dressed as Indians dumped British tea into Boston Harbor to protest. The colonists are further angered by the Québec Act. It again forbids further settlement west of the Appalachians. They see this as punishing the eastern colonies. In June the British passed the Quartering Act allowing the British Army to quarter troops in colonial homes.

"War is imminent. Even as we speak, Samuel Adams is meeting in Philadelphia with the likes of George Washington, Patrick Henry and John Hancock. They are calling it the First Continental Congress. All colonies but Georgia are being represented. There are no more British Colonists, only **American Colonists.**

"We have the resolve and manpower necessary to prevail, but not the talent. Most are simple farmers who have only used a musket to shoot game. Washington has said we need the type of fighting he faced unsuccessfully with Braddock. In short, our troops need training from you men. I have been asked to return with a small group to give instruction to a group of militia leaders who will be gathering near Boston. We should have enough time to help finish your harvest. With luck you can return home with time to do some winter trapping."

Toussaint spoke for the group. "It will be necessary for Monsieur Rivard to stay in Détroit, but the rest of us can go. We have two Sauteuse and two Ottawa men who have English skills and are willing. We can get some local help with the harvest and be ready to leave within two weeks." That being agreed the group broke for the evening. Pierre Drouillard held back to speak with the family as the others left, "Assounderchris has returned with me. We have a child, Pierre-George Drouillard, now one year old. It is not safe for them in the east so they will stay with my family. Monique, could you please look in on them while you are in Assumption this winter?" Monique congratulated him and agreed, and he too departed.

When the guests had left, Jacques*, Henri-Pierre, and Toussaint sat on the porch. Henri-Pierre said to his father, "You know it is not necessary for you to go."

Toussaint looked out over the moonlit lake, "Killing in anger has never been the Algonquin way. But I have killed in anger and it was the British who died. I was also angered with the French government for not using the Indian way to defeat these British. It was for this reason I took you, your mother and sister away from our home in Québec to this place. Now I see the opportunity to chase these people from our land with the Indian way. I would not miss this for the world."

Two weeks later they met at Cadillac's old docks, and after supplying at Rivard's they were off. They had said they were going to trap. As anticipated, the British on the docks were oblivious to the fact that they were supplied much too lightly. They made good time to Lake Erie, then on to Niagara where they made the downstream portage in record time. Turning at Oswego on Lake Ontario, they followed the Mohawk River system to Albany. There they were met by men with horses and proceeded quickly toward Boston.

That night at camp Toussaint remarked to Samuel Price, "Your people are much more organized and equipped than I had imagined. I now see that with some help from us, you shall prevail."

Massachusetts Back Country - October 1774:

They met in a remote clearing in the woods. Surrounding landscape was hilly and crossed with streams. Heavily forested, it was awash with autumn color. The Americans had assembled a group of 20 militia leaders. Their commander was introduced as Richard Montgomery who explained, "These men represent all the colonies. We hope to have them form clandestine forces to disrupt the British military much as the French and Indian did in the last war."

The men from Détroit had formed a plan, and Toussaint took the lead, "I have been told that all of you have experience in the wilderness. This is the same as hunting, only more serious. We have broken Indian warfare down into a few categories. We will have a demonstration, then proceed in groups to practice.

"Our first lesson is on moving through the woods; the concept is to be as quick, quiet and undetectable as possible. I will take one man one mile down this road. We will race back to you men at this point, but through the woods. At no time can we come to the road until we find this position. You, sir."

The man indicated was about twenty years Toussaint's junior. He stepped forward and introduced himself, "Captain Thomas Sumter from Virginia." The two men went quickly down the road at a slow trot. Toussaint learned Sumter had much experience in the last war and had been with General Braddock at Fort Duquesne. Toussaint chose not to use this time to tell Sumter about his connection with that battle.

One mile down the way they left the road and went a distance into the forest. Toussaint said, "I will give you a head start. Remember, quick, silent, undetected." Sumter left moving skillfully through the woods. A seasoned veteran of the back country he was certain he could beat this old man. His first surprise was seeing Toussaint sitting on a log in front of him about halfway through the course. Then, as if by magic, he was gone. The second surprise was when someone took his hat off his head. He looked around and saw no one. The final blow was arriving out of breath at the destination and seeing Toussaint talking to the others and holding Sumter's hat.

Toussaint threw him his hat, "Not too bad." Then he began, "You look at this as the woods, but the Indian sees it as a network of roads, much like a city. The Indian has been using these roads for years, always single file and always with limited damage to the surroundings. The secret is discovering the Indian roads. Once you learn, it is simple. Don't look at the trees, look at the spaces." They then broke into small groups.

A few days later Toussaint began, "Silence is the key. Who will volunteer?"

A young man raised his hand, "Captain Andrew Pickens from Pennsylvania."

"Captain, I want you and Jacques* Allard to go to the top of the hill. I will give one whistle; you are to return down to us as quickly and quietly as possible. On my second whistle, Monsieur Allard will do the same. We will all listen."

The men went to the top and Jacques* whistled to indicate they had reached their destination. Toussaint returned the whistle and Pickens started down. He was fairly quiet but occasionally the men could sense his position. He had done rather well until he was almost to the road and tripped with a terrible crash. He appeared red-faced to gales of laughter. Toussaint then gave the second whistle. The men listened intently but heard nothing. They stood peering into the bracken. Then Jacques* cleared his throat. He was standing behind them.

Two days later, "Deception is critical and frequently your best tool. You want your enemy to think you are where you are not and the opposite. When you want to encounter him, you make him think you are vulnerable. When you do not, make him think you are strong."

Finally, "Terror. It has not been the way of the Indian to kill as many as possible as it is with the Europeans. For the Indian it is how it is done. Many men killed with musket balls are less discouraging than one or two killed brutally. At the beginning of the siege of Québec, Wolfe camped on an island. He had a group of men in a house and two guards outside. The remainder of his men were on shipboard in the river. That night we killed the two guards and put their heads on pikes on the beach. We could have easily killed all the men in the house, but this was more effective."

Later that evening, a man slightly older than Jacques* stopped to chat. He began in surprisingly good French for an American colonist, *"Bonsoir, Monsieur Allard."*
Taken a little aback, Jacques* replied in English, "Good evening sir, you speak French."
The man sat by the fire. "My great grandfather came from the Larochelle region of France over 100 years ago. He was Huguenot and forced to flee south. He landed in the colony of South Carolina where I was born. We spoke French at home. I saw action against the French in the last war. I was impressed then that this style of Indian fighting was the only way to defeat the British Empire. I thank you for your instruction and hope we can do as well as the French and Indian often did against us." As the man rose, Jacques* asked his name. The man replied, "François, but here I am called Francis, Francis Marion."

By the end of November, the militia had learned a great deal and were able to move and maneuver Indian-style in the wilderness. As they left to train their troops, the Détroit men left to begin trapping the muskrat. Price said goodbye to Toussaint, "I suspect the next time you see me I am going to need you for more than instruction, thank you, my friend."

Chapter 25

Saint-Clair Flats - January 1775:

Unaware of events in the east which would forever change their lives, the men had returned to the life they loved the most. Détroit winters were balmy compared to those of Québec or the Great Falls. The lighter snow cover was ideal for their activities, even allowing them to maintain an open area of ice for ah-key. They set their camp next to the Sauteuse village. Since Marsac and Andrews had taken Sauteuse women, they were regarded by the Indians as family.

By a bright warm fire the men smoked while Toussaint sat carving a board. Henri-Pierre had learned the skill from his father and worked on his own piece. Jacques* broke the silence, "Why don't we just stay here, away from the troubles of governments and wars?"

Toussaint looked up from his work. He had changed from the impulsive man he was once and was becoming his father. Jacques* could see old Joseph in him more each day. "This land," sweeping his palm in front of him, "is ours. OURS! No one is going to take it away so long as I live." As he went back to his work, Jacques* realized that the impulsive young man had not left entirely.

Détroit - Spring 1775:

A flurry of activity was evident as the men reached Cadillac's old docks. Two crews worked hard rebuilding the fort's exterior. Jacques* and Henri-Pierre left the others with the canoes and furs and went to Rivard's. Entering, they saw two British officers dealing with Baptiste Rivard. The shopkeeper acknowledged them with a glance but did not speak until the two officers had left, "Things are heating up. You'll hear more tonight." They then fell to business and transfer of the furs.

Leaving the docks, they continued home to the Milk River. Monique had returned from Assumption and opened the house. As they finished dinner and a summary of the winter's activities, a knock came. "Welcome home." said Pierre* Saint-Aubin as he entered. They knew they would now hear the news. "Things have livened up since you left. The colonists in the east have seized control of each of the thirteen colonies. Fighting has already broken out around Boston.

"The new commandant at Détroit, Captain Richard Lernoult, has started to strengthen the fortifications in anticipation of an American attack. There is even talk of a new fort. Many are silent on the subject of politics. Most of the French favor the Americans, but not all are ready to fight with them. Even some of the English citizens seem sympathetic to the colonists. We receive word regularly from Samuel Price. For now, sit tight and keep your head down and your mouth shut in public."

Sunday the family took the cart to Sainte-Anne for mass. Simple Bocquet gave an uninspiring sermon on peace and love in the wilderness. Because there was surprisingly little socializing afterward, the French families headed directly home where things were different as the Milk River Settlement had taken to the old tradition of picnics after mass.

Today's festivity was at the farm of Michel Yax. A beautiful spring day, the trees were budding, the sky clear and warm. A soft southwest breeze turned the bright blue water into a plate of glass. The settlement had grown to twelve families with over forty children. Boys fished and wrestled by the lake while girls played games on the lawn. The women worked and the men gathered to discuss the topic that would dominate these picnics for some years to come, the war in America.

Baptiste Rivard was the most *au courant*, "There have already been battles in Boston, and the British are tightening down on all American enterprises, which is making Americans fight harder. The colonists have even tried to get Québec to join them. Many of the French are in favor, but the British have prevented it so far. In town it is difficult to read any man's sentiments. Some like Navarre feel that we are better with the British; others disagree but most are reluctant to take a side publicly."

Toussaint added, "The Indians have moved their camps away from the fort. Lernoult thinks he can use them to raid the American colonies. I doubt that he will convince the Algonquin, but I hear he has also made advances to some of the Iroquois in the east."

As the season passed the French remained quiet. In the Keg Tavern, the British were vocal on the subject of the upstart Americans. Lernoult felt that all his British citizens supported the crown. A more astute observer would have noticed that a number of the English farmers avoided the pub. At the Pontchartrain Tavern, the French were generally apolitical especially when anyone else was watching.

News trickled in slowly. The colonists had formed a colonial militia and appointed General George Washington as its head. The British had started to stage Indian attacks on Virginia from the Fort Détroit. As Toussaint had predicted, those using local Indians usually failed, so the British had taken up their old alliance with the Iroquois tribes to the east. At the end of August, the big news came.

Pierre* Saint-Aubin rode up one morning as the harvest was progressing, "Meloche's mill tonight at dusk. I have been asked to invite the head of each farm."

Toussaint climbed down from his wagon, "Jacques* and Henri-Pierre are now in charge. They will come. I will as well if that's acceptable."

"I wouldn't want it any other way. See you tonight."

The mill was filled, as expected, Saint-Aubin arrived with Samuel Price, "Gentlemen, we are needed in a strategic maneuver by the Americans."

Rivard questioned, "And what would that maneuver be?"

Price surveyed the room, "My friends, we are going to take back Québec." Pandemonium reigned until Price could get order, "General Montgomery is going to march north to Montréal and then on to Québec. You have been asked to supply the French and Indian support as well as liaison with our French friends in the north. We will leave immediately. I propose we take mainly voyageurs whose disappearance will not be so apparent. Older boys from nearby farms will help those families finish the harvest. I propose making Jacques* Allard and Henri-Pierre the group leaders. Jacob Andrews has already secured a number of men from the Sauteuse camp."

Arrangements were quickly made, and two of the Yax boys were hired to help with the harvest at the Allard farm. The voyageur group and the Indians took their canoes and obtained provisions from Rivard before heading to Lake Erie. The British were oblivious to the fact they were not going to head down the Maumee but continue on to Lake Champlain, to the old French fort now called Ticonderoga and held by the Americans.

Chapter 26

<u>Fort Ticonderoga, New York - September 16, 1775:</u>

The Frenchmen had made their way to the Hudson River Valley and north to the bottom of Lake Champlain. Ticonderoga sat on the western bank on a prominent point with a grand view of the countryside. Once the French Fort Carillon, it had been restored and strengthened. The Americans had taken control of it and used it to stage attacks in the region. The men were greeted, and Jacques* and Henri-Pierre were invited to a meeting of the leaders.

They had met General Richard Montgomery at their training sessions in Massachusetts. "Men, we plan to move north tomorrow and set siege to Fort Saint John on the Richelieu River. Once we prevail, we will proceed to Montréal and then on to Québec City. General Benedict Arnold is leading a second force from the east and hopes to meet us there to take Québec and all of French Canada. At that time we will control the British on several fronts."

Following the meeting, Jacques* approached Montgomery who remembered him from Massachusetts, "Pardon me, General, but are your men adequately fitted for Québec? I was born there and the winters are quite different from those in New York."

The general regarded Jacques* carefully, "Thank you, Monsieur Allard, but I assure you that we shall be done with this before the snow flies."

Later that night Jacques* voiced his concern to Toussaint who replied, "Americans or not, they are still British, arrogant and stupid."

At dawn they proceeded north on Lake Champlain with 1700 men and soon entered the Richelieu River. One night at camp Toussaint observed, "Long ago, the Five Nations of the Iroquois travelled this river to raid French settlements. Later the French and Abenaki used it to raid English settlements. Your father and I took it to fight at Fort William Henry. Now we are going back up the river to take back Québec. It would be better named the river of war."

The next day they arrived at the old Fort Saint-Jean, now renamed Fort Saint John. Montgomery set the siege and the Frenchmen were deployed to stop anyone from entering or exiting the fort. It was easy work. Six weeks later the flags of surrender went up. Montgomery had achieved his first objective and proceeded north. Though successful, this stage of the campaign had taken longer then expected.

Soon they reached Montréal. Word of their arrival had been received and the British governor, Major-General Guy Carleton, had fled with his troops to Québec. Montréal was taken without a fight. That evening Montgomery boasted, "This has gone better than I had hoped. Our goal is now in sight."

Jacques* had to reply, "Québec is a formidable structure, and it is now November 13th. I fear we cannot last the winter as supplied." Montgomery regarded him strangely and departed.

The following day, Montgomery sent Jacques*'s group downstream to scout safe areas to camp on the way to Québec. When they reached the town of Sorel, they took a short detour to *Ile Dupas*. Jacques*'s family could scarcely contain their surprise and glee at the unexpected arrival of the men. All work stopped and the group filled the farmhouse for dinner and news.

After dinner Jacques* explained their activities. His stepfather, Louis Jacques, exclaimed, "There are many French in the area who would be willing to join. While you go on, your brother Joseph and I will find recruits and join you on the Ile as you pass to Québec. Your brother Pierre has married and has returned to your father's farm at Charlesbourg. Contact him. He will find some locals to help."

In the morning, Marie-Angélique* walked her son to the river bank. There she stared into the different colored eyes of this strong man, once the young boy who fifteen years before had left her for adventure, "I don't know why men must always make war, but I suppose it has always been so and will always be so. I will pray nightly for your survival." And with a mother's kiss, Jacques* Allard and his band of French Americans left for the city of his birth.

Like Détroit, Québec had grown only a little, and its population remained predominately French. Realizing that the British would be oblivious to their aims, they simply walked into the citadel and took a look around. Later they crossed the bay to Beauport, then up to Charlesbourg. After a joyful reunion with his brother, Jacques* told of their

202

mission. Pierre Allard had indeed returned to their father's farm and married. He told Jacques*, "I will be able to rally several men. We will wait for your return and join you. We can live with the British but would much rather live without them."

The last week in November, they arrived back at Montréal. Jacques* reported to Montgomery, "Carleton did not abandon Montréal out of weakness. He realized he would do much better fortifying Québec and making his stand there. He has a full force and is well supplied." As Montgomery pondered this information, Jacques* continued, "There are many French along the way who will join us. This should greatly enhance our chances."

Montgomery finally replied, "In this light it is imperative that we join with General Arnold's forces from the east. As we make our way to Québec, we will send scouts ahead to find them and coordinate our efforts."

Montgomery secured the fort with a small force under General David Wooster, commandeered two sailing vessels and left for Québec on November 28. Jacques* had become severely concerned about the group's ability to withstand the Québec winter, but Montgomery had other things on his mind. They stopped at *Ile Dupas* for Louis Jacques's men and Jacques* Allard's group proceeded ahead planning to meet General Arnold and return to Montgomery who would camp at Saint-Foy. Jacques*'s men made good time to Québec where they headed south on the Chaudière River toward New Hampshire. Two days later, they came upon Benedict Arnold and his confused men.

Jacques* and Henri-Pierre found the General and related Montgomery's progress and plan. They were surprised to see Samuel Price in Arnold's command. That evening, Price met privately with Jacques*, Henri-Pierre, and Toussaint. "This is the most incompetent group I have seen. They used green-wood flat bottom boats rather than canoes. Most were sunk or destroyed by the time we found the Chaudière. They brought obviously sick men and the pox broke out and we lost two hundred in a week. They are not dressed or outfitted for Québec. I hope you have had better luck with Montgomery."

Jacques* sighed, "Montgomery is capable enough, but he too equipped his men as though they were to fight in Ohio rather than Québec. I tried to explain this, but as Toussaint has observed, you Americans are still English in your brains." Price could only nod in agreement.

They made Saint-Foy by the last week in December of 1775. Arnold and Montgomery met with the officers for a few days and devised a plan. "We are not equipped for a long siege. We will mount a frontal assault beginning with surprise. We will send some of our American frontiersmen who are not known into the fort and start from within."

Toussaint objected, "We have been sitting here two weeks with two sailing vessels; I suspect they have some idea that we are here." Montgomery assured him the plan would work. On the morning of December 31 they set off to take the city.

The battle seemed doomed from the start. The ruse of surprise failed and those men were killed or captured in the first day. Carleton mounted a strong and well-designed defense and within a few weeks the end was certain to be a British victory. Arnold was among the wounded, and Montgomery was among the dead. Several men and many officers were taken prisoner. General John Thomas arrived with some reinforcements and met with Jacques*. "Monsieur, you know this country. How do you see our prospects?"

"General, these men are not equipped for the winter which is only beginning. If you stay where we are, the French traders will be the only survivors by spring." One week later, Thomas was forced to admit Jacques* was correct and began a slow withdrawal south.

Carleton proceeded to retake Montréal and Fort Saint John. French Canada remained firmly in the grasp of the British. General George Washington decided he did not have the forces to make another attempt.

BATTLE OF SARATOGA 1777

Chapter 27

<u>The Pontchartrain Tavern, Détroit - Summer 1776:</u>

Life had returned to near normal in the city in the wilderness. Henry Hamilton, the new Lieutenant Governor, had been a bit overbearing, but the French handled him as always. They ignored him. He had reputedly told the local natives that he would pay them for rebel scalps. The local Indians did indeed cash in the occasional scalp, but as the Sauteuse chief had told Jacques*, "Scalps do not come with identification." He had further confessed that Hamilton was generally buying scalps of people long dead or of his own supporters.

Jacob Andrews entered with a scrolled document under his arm, and announced, "This has been sent from Samuel Price. It is being circulated throughout the American Colonies. It was written by a man named Thomas Jefferson and is a declaration by the colonies of their independence from Great Britain." He stood and read it in French.

It was enthusiastically received, although at the end Pierre Drouillard stated, "Obviously stolen from Rousseau."

Paul Marsac came and took the document. "I think I will hang this behind the bar." One of his customers asked, "Aren't you afraid that Henry Hamilton will see it?"

Marsac replied, "If he does I'll tell him I didn't know what it said. I just hung it to cover the hole in the wall. At any rate, when was the last time Monsieur Hamilton graced my establishment?"

The season of 1776 progressed with good crops. After the harvest, Jacques*'s men went to trap and trade the Saint-Clair Flats. Hamilton organized the occasional raid with the help of eastern Iroquois to the frontier areas of Kentucky and Ohio, but for the French *habitants,* life proceeded as usual until June of 1777.

The Pontchartrain Tavern - June 1777:

Jacob Andrews entered quietly and proceeded to a table where Jacques* Allard and Henri-Pierre were seated. He spoke softly and quickly, then left immediately. "Meloche's Mill, dusk tomorrow."

The old mill in north Assumption was crowded. All the men were well known to each other and all well trusted. Samuel Price arrived and began to explain. "Things are not going well in the east. The British continue to hold New York City and are planning an attack from Québec to take control of the entire Hudson River Valley. We need a French and Indian force that will allow us to use Indian tactics. Without this, I fear our revolution will be doomed."

After the comments died down and Marsac had passed around a jug, Price continued, "I would like to take as many of the voyageurs as possible and some of the other men without making things too obvious to Lernoult and Hamilton." The group decided who would go and fight and who would stay and farm. Jacques*'s entire voyageur group was among the fighters. They left one week later.

Departures were gradual and in small groups. Jacques* Allard's men indicated at the dock they were leaving early because they hoped to trap at the Great Falls.

Mohawk River Valley - July 1777:

As night fell the full moon shimmered off the slow flowing Mohawk River. Jacques* Allard and Jean-Baptiste* Laforest had made camp just short of the junction with the Hudson River. Henri-Pierre had taken the others to scout Hudson River Valley north of the Mohawk River. Two canoes appeared at the bank. The men remained seated but certain of the position of their weapons. Four frontiersmen landed the canoes and approached the fire. The largest of the four called out in English, "Can we join you? We mean no harm."

Jacques* grunted a disinterested approval in English and the men approached. The voyageurs knew to remain quiet, and totally apolitical in such an encounter. The men came and sat, "You boys must be French," and stating the obvious, "We're colonists. British that is, not them Americans." As was always a part of the plan, Jacques* offered them something to drink. They accepted enthusiastically. "You boys from up north?" Again Jacques* grunted in the affirmative. "Well, we been scout'n for General Burgoyne. He's going to finish these rebels. We figure if he can stop them, they'll leave our frontier and trading alone. If not, there'll be a farm on every inch of this land." Jacques* offered more corn whiskey.

After a few pulls on the jug, the leader continued, "Yea, Burgoyne has taken Fort Ticonderoga and he's leaving soon down the road south to Albany. St. Leger is going to set the siege on Fort Stanwix west of here and General Howe is going to approach from the East. They'll take Albany and the Americans will be stuck. Washington will have to surrender." The evening wore on as the English trader talked and Jacques* grunted in reply always keeping the jug available. The visitors eventually fell sound asleep. Jacques* and Jean-Baptiste* then quietly took their packs to the beach and launched their canoe in the moonlight. They began quietly and once they were out of earshot, they quickened their pace. Jean-Baptiste* remarked softly. "This information should come in handy. Nothing like handing your plan to the enemy."

They turned north as they reached the Hudson River, and by noon two days later, they found Henri-Pierre and the others at the top of Lake George, a short way from Ticonderoga. Henri-Pierre reported, "All the British are concentrated at the fort. Apparently they took it earlier this month."

Jacques* replied, "We met these English traders who are working for Burgoyne who is at Ticonderoga. They said he was soon to set off on the road south to Albany."

Scratching his chin, Henri-Pierre added, "We have been to that road. It is dry and clear. They will make excellent time with horses."

Jacques* suddenly smiled, "Maybe we need to do one of the things French-Canadians do best."

"And what would that be."

Smiling more, "Start cutting trees."

Henri-Pierre understood immediately. They went to the road which was at certain points just at the bank of the river. The voyageurs always travelled with axes and two good saws for cutting wood to build shelters in the winter. They began to cut trees falling them over the road in a crisscross pattern to make moving them quite difficult. As they finished one area they returned to the canoes and moved rapidly south to another strategic place to set yet another roadblock. Within a few days they had blocked the road periodically all the way to the small village of Saratoga. They then proceeded quickly to Albany where they were to meet the Americans.

<u>Albany, New York - Late July 1777:</u>

One hundred miles up the Hudson River from the City of New York, Albany was easily accessed by small boats. As a result a large village had grown on the banks of the Hudson close to the entry of the Mohawk River. It was more like Montréal than Détroit in size and character. Samuel Price knew many of the people who in large measure were sympathetic to the revolution. He was directed to the camp of General Horatio Gates.

Gates greeted the men with enthusiasm, and when he heard the intelligence gathered by Jacques* and Jean-Baptiste*, he could scarcely contain himself. He immediately called a meeting of his captains and included Jacques*, Henri-Pierre and Samuel Price. General Horatio Gates was fifty years old, on the tall side and spoke with a level of confidence but not arrogance. Born in England, he came in the 1750s to fight for the British Army in the

French and Indian War. Now he had sided with the Americans.

"Gentlemen, as you know, General Howe has taken control of New York City for the British. He plans to advance his control to Albany which will give him an almost insurmountable advantage. Fortunately Captain Price and his French allies have obtained excellent intelligence on the plans of General Burgoyne. In addition, they have clogged the Albany road in the north to impede his travel from Ticonderoga.

"Burgoyne hopes to hold Fort Stanwix in the west at siege and move on Albany while Howe advances from the southeast. We will send a group to aide Fort Stanwix and send Captain Price and his men from Détroit to intercept Burgoyne. We will wait here for Howe."

After the group was dismissed, Gates came to speak with Jacques* and Henri-Pierre. "Gentlemen, I am told your fathers fought at Fort Duquesne at the great defeat of General Braddock. I was a young officer in Braddock's ranks as were Generals Washington, Gage, Lee and Colonel Morgan. It was after that battle we foresaw the end of the British rule. We also saw how the British could be defeated. I cannot tell you how pleased we are to have you here. It is your style of fighting that will allow us to succeed." Going to a map of the region, he added, "As you have greatly slowed Burgoyne, he will likely run short of supplies before Albany. I anticipate he will have to leave the road for one of the nearby villages to restock. I am asking you to go and scout him. After he makes the turn east for supplies, you will be able to cut him off. If you can be half as successful as your fathers were with Braddock, we will prevail."

The Albany Road - July 31, 1777:

Recently General John Burgoyne had turned 55 years old. He had come to America like most British officers to fight in the French and Indian War. His duty in the past few days was far from what he had expected to be doing at this point in his life. A march that should have taken three days at the very most was now at the end of its second week. He didn't know who had cut the trees or how they even knew where to cut them as his plan had been secret. He had called his aide-de-camp, "Major Johnson, we do not have the supplies to reach Albany. My map indicates a small village named Bennington in Vermont, fifteen miles from here. There are farms there. We will deviate to the southeast at this point and commandeer some cattle and other provisions."

When Johnson gave the order, the group of 9000 including British and Hessian forces as well as 600 loyalist colonists left the main road for the smaller country lane. By evening they were in Bennington. The city fathers seemed surprisingly cooperative and by the next day they had supplied Burgoyne with the items he needed including many of the local cattle. The British returned to the lane leading to the Albany road. In the afternoon the column came to an abrupt stop. The General rode to the front to see what the problem was, and what he saw filled him with rage. "God damn it! Who can be doing this?" Another bramble of trees lay blocking his path.

By now his troops were rather skilled at clearing trees, but they had only nicely begun when the first shots came. Men started to drop in all directions. Burgoyne called for the men to fall into a defensive formation, but the shots continued, and the troops continued to fall. Shots came from all directions, and there was no sign of anything except the shots. A few men were sent into the brush to investigate simply disappeared. Finally the shots stopped, and Burgoyne ordered his men to continue clearing.

As soon as they began, the shots resumed. When they returned to formation the shots stopped. This happened three times when Burgoyne realized in his frustration he had lost sense of the time, and a dark moonless night descended with the rapidity typical of the mountains. As the British tightened their ranks, the fire arrows came. Soon many of the wagons were ablaze. Those carrying powder began to explode and the newly acquired herd of cattle stampeded back to their home.

The British tried to follow in retreat but were greeted by the same people who had been so helpful in the daylight. However in darkness they had turned into a disciplined and well-trained colonial militia unit. By morning, more than one-third of Burgoyne's force lie dead in the woods. Their enemy seemed to have vanished as quickly as it had appeared. They cleared the obstruction and made their way back to the road. To heighten the General's anger and anguish, four of his junior officers hung from trees at the entrance to the Albany road. They cut their comrades down and began the painfully slow march clearing trees as they proceeded south.

At the same time Jacques* Allard's men worked their way back to canoes they had left at the Mohawk River and rushed to the west. St. Leger and his British soldiers had made it to Fort Stanwix, but when they began their siege they encountered the American militia and Indian allies who had been sent by Gates. The fight seemed to be a stalemate when phantom shots began to ring out. St. Leger's men began to fall, and by the middle of August St. Leger's British and Loyalist troops withdrew to Montréal. They traveled lightly as most of their supplies had disappeared in the confusion.

Jacques*'s men returned to the Hudson River where they followed the rear of Burgoyne's diminished army as it cleared trees and made its way slowly toward Albany. On September 19, they came to the farm of a loyalist named Freeman by the village of Saratoga. Here the British saw their first real American soldiers. Burgoyne assumed they were the men of Horatio Gates, but they were actually the troops of General Benedict Arnold and Colonel Daniel Morgan who had come from the east to reinforce Gates.

Things began poorly for the British and deteriorated when their phantom nemesis began to shoot from behind. By the end of the day Burgoyne realized he was losing badly and marched south for two miles where he fortified his position and decided to wait for Howe. Jacques*'s men returned to Gate's camp between Albany and Saratoga at a place called Bemis Heights. Jacques* and Henri-Pierre were invited to meet with the General. When they entered his tent, he was laughing with Arnold and Morgan, whom Jacques* had met during the unsuccessful battle of Québec two years earlier.

Gates explained, "I have just been informed that General Howe has taken his British forces to Philadelphia where he is bottled up by General Washington. Burgoyne doesn't realize it but his help is not coming. We are going to wait for Burgoyne to make his last fatal move." They waited until October 7, 1777, when Burgoyne, realizing his reinforcements were not to be, formed three columns and led a direct attack on Gates at Bemis heights. It was a disaster from the start. They were stopped by Gates. Then Arnold's forces came from the east, while the Frenchmen came from the west and again remained invisible. By mid-afternoon, Burgoyne led a hasty retreat to his camp.

Gates visited him the next day with Jacques* and Arnold, asking for an unconditional surrender but Burgoyne held out, only agreeing to leave all arms and depart with his men to England. As they marched to the east unarmed, Burgoyne had lost over half his force. He had never injured or even seen one of the French or Indian under Jacques* Allard.

Jacques* paid a last visit to Gates to tell him they were returning to their farms in Détroit. During their visit, Gates received a pouch from a courier; he excused himself to read the letter inside. He then laid it on the table and said, "Monsieur Allard, I fear I must ask you one more favor." Jacques* was hesitant, knowing his men were anxious to return. Gates continued, "General Washington has an urgent need for a man of your talents. This is not for battle but for diplomacy."

Jacques* looked quite puzzled, and Gates went on, "It seems there is a very young French officer who has come to General Washington. This young man is apparently of high rank in France and has the ear of the King of France himself. He is interested in forming a formal public alliance between our two countries. Washington needs someone with battle experience, fluent in French and English, and with French roots. It seems you are made to order. I cannot overestimate what an advantage this would give our effort for independence. I suggest you and Henri-Pierre go meet with the General at his camp outside of Philadelphia."

Brandywine, Pennsylvania - October 1777:

Colonel Daniel Morgan and two of his aides accompanied Jacques* and Henri-Pierre on horseback and rode rapidly down the Hudson River Valley. They veered southwest avoiding New York City until they reached Washington's camp just south of the city of Philadelphia. Making inquiries, they were taken directly to the General's tent. George Washington was exceptionally tall, soft spoken and confident. They took an instant liking to him. As they shook hands he remarked, "I have been told that the fathers of you two men fought us at Fort Duquesne at the defeat of Braddock's army." Henri-Pierre answered in the affirmative and the General continued, "I learned a great deal at that defeat, and since that time I have had the highest regard for your type of fighting and your ability to use it so effectively. I understand this was highly significant at the recent victory at Saratoga. I cannot thank you enough. You have breathed the very life back into our cause."

Just then an aide entered with a gentlemen, at least ten year's Jacques*'s junior. He was a good deal shorter than Washington but carried himself with an equally confident air although he walked with a distinct limp. The General spoke, "Gentlemen, allow me to present Gilbert du Motier, the Marquis de Lafayette. Monsieur le Marquis, if I may, Jacques* Allard and Henri-Pierre de Baptiste. The Marquis helped us in our recent battle with General Howe here at Brandywine. I regret to report that he received a leg wound in the battle."

The younger man responded in English and Jacques* and Henri-Pierre answered in perfect French. Taking the cue, the Marquis de Lafayette continued in French, "Monsieur Allard, I am told your family is from France."

Jacques* replied, "*Oui, Monsieur,* although I was born in the new world at Québec, as were my father and grandfather, my great-grandfather came from the region of Normandie. My great-grandmother came from the region of the Loire."

"*Très bien, Monsieur,* I was born in the Haute-Loire and raised at Aix-en Provence in the south. Monsieur Allard, I cannot escape your eyes. It is said that Alexander the Great had such different colored eyes. I envy you."

"It runs in my family, Monsieur le Marquis."

"And you Monsieur de Baptiste, I understand you have Indian blood."

"That is correct, Monsieur le Marquis; I am what we call *métis.*"

"Excellent, Monsieur, this idea of equality is what the world needs. It is right from the writings of Voltaire and Rousseau. *Liberté! Bravo Messieurs, Bravo!* Are you familiar with the works of these men?"

Jacques* and Henri-Pierre could speak French and English well and even read some French, but not well enough to read these scholarly works. Fortunately their friend, Pierre Drouillard read constantly and had spent many evenings at the fire in the frontier extolling the works of these two Frenchmen. At this point they would have liked to kiss Drouillard. Jacques* replied, "Of course, Monsieur le Marquis."

They continued with a discussion of the works of the two French thinkers. Fortunately, Lafayette dominated the conversation. He asked of their accomplishments and Washington stepped in, "These men have just come from our great victory at Saratoga where the French and Indian fighters were decisive. With this type of assistance, we can control the ground battle, but as you know, America has only a few boats and no navy to speak of. If we were to have the aid of the French Navy, victory would be ours."

Lafayette replied, "General Washington, I shall write immediately to his majesty. I believe he will agree and supply the help you need." Washington poured drinks and proposed a toast. In the morning Jacques* and Henri-Pierre left for Albany where they found their canoe and proceeded toward Détroit.

Chapter 28

The Saint-Clair Flats - January 1778:

Jacques* Allard exited his tent into the clear cold morning. He was naked but for his deerskin boots. He found this ritual awakened and refreshed him. He also believed it made him stronger. He gazed across the lake. The opposite shore of the bay which formed above L'Anse Creuse was entirely ice covered. The rising sun behind him gleamed on the frozen wilderness. Most of the lake was white with snow-covered ice. Occasionally areas of the ice had moved and raised small mountain ranges of broken ice that glimmered in the sun as heaps of diamonds. In places the ice had cracked, water ran over it and refroze, creating strips of deep blue that were as smooth, well, as ice.

He had been pensive since he and his men returned from the war in the east to the peace of the flats. Here the only sound in the world was the occasional groan of the ice as some invisible disturbance moved it slightly. He pondered his life so far. It had been eighteen years since he left his mother and the family in Québec to become an adventurer. Since that time he had certainly experienced and seen more adventure than most men in many lifetimes.

He reflected on his lost love, an Indian maiden who had fallen prey to a disease of the Europeans. Both he and Henri-Pierre had lost their young loves in such a fashion. Now in the past year, the Indian wife of his friend Pierre Drouillard had fallen victim to the same pox. This left Pierre to care for his young son alone. As must be done in the wilderness, Pierre Drouillard had remarried to Marie-Angélique Labadie, the granddaughter of the old voyageur, Niagara Campau. She would care for young Pierre-Georges, now called simply Georges, and she would give Drouillard more children.

Earlier in the winter, two young Sauteuse women had come to the camp with the wives of Andrews and Marsac. They built an Indian bath which the entire group enjoyed. After a few days, they moved in with Jacques* and Henri-Pierre in an obvious attempt at matchmaking by their friends. For a few weeks they enjoyed one another's company, but eventually the ladies returned to the Sauteuse camp.

What should Jacques* Allard do? Should he marry? Should he become a full-time farmer? His solitude was broken when Henri-Pierre emerged and said, "If we are going to tend the traps, I think you would do better to dress more warmly."

As Jacques* started to dress, he asked his friend, "Do you ever think of marriage?"

"Frequently as a matter of fact. I plan to start looking in earnest when we return."

"Anyone in mind?"

"My mother and sister have plenty of ideas. I'll start my own research when we get back. I might even consider a French girl. Marsac and Andrews are happy with their Sauteuse wives, but I find them a little bossy. Being *métis* has always worked in French society, but I fear in English society, whether it be British or American, being too Indian will not be easy."

Jacques* had finished dressing, "Let's go get some furs. We can trap women this summer."

Détroit - Early Spring 1778:

From the view from Cadillac's old docks, one would never guess that a revolution was raging. Indians, *habitants,* a few British colonists and soldiers went about their business as they had for the past fifteen years. The city's two official leaders, Henry Hamilton and Colonel Lernoult walked about the exterior of the walls with two other men pointing and making notes.

Baptiste Rivard was busily putting out merchandise, but he stopped abruptly to greet his friends. After they quickly settled the question of the furs, Rivard lowered his voice, "There have been issues regarding the militia. Play dumb for now, Saint-Aubin or I will try to come by this evening."

That evening after a joyful reunion and real dinner with Monique, they found Pierre Saint-Aubin on their porch. They sat to smoke and watch the white-caps on this cold spring night, "Hamilton was concerned with the lack of French participation in the local British militia. Now enough of the *habitants* have joined him to make appearances. The Reaume family has sent the most men. Those appointed as officers serve for a short while and then ask to be relieved due to issues on their farm. This way the British don't have a good opportunity to observe anyone carefully for a long time. I'm afraid at least Jacques* will have to make an appearance. They aren't sure of the *métis*, so Henri-Pierre you are probably safe."

Sunday the family took the cart to Sainte-Anne. *Père* Simple Bocquet gave a disjointed sermon on loving your fellow man during the time of war. Jacques* found this a bizarre concept. After mass the locals gathered and welcomed the voyageurs home. A well-dressed man of Jacques*'s age approached him through the crowd. Jacques* knew Alexander Macomb but not very well. Alexander and his brother William had come to New York with their father some years ago. Later the boys settled in Détroit. An Irishman, Alexander Macomb married Marie-Catherine Navarre, the daughter of Robert Navarre, an early French settler of Détroit.

The Macomb brothers had been sent to Détroit to deal in the fur trade and had enlarged their father's fortune. They lived on large farms on the south side of the Fort and had recently purchased Grosse Ile in the southern river. "Good day, Jacques* Allard, how good to have you back. Did you have a good season?"

Jacques* replied, "Good day to you, Alexander. Yes, quite good, thank you."

"I have been waiting for you to return. I would like your thoughts as a leader of the French community on the issues of the day. I wonder if you could join us for dinner next Sunday after mass."

Jacques* was pleased to see himself elevated to a "leader" and he replied simply, "Yes, Alexander, that would be fine. I will look forward to it." After some pleasant chatting, they parted ways.

On the way home from mass he discussed it with Toussaint and Henri-Pierre. "Normally an invitation like this means I'm to meet an eligible daughter, but Macomb is just my age and his children are quite young. Perhaps it is to discuss this thing about the militia." This Sunday the first picnic of the year was to be held at the farm of Louis* Renaud. Most of the Milk River Settlement farmers were in attendance.

The Milk River community continued to grow. There were no new families but there were more children. The Sauteuse wives of Paul Marsac and Jacob Andrews were accepted into the group. They each had one child. Therese Andrews was two years old and Jean Marsac four. They both resembled their fathers, and the families were definitely raising them in the style of French-Canadians.

During dinner the women had large doses of advice for Jacques* and Henri-Pierre on the topic of marriage and suggestions of prospects. Each wife had made it her mission to see these two married. After dinner the men fell to the discussion of the war. They had all heard the news of the success at Saratoga in the fall and were anxious to hear the first hand accounts. It was tacitly understood, however, that this was information to stay within the community. Henri-Pierre reported, "Fortunately the British learned little from the Seven Years War. This continues to be the way to success for the rebellion."

The following Sunday, Jacques* rode a horse to mass so that he could continue on to visit Alexander Macomb. The large Macomb farm was about five miles south of the fort, where the river had turned due south to Lake Erie. The road along the river now stretching from the Milk River half way to the level of Lake Erie was well maintained. A more primitive trail continued along L'Anse Creuse for a short distance, so the road now allowed Jacques* to make better time than he would by canoe.

The Macomb farm was large and prosperous. The great house was as fine as the Saint-Aubins' or any house in Détroit. Jacques* was graciously greeted by Alexander and his wife. Macomb was about Jacques* age and Madame Macomb was about ten years his junior. The couple had five small children. After the greeting, they entered the great room of the house and Jacques* saw the reason for the invitation. Madame Macomb announced, "Monsieur Allard, permit me to present my cousin, Charlotte Navarre."

Charlotte was obviously older than Madame Macomb, somewhat plump and rather homely. Jacques* responded with his most gallant, *"Enchanté."*

They sat and visited and had a glass of wine. Jacques* knew about the Navarre family. Madame Macomb was born Marie-Catherine Navarre whose father, Robert Navarre, had come directly from France as head notary of Détroit. He was descended from Antoine Navarre, who was half-brother of Henri Navarre who became Henri IV King of France.

Jacques* had been instructed as a boy by Toussaint that in this world, people with these histories deserved only the same consideration as anyone else. Jacques* handled himself well with these people. After dinner, Alexander invited Jacques* to take a cigar and a walk about the "park" as he called the yard about the house. "My brother and I have purchased the *Grosse Ile* south of here. I believe land is to be the true source of wealth in this country, and I understand you have obtained some parcels in the northern part of the city."

"Jacques* inhaled the cigar mimicking Macomb. It was very strong, but mild compared to the tobacco he had smoked with the Indians. "Yes, I have been able to purchase some land with the money I have earned trapping."

"Yes, I have heard that you are well respected among the *habitants*." Jacques merely shrugged. "I believe that land owners should be acquainted." Then with a less than subtle turn, "Tell me, Monsieur Allard, how do people on the north end of the city view this rebellion in the east?"

Realizing "people in the north" was simply a way of saying "French", Jacques* replied, "Guess I would say they are rather neutral. They have seen little change with the British control of the fort and don't see how any other change will make things much different."

Macomb continued, "At first, I thought this was to be a short affair, but now with this news from Saratoga this fall, I wonder if these Americans could actually win."

Jacques* feigned surprise, "Against the British Empire?"

Macomb stopped by a bench overlooking the river, inviting Jacques* to sit. "There is rumor of a possible alliance of France and the rebels. Monsieur, these rebels may win. In fact, I believe they shall win. Let me be frank. The King of England is a fool. He has no grasp of the situation here. Although many landowners seem to be loyal to the crown, like you they do not see a great change with the rebels and not necessarily a bad change. If the rebels prevail, the predicted mass exodus to England will not occur. I for one have no intention of returning to Ireland."

Jacques* replied, "As I said, I think most of the French are neutral."

"As am I Monsieur. I thank you for the visit and apologize for my wife's attempt at matchmaking. I suppose you encounter this frequently."

Jacques* chuckled, "It has occurred."

"Well Monsieur, perhaps I will see you at the militia meetings." Jacques* looked surprised. "Yes, like some of the *habitants,* I show up occasionally. It gives me the opportunity to drink to excess. Madame Macomb frowns upon it at home. Well, good day sir."

"Good day sir and thank you for dinner." Jacques* returned to his horse and as the sun set behind him, he rode home pondering the meaning of this meeting.

Jacques* attended his first militia meeting two weeks later. It was held in the meadow behind the fort. On his way, Jacques* met Pierre Drouillard who had crossed the river with Bonaventure Reaume. It was Pierre's first meeting, but Reaume had been a member and was now a lieutenant.

The meeting was an altogether disorganized affair. Colonel Lernoult spoke, they practiced marching and formations, and then had shooting practice. The group was evenly split between French and English members. The English were even more pathetic. At least the French could shoot. Alexander Macomb and his brother William came by and said hello to Jacques*. At the end of the ordeal, Lernoult addressed the men, "We have news of rebel activity to our west. George Rogers Clark is leading a group to attack Kaskaskia in the Illinois country. If he succeeds, we have reason to believe he will turn on Détroit. Our current fortifications are entirely unacceptable. Lieutenant Hamilton and I have plans for a new fort where we stand which will be included in expanded fortification of the city. Construction soon will begin and I am asking each of the residents to donate three days a week to work on the building."

Following dismissal, the group split along ethnic lines and headed to one of the city's two taverns. The conversation was less subdued than usual. Pierre Reaume began, "It's bad enough that we have to march with this group, but now we must give up farming to build the new fort. I told Lernoult I'm retiring; I've been coming almost a year."

Baptiste Campau spoke up, "We must maintain an air of cooperation. Do not forget, the English are powerful, they may win. The new fort will benefit the city. We must consider our best interest in view of our options. At any rate, I have met this man Clark, and if he attacks Détroit, a bigger fort will not stop him."

The next Sunday marked the first time the Allard farm would host the Milk River picnic. Monique was busy all week long and her daughter even came from Assumption to help. On the big day, as the *habitants* returned from Sainte-Anne, Monique's son-in-law arrived with two female guests. Marie Saint-Jacques was a *métis* friend of Henri-Pierre's sister and the other lady was Agathe Saint-Pierre. Agathe was a young widow in her early twenties. She and her husband had come from Montréal one year ago, but he had drowned in the early spring.

228

There was little doubt why these two were invited, as the hunt for wives for Jacques* and Henri-Pierre had become a full-time job for the ladies of the settlement. Henri-Pierre confided in Jacques*, "I'm afraid to go to bed at night for fear my mother has planted a prospective wife under the sheets."

The two couples sat politely on the lawn and dined and visited. Marie Saint-Jacques was all of sixteen and very shy. Agathe was quite the opposite. Twenty years old she had a three-year old daughter who was off playing with the other children. Agathe was also very attractive, animated and intelligent.

At home that evening Henri-Pierre asked his friend what he thought of his date. Jacques* replied, "Pretty enough, smart, but I don't know. She's not for me."
Henri-Pierre replied, "You're certain?"
"Quite certain." The next Sunday, Henri-Pierre visited his sister after mass and also visited with the young widow Saint-Pierre. As the summer progressed they kept frequent company, but Henri-Pierre's friend Jacques* Allard continued as available as ever.

Détroit, Autumn 1778 - The Pontchartrain Tavern:

Jacques* and Henri-Pierre with some of their friends were relieving their thirst after a day laboring on the new fort. Work was progressing slowly reflecting the lack of interest of the French farmers. In fact, although Lernoult had suggested three days work a week for each resident,

Jacques* and Henri-Pierre had only worked three times all summer.

Just as Marsac had brought a round of shots and beers, the door burst open and Pierre* Saint-Aubin entered. He quickly joined the men at the table, and as soon as he could order a round, he began, "News has just arrived. General George Rogers Clark has raided the Illinois territory and taken the fort at Kaskaskia from the British. He is said to be planning to stage an attack on Détroit. Lernoult has heard this and is in a panic. He is calling for rigid work details to finish the new fort."

Henri-Pierre took a drink and replied. "Looks as though we have just enough time to finish the harvest and head north before our next work detail comes up."

Within the week the men were at Rivard's picking up their supplies for the winter. As the shopkeeper piled up their goods, he asked Jacques*, "Could you do me a great service and deliver this package to Tucker on your way up?" He produced a large package and placed it along with the other items. "I don't know what it is but he asked about it last time he was in. Now I hear he has gone up to his property and I don't know when he'll be back." Jacques* agreed and loaded it with the rest.

They loaded and departed. The next evening they reached the point marking the northern end of L'Anse Creuse. At the mouth of the River of the Huron they headed inland and beached the canoes. It was a glorious early autumn evening. The colors were just changing and the warm offshore breeze kept the lake flat. Jacques* reported, "This is his land. Now all we have to do is find him."

William Tucker was possibly the strangest man in Détroit, and that was no small accomplishment. Tucker was a few years younger than Jacques*. His father had been a Virginia colonist, but when William was eleven, Chippewa Indians raided his father's farm, killed his parents and kidnapped William and his brother Joseph. The boys lived with the natives for some years and eventually landed in Détroit. William had worked for the army as an interpreter but had recently occupied this land in the middle of nowhere. What his plans were was anyone's guess, but no one had ever had a clear grasp on what William Tucker was thinking.

They beached by a small wooden shelter that was probably Tucker's as it was the only structure in the area. The only trees that had been cut had been used for the shelter or fires. No one was in sight. They sensed a fire farther inland and proceeded toward it. Eventually they came upon a small Chippewa camp. There was dancing at the fire by the Indians and William Tucker in full Chippewa dress.

The men stood in the background until Tucker noticed them and came out of the dance. He shook hands with Jacques* and Henri-Pierre, "We are asking the Great Spirit for a good hunt." Although Tucker was younger than Jacques*, he appeared older. His forehead was balding. The hair he had was very long and tied in back. It had taken on a salt and pepper character. Naked to the waist with Indian style deerskin trousers. His body was fiercely painted. His heritage was betrayed only by a two day growth of beard and his deep-set blue eyes, the sort of eyes which made one wonder what was behind them. Old Joseph would have described them as the eyes of a tormented soul.

Jacques* explained the purpose of their visit and presented Tucker with his package. Tucker merely took it without comment other than inviting the men to stay and eat. They were seated at the fire and when the dancing ended, women brought food. Tucker sat next to Jacques*. Breaking a piece of corn bread, "Not even the French can make corn bread this good. My people are relying more and more on crops. The westward expansion of the European is making subsistence by hunting impossible.

"We are planting a large area behind us. I say 'my people'. As you know I have two people. In town I wear a red coat and translate for the British, but here I am with the people who raised me to a man. It is here I feel at home. We occupy an enormous segment of land. British or American, it makes no matter. Here we have our own country and I shall be king." He gave a laugh that fit with his deep set eyes. "The Chippewa are not the best farmers. I may have to go back to Virginia and bring back slaves." He gave another shrill laugh.

The men departed for their winter camp at dawn. Once away from shore, Henri-Pierre said, "I wonder what was in the package."
Jean-Baptiste* Laforest replied, "Perhaps a tool to tighten the loose screw in Tucker's head. Do you think he is serious about slaves in the Indian camp?"
Jacques* stopped paddling momentarily, "With Tucker, who can say. I hear slavery has been all but ended

in the British Isles but it is still common in the southern colonies."

In fact there were African servants in Détroit. Most had British owners. Even Campau had a few that worked his farm. Their relationship was more servant than slave. Although they were owned by law, most travelled rather freely and were occasionally allowed to leave as free men. The men had heard the situation in the south was quite different.

The winter was fine, just enough snow and ice, and the trapping was as good as ever. They returned to Détroit in the early spring. This season no Indian ladies came for Henri-Pierre and Jacques*. The word was out that they were looking for French wives.

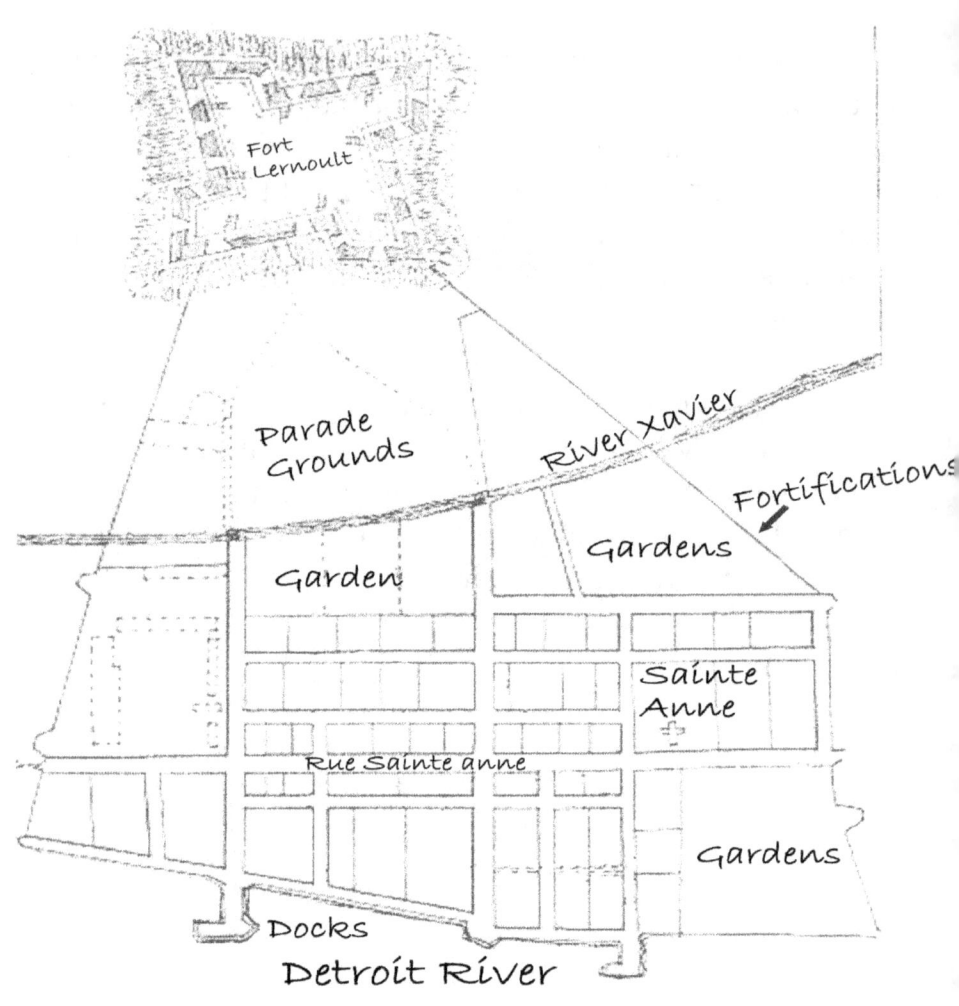

Fort
Lernoult

Parade
Grounds

River Xavier

Fortifications

Garden

Gardens

Sainte
Anne

Rue Sainte anne

Gardens

Docks

Detroit River

(Detroit After Completion of Fort Lernoult

Chapter 29

Détroit - Spring 1779:

As the men landed at Cadillac's old docks, a few changes were evident. The docks had been enlarged and improved. The small sailing vessels that plied the lakes could now easily unload directly onto the dock. In addition, considerable progress had been made on Lernoult's new fort. The fortifications of the town stretched all the way back to and included the new fort. The new fort itself was also taking shape.

Rivard's store was unchanged as was Rivard. "The construction is progressing. A few new British soldiers and officers have arrived and we are expecting a new commandant in the next few weeks. Hamilton was recently taken captive at fort Vincennes by George Rogers Clark and the American Militia. Lernoult is to stay until the completion of the fort which is to be called 'Fort Lernoult'."

After unloading their furs to Rivard's, Toussaint, Jacques* and Henri-Pierre took a walk around the expanded town. The interior walls of the old Fort Détroit had been removed and the official quarters moved to the new fort. The streets of the village remained the same. The northwest wall had been removed and between the old fortification and the new fort was a large meadow almost one-half mile long. Gardens to feed the fort were planted on the sides while the center was a parade and military training ground. The meadow was crossed by the stream the French called the Xavier River, which had previously flowed behind the fortification before turning to empty into the Détroit River. The new Fort Lernoult was taking form at the northwestern edge of the new fortification.

A small gathering of men in the meadow were listening to an animated speaker who stood with a much younger man. They both had the look of *métis* but darker. They wore the typical dress of British businessmen. Just as the voyageurs approached them the presentation ended and the crowd slowly began to disperse. Toussaint suddenly called out "Georges! Cousin Georges!"

The speaker looked over and replied, "Toussaint!" going quickly to meet him. After a brief conversation and introduction of the young man as his son Thomas, Georges said, "I am afraid we must run. We have a meeting in Assumption. We are however free Sunday after mass."

Toussaint replied, "Excellent, we always have a picnic after mass. Like the old days in Québec. We will meet you and Thomas at the church."

When the family entered Sainte-Anne that Sunday, they were surprised to see Georges and Thomas sitting in the front of the church talking to Simple Bocquet. After the Gospel reading, Bocquet turned to his congregation and said, "This morning in lieu of my usual sermon, I have asked a visitor who is no stranger to Détroit to say a few words. He can probably introduce himself better than I. Monsieur de Baptiste."

Georges rose to the pulpit. He was as old as Toussaint, and his white hair tightly curled. His son Thomas remained seated, a younger version of his father with dark black hair. Georges surveyed the group and began to speak in excellent French, "I am the only son of an African slave and a Québécoise *métis* woman. My family name is the same as Toussaint de Baptiste of Détroit. He is my cousin.

"My father's name was simply 'Tom'. He was born of African parents in the English colony of South Carolina. Over seventy years ago he was purchased by an English officer sent north to fight the French, and he was serving as personal servant to this man when they encountered a group of Québec militia. My father and the officer were taken captive along with an English soldier. The English officer died. My father and the soldier named Jacob* Thomas were taken prisoner by Jean-Baptiste* Allard, whose grandson Jacques* is among you today and his Algonquin friend, Joseph, who you may remember as the father of Toussaint de Baptiste.

"My father remained and became a free citizen of Québec. He married a *métis* woman named de Baptiste and took her family name. Joseph married her twin sister. As a result we share this name. Later my father went with Jean-Baptiste* Allard, Joseph, and Jacob* Thomas to help Antoine Cadillac build the city of *le Nouvelle Orléans* in the Louisiana territory. It was there they had the good fortune to rescue a family of escaped slaves who remained in the new city. They also rescued a ship of African slaves from slave merchants on the island of Cuba. This experience led my father to a life of fighting slavery. He moved to Détroit where I was born and later to Virginia where my son Thomas was born. All three of us have devoted our lives to this mission.

237

"I know that many of you are aware of the evils of the slave trade and the evils of the slave owners to the south. Great Britain has banned slavery on the British Isles, and the territory of Vermont has banished the practice as well. In the next few years we hope to have banished it in all the northern colonies regardless of the outcome of the current revolution."

Georges continued for a while on the evils of slavery and movements afoot aimed at its demise. He was an excellent orator and spoke English as perfectly as French. Although he exceeded the usual time of Simple Bocquet's sermons, the congregation's interest did not wane. Following the conversations after mass with parishioners, Georges and Thomas loaded into Jacques*'s wagon and headed for the Milk River.

The guests were greeted with enthusiasm, many of the older residents remembered Georges from when he lived in Détroit with his father, Tom. His son Thomas was about twenty, but as elegant and persuasive a speaker as his father. Realizing he now had a more discreet and sympathetic audience, he expanded on the mission. "For years, my father and grandfather have aided slaves who are free," then quietly, "Or who have escaped, traveling to the Québec territory where they have been allowed to stay as free men. We hope to increase this program.

"We fully expect Americans to prevail in the war, and are concerned that although the Americans to the north are sympathetic, those to the south are not. They are less sympathetic than the British. We look to this to be an ongoing and uphill struggle. However, we are certain that slavery will not continue indefinitely. Abolition, as we call it, movements are afoot in many modern nations today."

The picnic commenced and as Thomas sat enjoying the meal, Marie-Françoise* Balard came and sat beside him. "Monsieur, I am, as you are, *métis*. I have much interest in this plan of yours. Have you considered housing slaves secretly here, near the river, then moving them across where they are safer? You could make a network of such places with sympathetic citizens." The idea struck Thomas and his father, and as they sat with this young lady, a plan to have great importance began to take form.

Jacques* was walking across the lawn when he noticed a beautiful young lady whom he did not recognize. Suddenly pleased that he had been able to shave, cut his hair, and bathe properly since his return, he followed her. He saw Jean-Baptiste* Laforest and asked, "Baptiste? Who is that girl?"

His friend laughed, "Charles* Saint-Aubin's youngest, Marie-Louise*. She's been at the convent in Montréal for the past three years for schooling."

Jacques* whistled low, "Didn't she have a big butt and bad skin?"

"I guess the convent agreed with her. If you like, I will help you renew your acquaintance. I talked to her at mass today. I think she is too educated for you, however." Having lost interest in the issue of slavery, the two men made their move.

Three weeks later, Jacques* and Henri-Pierre sat at another Sunday picnic but this time both in the company of enthusiastic, marriageable young women. Henri-Pierre and Agathe Saint-Pierre were becoming serious. It was not well concealed that they had kept overnight company occasionally. Although they would not flaunt this at church, this had always been accepted in Québec society when the lady in question was a widow with children.

Jacques* and Marie-Louise* Saint-Aubin, on the other hand, remained strictly celibate. Charles* Saint-Aubin had only three children. Marie-Louise*'s older sister, Madeleine had already married, and their only brother had died young. Having spent three years at school in Montréal, Marie-Louise* was much more educated than her peers, and she was now the only remaining child of a very rich father. She and Jacques* related well although frequently he had no idea what she was talking about. On the other hand, Jacques* Allard was on the short list of eligible men of all the young girls in Détroit.

At the end of July, Henri-Pierre made an announcement. "Agathe and I have been to see the priest and register our banns. We will be married in three weeks." Three weeks later they were married at the Church of the Assumption and moved into the Allard farm house. Henri-Pierre and Jacques* had started a new house for the new family and would have it finished before winter. This caused Jacques* to seriously consider his situation. Two weeks later at the picnic following mass, he broached the subject. Marie-Louise* seemed delighted, "It will be wonderful. You can begin at the mill and soon assume my father's role. Jacques*, we will be rich!"

Jacques* had not foreseen this complication. Although she was correct that she would come with a great dowry and there was no one else to take Charles* Saint-Aubin's position, Jacques* had never seen himself as an indoor businessman. "Well, actually I was planning on continuing the farm. I do have a good deal of property and I am certain it will continue to grow."

"Jacques*, my father did not have me educated to be a farmer's wife. Think about it, you'll agree."

That night he saw the bear in his dreams. The bear came around in times of crises. Jacques* had no actual memory of the bear he had met as an infant when it killed his grandparents. But the bear came at times and he always had good advice. *The old bear looked into Jacques*'s different-colored eyes with his own dark red eyes, "You are correct. You are meant for the outdoors and the frontier. You still have work to do."*

A few days later he went to call on Marie-Louise* after dinner. They took a walk down to the beach and walked across the sand looking at the moonlight glimmering on the ripples of the lake. "Marie-Louise*, I think I need to stay on the farm. Jean-Baptiste* Laforest can run the mill. You will like the farming life once you get used to it."

She stopped suddenly and said, "Let's go for a swim!" And as though it was a daily ritual, she removed her clothes and stood naked in the moonlight, saying, "Well, let's go." She walked slowly into the lake under the bright moon. Jacques* undressed and followed her in. He was amazed at her beauty. Even Quiet Stream did not have this beauty. They splashed about for a while and she embraced him closely with a long passionate kiss. She then left the water slowly and picked up her clothes. Standing before him, she said, "Well then, I guess it is not to be." And with a platonic kiss on the forehead, she walked away naked, carrying her clothes, up to her father's house leaving a confused Jacques* Allard in the moonlight.

Chapter 30

<u>Détroit, - September, 1779:</u>

The next day the big news arrived. The new commandant had come to town. Major Arent Schuyler DePeyster was a native of the new world. Born in New York and educated in London, he had been a junior officer in the Seven Years War. He had been taken captive and held prisoner in France. Well schooled in Indian warfare, he had just left the commanding position at Fort Michilimackinac. As members of the militia, Jacques* and Jean-Baptiste* Laforest had been asked to attend the ceremonies. At their conclusion they headed north in Laforest's cart to do some hunting behind Jacques*'s farm.

Along the way, Jean-Baptiste* broke the silence, "Well, anything has to be better than old Hamilton. By the way, I have started seeing Marie-Louise* Saint-Aubin."

Taken by surprise, Jacques* replied, "OK by me, I guess we're through." He thought it would be best not to mention the swim.

Laforest continued, "We are going to be married this winter. I'll take over my father's as well as her father's role at the mill."

Jacques* said awkwardly, "OK by me."

"Oh, and Jacques*."

"Yes?"

"She told me about the swim." Jacques* began to laugh and soon Jean-Baptiste* had to stop the cart for them to get over their fits of laughter.

Jacques* held out his hand, "Congratulations."

They returned to small talk as they pulled into Jean-Baptiste*'s house by the mill. "I seem to have forgotten my things for the hunt." Baptiste* went in the house while Jacques* waited in the cart. A lovely young lady approached, and Jacques* began to think furiously, "Who could this be?"

She looked up and asked, "Jacques*, have you seen Baptiste*?"

He stuttered, "Up to the house." She thanked him and skipped off. He could not take his eyes off her.

Soon Jean-Baptiste* returned with his rifle and gear. Jacques* croaked out, "Who was that?"

"My little sister."

Jean-Baptiste* had five little sisters, so Jacques*started mentally to do the inventory, "Jennie*?"

As the cart jolted forward, "Yeah."

As they proceeded north to the Allard farm, Jacques* couldn't get the young woman out of his mind. He tried to remember more about her, particularly her age. He had never thought of her before as an adult. Upon reaching the farm, the two men and Jean-Baptiste*'s bird dog walked past the fields and into the woods. They came to the pond and beyond where a fire some years before had caused a meadow perfect for pheasant on this gorgeous early autumn afternoon. The dog started to flush out birds easily. Jean-Baptiste* shot five. Jacques*, on the other hand, had missed two and seemed to ignore four more.

They came to an old fallen oak tree where Jean-Baptiste* sat and lit his pipe. "Is this about my little sister?"

Jacques* responded, "How old is she? I was trying to remember."

"Old enough I suppose, sixteen." Jacques* realized that this was considered prime marrying age in Détroit, but it did mean he was exactly twice her age. Realizing this was why his friend had lost his hunting interest, Baptiste* decided he needed to say more. "I have to warn you, she's a handful. She was only four when our mother died. When father remarried three years later, Jennie* was kind of taking care of herself. Our stepmother started having her own children and Jennie* kind of remained independent. She's smart but very headstrong and a little wild. She will definitely go swimming with you. Now that I think more about it, she might be just right for you. Why don't you come to the mill after mass Sunday? I know my stepmother would love to get her out of the house."

Windmill Pointe - October 1779:

Jacques* attended mass on horseback so he could stop at the mill on his way home. Windmill Pointe had been settled by four young interrelated Tremblay and Laforest families in 1750. Today it was almost a small village in itself. The point was a right angle of land protruding exactly at the junction of Lake Saint Clair and the Détroit River. The Fox Creek, named for a tribe long absent from Détroit, ran directly through the point exactly where the city fathers would later declare the border of the city of Détroit.

Today in full autumn splendor it was at its best. The four mills sat at the end of the point. They were stone towers with graceful vanes, all in excellent repair. The extended families now had six houses that formed a half-ring around a central green with the mills at the end. Farms extended back like slices of a pie reminiscent of Charlesbourg in Québec. The four original young families had produced a total of forty-four children. The original houses had been rebuilt and added to. These were all large by Détroit standards of the day.

The Laforest house was the largest and grandest. Jean-Baptiste*'s father, Guillaume* Laforest, had been the head operator of the mill since its inception, and no one disputed that it was he who was responsible for the enterprise at it existed today. Today he owned it jointly with Charles* Saint-Aubin. This relationship was about to become stronger with the pending marriage of Jean-Baptiste* Laforest and Marie-Louise* Saint-Aubin.

Red and yellow maple and oak trees checkered the green, and graceful willows in the full gold of autumn graced the banks of the rivers and lake. Directly off the point, one could see *l'Ile du Pêcheurs,* or as the English had renamed it Peche Island. Looking to the right, one saw the tip of *Belle Ile* and to the left the expanse of Lake Saint Clair as the English now spelled it. In back of each house was an orderly grape arbor and orchard followed by vegetables and fields of grain and corn. Work at the mill did not prevent these families from being successful farmers.

Jacques* Allard rode his horse up to the Laforest barn as he had many times before and dismounted. As a long-term friend of Jean-Baptiste*, he had been here innumerable times over the past several years, but today it was apparent that something was different. The women were hard at work preparing an outdoor lunch. Trying unsuccessfully to be casual, the adults all drifted over to greet him. Jennie*'s stepmother, Genevieve Bigrass-Laforest, came over and welcomed him graciously. Jacques* could not fail to realize that she had hardly said two words to him in the twelve years she had been Jean-Baptiste*'s stepmother. Guillaume* Laforest came and greeted him as though Jacques* was George Washington himself. Finally Jean-Baptiste* came by and rescued him.

Chuckling, his friend said, "I think the cat is out of the bag." Not long after, he saw Jennie* helping the ladies with preparations. Marie-Genevieve-Madeleine* Laforest was the seventh of eight children born to Guillaume* Laforest and Marie-Marguerite* Tremblay and their fifth child born in Détroit. When angry, her father would call her Genevieve* but at all other times and to all other people, she had always been Jennie*. Her mother died when Jennie* was four. Her oldest sister cared for her and the younger children until her father remarried three years later.

Her stepmother was a widow with no children. She was however, only five years older than Jean-Baptiste* and overwhelmed by the sudden large family. Jennie* became very independent at a very young age. Jacques* was wondering how she had gone from a friend's little sister to spectacular young woman so quickly and without his notice.

Jacques* did not have to worry how to handle this situation. Everything seemed to have been prearranged. Soon he found himself conveniently having his first actual conversation ever with Jennie*. He wasn't even aware of how it happened. Although women her age were thought ready for marriage, they generally came with a certain degree of immaturity. This girl had more poise than any other young lady he had met regardless of age. They ate together at a table seated with others who had obviously been cast for the part. After dinner her older sister, Madeleine suggested they take a walk.

The threesome strolled northward on the beach. As they approached a more isolated area, Jennie*'s youngest sister, Archange, appeared suddenly and asked Marguerite to help her with something, conveniently removing the obligatory chaperone. As they went a little farther, Jennie* said, "You know we planned that."

"Oh?"

"I just want to be honest. I don't like deceit." She sat down on a rock and took off her shoes and stockings. She rolled up her skirt and continued the walk wading on the beach. Jacques* followed suit. Soon they came to a beached canoe. "This is mine. Would you like a ride?"

Becoming more impressed, Jacques* answered, "Sure."

She easily pulled the craft into the water and entered the canoe as well as any voyageur. "You don't mind if I steer?"

"Not at all." Jacques* was certain he had never seen a woman handle a canoe like this.

As they left the shore she said, "I have nightlines here." She took a large hook on a rope from the floor of the canoe and threw it overboard, then continued on until the canoe slowed. She retrieved the hook with another line on it. As she pulled it up it was evident that it contained small

248

hooks and the first few contained pickerel. She lowered the line back into the water, "I'll get them in the morning."

More and more amazed, Jacques* asked, "What else do you do?"

"I like to hunt birds. I'm a good shot. I trap rabbits, too. Baptiste* taught me. Baptiste* taught me everything. When our mother died, my world ended. Archange was youngest and got all the attention. My father thought I was old enough to do for myself, but he was wrong. It was Jean-Baptiste* who came and told me everything would be all right. He took me everywhere, hunting, fishing, swimming. My father said I was becoming another son. By the time he remarried, I was all right. I was independent, and I always had Baptiste*.

"As I said, I do not like deceit. When you saw me the other day, it was not by chance. I started noticing you as soon as I was old enough to notice boys. I have always adored your eyes. I asked Baptiste* what you were like. He said that you were the finest man in Détroit. I waited until I was old enough, and this is it. The other day I hid Baptiste*'s gun so he would return home to find it. I was waiting. Was I terrible?"

"Not so far."

"We should return. My father trusts me, but only so far." She deftly turned the canoe and they were soon back at the picnic. As Jacques* went to leave, Guillaume* Laforest approached. "Thank you for coming, Jacques*. Will you join us next week?"

Trying not to look too eager, "Yes sir, thank you." Jacques* Allard returned to the mill three Sundays in a row. Each time he found Jennie* more interesting and more attractive.

249

Chapter 31

Jacques* sat on a large log overlooking the lake. The sky was ominous as a storm approached from the north. He heard something from behind. He turned to see the bear, now getting grey around his whiskers as old grizzlies do. He looked at Jacques*, "This is the one, young Allard. Now is the time."

Jacques* waited for a second when the first bolt of lightning struck. "I worry she is too young."

As the wind began to howl he noticed a girl by an old birch tree. It was Quiet Stream. She gazed at him a long while as the rain began to fall, "And how old was I?"

Jacques* Allard awoke with his heart racing. He was drenched in sweat. The following morning he rode to Windmill Pointe.

As he entered the grounds, he saw Louis-Michel Tremblay hauling sacks. "Louis-Michel, where might I find Monsieur Laforest?"

His friend lowered his sack and pointed, "Second lumber mill."

Entering the mill, the sound of the saw was deafening. He saw Guillaume* Laforest talking with two of his laborers. When Laforest saw Jacques* he came over. Jacques* shouted, "May I speak with you, sir?"

Guillaume* pointed to the door and they went out walking toward the beach. "Is this about my daughter?"

Unsure of the meaning of this direct question, Jacques* gathered his courage and said, "Yes sir. I would like your permission to marry her."

250

"Praise God! Have you asked her?"

"Not yet sir, I wanted to ask you first."

Laforest motioned, inviting him to sit on a large log. "I would advise it. She is one headstrong woman. However I am certain she will be thrilled." Then smiling, "In fact, had you not moved soon, life around here may have become difficult." Then becoming serious. "I knew your father well in the old days in Québec. He was as fine a man as I have known. I have seen a great deal of him in you. Jennie* is my most precious child. I could never have imagined anyone better for her than you."

As they walked back to the mill, Guillaume* asked, "What would you expect for a dowry?"

Totally unprepared for this question, Jacques* stuttered, "Well… I…don't…"

Laforest rescued him by saying, "Well, I guess I should do at least as well as Charles* Saint-Aubin is doing for Jean-Baptiste*." He took his carpenter's pencil from behind his ear and wrote something on a small sheet of paper he had in his pocket. He handed it to Jacques*. Jacques* looked at it and his jaw almost hit the ground. Laforest again rescued him. "You have always been a good steward of money. I am certain you will use it wisely. Come this Sunday and we will announce it, but you had best tell the bride first. I believe she is at the house."

Guillaume* returned to the mill and Jacques* went to the house. He was pleased to see Jennie* sitting alone on the porch swing, busy with some project. He came up the steps and cleared his throat. She looked up and said, "Why Monsieur Allard, what a surprise. What brings you to the mill on a Tuesday?"

251

Jacques* joined her on the swing, "Genevieve* Laforest, will you marry me?"

She looked up calmly, "Only my father calls me Genevieve*, and he will never consent."

He persisted, "I've just come from talking to him. He has agreed."

She quietly put down her sewing and replied, "I know. I've been watching since you arrived." She put her arms around his neck and kissed him passionately. "Of course I will!" As he recovered, she went into her organization mode, "When will we do it?" Thinking for a second she continued, "Baptiste* and Marie-Louise* are planning to wait for *La Chandeleur.*" referring to a traditional French holiday of the candles on February 2. "Marie-Louise* has some silly idea from the convent. However, I think we must wait until after their wedding, but only a few days. My father will be pleased with the wait so people won't think either of us is pregnant."

Jacques* was beginning to realize his bride was not one afraid of speaking her mind. After a while he excused himself to return to his farming. They embraced one more time and he made his way to his horse. He found Henri-Pierre and Toussaint in the field but waited for dinner to make the announcement. There was much excitement, mostly on the part of Monique and Agathe who began planning in earnest. Henri-Pierre and Agathe were almost ready to move to their new house, and Toussaint suggested that he build a small one for him and Monique.

Jacques* announced that they should stay in the current house and he would build a new one for himself and

Jennie*. He confessed he would be able to easily fund it with only part of the generous dowry from her father.

The following Sunday, the picnic at Windmill Pointe was a good deal larger than usual. In fact most of Grosse Pointe, Milk River and eastern Détroit were present. Guillaume* Laforest had spared nothing. Food, wine, and beer abounded. He gave a wonderful, if not short announcement. Jacques* and Jennie* spent the entire day being congratulated. Even Simple Bocquet was in attendance.

The gangly priest came to pay his regards as the couple was talking to Jacques*'s neighbor, Louis* Greffard and Marguerite* Saint-Aubin-Greffard. "Well Monsieur Allard, congratulations. I remember the day I baptized Genevieve*. Loudest screamer I ever had. I think some of the echoes are still ringing in the belfry." Laughing at his own joke, he added, "In fact Monsieur Greffard, were you not *Parrain*?" Confessing his role as godfather, Louis* agreed. Bocquet continued, "Yes, well, are we not all one happy family? One thing about the parish of Sainte-Anne, we are indeed one happy family."

After the festivities had calmed down, Jennie* took Jacques* to escape down the beach. As can happen in Détroit, although it was late November, it was actually hot. Jennie* removed her shoes and stockings and they waded in the chilly water. When they were well out of sight she said off-handedly, "Marie-Louise* told me she went swimming with you." Jacques* had the good judgment to remain silent. "I don't mind, really." Then turning and staring her dark brown eyes into his different colored pair, "Would you go swimming now with me?"

After pausing, "I think we should wait."

"But how will you know if you like me?"

"Oh, I will like you."

"No, I mean how will you know you will like *all* of me?"

"I know I will."

"But how?"

"An old grizzly bear told me." She stared for a while and then embraced him with a long kiss. Jacques* felt his resolve slipping and suggested they turn back.

The next day it snowed six inches. The farmers finished the necessary chores of the harvest and began clearing land in earnest. At Windmill Pointe, they began to get ready for the onslaught of trees to be turned into lumber. Fortunately Guillaume* Laforest gave precedence to the Allard trees so his daughter's house could be completed by February. Jacques* and Henri-Pierre had given up trapping for carpentry and marriage. In early December Henri-Pierre's first child, a daughter, Lucille de Baptiste, was born.

Sainte-Anne Cathedral - Détroit, February 2, 1780:

Simple Bocquet came to the pulpit; the gangly priest was beginning to feel his age and moved more slowly. His level of enthusiasm had, however, not weakened and his sermons were as boring as ever. "The feast of *Chandeleur* marks the midway between the winter solstice and the beginning of spring. In France it is the traditional blessing of the candles. Also in the old country it was believed that

254

the wolves left their winter dens on this day. If it was sunny and they saw their shadow, spring would be late. If it was cloudy, spring would be early. Today was chosen as the day joining two of Sainte-Anne's oldest families. The marriage of Jean-Baptiste* Laforest and Marie-Louise* Saint Aubin. This will mark the 317th marriage in the 79 years of our parish."

Following the ceremony, there was a grand celebration at the farm of Charles* Saint-Aubin. Winter had been harsh and the snow was deep. All the *habitants* had installed runners making their carts into sleighs. However, the day was overcast and the city in the wilderness hoped for an early spring. After dinner, Jacques* and Jennie* walked along the path leading into the woods on the side of the Saint-Aubin farm. They walked hand in hand contemplating their marriage a few days hence.

Suddenly Jennie* stopped, "Look, just as Father Bocquet said." Two small wolf cubs stood at the clearing. She cautiously approached them when she heard a low growl behind her. Her heart raced as she realized she had committed a cardinal sin of the woods. She turned slowly and came directly into the gaze of the yellow eyes of their mother. The only thing more dangerous than meeting a wolf, bear, or lion in the wild, was being between a mother and her young. Having no weapons, she knew she was doomed. She began to sob knowing due to her foolishness she would never see her wedding day.

Softly Jacques* said, "Don't move, and be silent." Jennie*'s mouth dropped as he walked slowly to the she-wolf and softly touched her nose. He then went to the cubs, and to his fiancé's horror, he picked them up, one by one and brought them to their mother. The wolf sniffed her cubs, turned and returned slowly to the cover of the forest.

Jennie* threw herself into his arms and half laughing, half sobbing said, "Jean-Baptiste* told me about this, but I thought he was joking. But it is true. You are an animal charmer."

Jacques* replied calmly, "I don't know why or how, but it has always been. If I do not threaten an animal, they will not threaten me. An old Indian once told me that it was a gift from the Great Spirit and if it is used to hurt an animal, it is taken away. Anyway, I don't know how this will bode for an early spring." Understanding the joke, Jennie* began to laugh and suddenly the fear of the wolf was gone.

<u>Sainte-Anne Cathedral, Détroit - February 7, 1780:</u>

It would appear that the wolf had seen her shadow, as the weather remained extremely cold. Fortunately the day was clear and sunny as Simple Bocquet stood for the second time in a week in front of the same members of his congregation as he joined Jacques* and Jennie*. In spite of the weather, a grand celebration was held at the mill. Due to the cold weather, their friends from Assumption were able to cross the frozen water to attend the ceremony. Pierre Drouillard was there with his son Georges now seven years old.

At the mill Jacques* climbed down from the sleigh. He saw a man approaching on crutches. To his amazement it was his old boss and teacher, Jean-Baptiste Charbonneau. Jacques* rushed to greet him and introduce him to Jennie*.

Jean-Baptiste explained, "We were headed west for the winter when I broke my leg at Niagara. We were through the portage, so we continued to Détroit and have held up with André* Peltier. I am with two of my boys, Jean-Baptiste Jr. and Toussaint." The men shook hands. Baptiste Jr. was a copy of his father as a young man. At twenty he was soft spoken and thoughtful. He exuded his father's gracious confidence. His younger brother, Toussaint, was only thirteen but seemed much more impulsive than the other Charbonneaus.

As the day progressed, Jacques* had the opportunity to visit with his old mentor. "This broken leg has helped me with a decision. I am going to move my family to Assumption in the spring. No matter the outcome of the war, Détroit is going to become the center of the fur trade. There are enough portages in life without Lachine or Niagara."

Jacques* noted, "Your boys have grown nicely."

"Yes, young Baptiste is a fine level-headed man and will do well. His young brother, however, remains a mystery to me. He is more skilled in the ways of the wilderness than I was at twice his age. But for him, the hunt is everything. The business means nothing. He reminds me of old Pierre Roy. He will pick a fight with a grown man and frequently take a licking, but it has no effect on the lad."

At this point an older man unknown to Jacques* joined them. He shook hands with Charbonneau who introduced him, "Jacques* Allard, meet Jacob Harsen from New York." The men shook hands. "Jacob has recently taken a small place down the point from here."

Harsen added in passable French, "My wife is French. We married in Albany where I lived before. I had knowledge of Détroit from dealings in furs with John Jacob Aster. Now I am a blacksmith by trade but not presently employed. Monsieur Allard, I understand you have knowledge of a great marsh at the upper end of this lake." When Jacques* affirmed, Harsen added "I wonder if when the weather breaks, I could hire you to guide me there."

Jacques* replied, "I could do it if it does not interfere with my farm and new marriage."

"Of course, it would be at your convenience. I will come discuss it with you when the weather is better." And rising he took his leave.

At the end of the day Jacques* and Jennie* left with Toussaint, Henri-Pierre and their families. The new Allard home had been finished for a few weeks. Jennie* had been by to plan but there was still work to be done. The three houses faced the beach with a wonderful view of the lake. The new house was larger than the first two and was a typical French-Canadian farm house with room for a very large family.

After bringing the fire to life, Jacques* poured a toast of Québecois Calvados. The wind shifted violently to the north and a blizzard began to howl. Jennie* exclaimed, "Good, my sister said that a storm during your wedding night is good luck." Jacques* seemed awkward and she continued, "Don't worry, I have three older married sisters. I have been well instructed." In the morning, Jacques* arose exhausted. He realized that his bride had been well instructed, and his old grizzly bear had been correct.

In the morning there was a knock on their door. Jacques* opened it and found Toussaint who had braved the large snow drifts that had collected overnight. He held a package wrapped in a leather cover. "I said I would give you this as soon as you had a wall on which to hang it." Jacques* unwrapped the carved panel.

Jennie* looked it over, "Whatever is this?"

Her new husband replied, "My father's ice boat. Maybe someday I can really show you."

Chapter 32

As winter wore on the new Allard family began plans for the future. At this point the complex including Toussaint, Henri-Pierre, Jacques* and their families had enough crops to fulfill their personal needs, two cows, three horses, three pigs and some chickens. Their livelihood to date had been mainly trapping, but the men now spent the day clearing land to plant and add livestock in the spring. Jennie* used her fishing skills to provide food. Each morning she took Henri-Pierre's two sled dogs onto the lake and fished through the ice, returning each noon with more than enough fish to feed the three families.

In March, as spring was finally in the air, Jacques* went to Rivard's for supplies. As usual, the shopkeeper was up on local happenings. "DePeyster has sent a group of soldiers with two hundred Indians to the Maumee River. Rumor has it that a regiment of Americans is approaching to attack Détroit. DePeyster plans to stop them before they reach Lake Erie. I would stay close to your farm until we see what happens."

As spring came there was no word of the proposed battle in the Ohio country. The French ignored it enough to continue their farming. The Allard complex planted larger fields and added livestock as it began to evolve into one of the area's large farms. Jacques* used some of his money from trapping and Jennie*'s dowry to hire enough help to allow himself and Henri-Pierre time for some local hunting, trapping and fishing.

Lieutenant John Douglas stood staring at his feet while DePeyster stormed around the room. "What do you mean they left?"

Douglas thought he would try to explain one more time, "As I said, Major, we encountered the Americans as we neared the Ohio River. I sent an Indian party to scout. They returned and reported it was a regiment led by a man named LaBalme. The Indians claimed the regiment contained many Frenchmen and refused to fight them. Then they simply left."

"Where in hell did they leave to, Lieutenant?"

"Well, sir, they are Indians. They simply disappeared into the woods. We were hopelessly outnumbered without them, so we returned home."

"DePeyster hit his desk with his riding stick so hard the stick broke. This only served to enrage him further. "God damn the French. And God damn the Indians. Blasted savages can't be trusted. First they are with you, then they are with the enemy. How can I fight a war like this?"

His aide spoke up sheepishly, "Sir, our intelligence continues to tell us we cannot prevail in the frontier without the allegiance of the natives."

"Well, gentlemen, we had better double the guards on the fort and prepare for an attack. I have been told that George Rogers Clark is returning from Vincennes and may be planning to meet with this LaBalme." The lady cleaning the room next to DePeyster's office finished quickly and left the fort for Rivard's store. Soon the news was out in the French community.

Détroit, the Pontchartrain Tavern - Three Weeks Later:

Having finished the planting, Jacques*, Henri-Pierre, and Toussaint went to town for supplies, information and a few libations. Rivard came in and the group huddled closer to hear the news. "Scouts have returned from Ohio. DePeyster doesn't know it, but Clark has met with LaBalme to take Détroit. However, it seems General Benedict Arnold has had a change of allegiance and has joined the British. He is causing problems in New York at a place called West Point. Clark and LaBalme have been called back to fight him. It looks like Fort Lernoult will go untested for now."

As Marsac brought another round, Toussaint said. "If General Washington plans to win his war, I hope he is a student of old Cadillac."

Pennsylvania - The Same Day:

By chance Washington was familiar with Cadillac and at the same time was discussing it with his officers in a tent in the Pennsylvania countryside. "Gentlemen, once we have some control here, we must take this," pointing to a place on the map.

One of his officers replied, "But sir, this is a place of a few hundred souls most of whom are French peasants who have no interest in anything but farming."

"That may be so, Mr. Johnson, but nearly one hundred years ago, a man named Antoine Cadillac realized what is still true today and will be true again tomorrow. We may hold the Atlantic coast, but unless we control the straits at Détroit, we cannot hold the frontier. If we cannot hold the frontier, we cannot hold the country."

Washington had no idea this fact would haunt him the rest of his career.

DePeyster waited anxiously, but the attack never came. The French went back to farming and ignoring the British.

Milk River Settlement - Summer 1780:

The tradition of the Sunday picnic continued. Today was the first turn for the new Allard family. Jennie* had planned everything in her typical meticulous detail. Beside the settlement neighbors, the Tremblay and Laforest clans had come to lend support and drink Jacques*'s whiskey. On a beautiful summer day with a gentle breeze from the lake, most of the children were swimming or fishing at the beach.

As the party was winding down and the sun beginning to set, a carriage appeared with an unusual group of three men. Jacques* knew Robert-Jean* Jeannes who had come to Détroit from the area of Montréal in the early seventies and lived to the south. He had always been called Robert-Jean* and that had become his official family name. Accompanying him was Jacob Harsen whom Jacques* had met at the wedding in the winter and an English trader named John Askin whom Jacques* had not met.

Robert-Jean* spoke for the group. "We are interested in land on L'Anse Creuse. We have been told that you are familiar with it and the land along the entire lake."

"It is true I have trapped the area for some years."

When Askin spoke up, obviously the leader of the group, he could not hide his British assertive nature. "It is clear that this country will not remain the frontier. Regardless of the outcome of this war, people will come and land will become valuable. It is now readily available and we wish to consider it as an investment."

Harsen added, "I asked if you could guide me to the top of the lake and this is what we are after. That is if you are for hire."

Jacques* thought for a moment, "This is the slow time of the summer. I could go soon if you like."

Askin answered, "How is Wednesday?"

"If you like. I should like to bring my neighbor Henri-Pierre."

"Excellent. We will be here in Monsieur Robert-Jean*'s canoe at sunrise."

Chapter 33

As promised the men met at sunrise Wednesday. Jacques* and Henri-Pierre knew they could travel light as the weather would remain fair and food would be plentiful along the way. They took their time as they headed northward. The men wanted to make many stops along the way to examine the terrain. Askin drew maps while Harsen examined the nature of the soil and the contour of the land, making comments to Askin who made notes. Jean* Robert-Jean seemed to be only along for the ride. By nightfall they had only made it to the northern portion of L'Anse Creuse.

Harsen and Askin turned in early. Robert-Jean sat up with Henri-Pierre and Jacques*. Once the men were asleep, Jacques* took the opportunity to question Robert-Jean. "Exactly what is this expedition about?"

Robert-Jean had been expecting this, "John Askin is an Irishman from New York. As he says he was in business with John Jacob Aster and I assume has acquired some wealth. He has great interest in gaining control of land. He fell in with Jacob Harsen when he learned Jacob was Dutch. I think he is interested in control of the marshy shore and making it more habitable and cultivatable. Harsen is an odd one. He has a great interest in the Flats although he has never been there. They heard I had some interest in the land in L'Anse Creuse and came to me as they thought having a French-Canadian would make things easier for them. They also knew I could bring them to you and Henri-Pierre who have first hand knowledge of the area and the Indians."

In the morning, Askin approached Jacques*. "I hear there is an Englishman named Tucker who occupies land near here."

"Yes, there is."

"Do you suppose we could meet him?"

"We can meet him if we can find him He lives with the local Chippewa tribe. He is a bit of an odd fellow."

"How so?"

"If we find him, you'll see."

They broke camp and headed east along the point that formed the northern edge of L'Anse Creuse. Coming to the mouth of the River of the Huron, they turned upstream. A short while later, Henri-Pierre sensed the camp. "I think we will find the tribe near here." They beached the canoes and hiked to a clearing where they found the Chippewa camp. Taller than the Indians and much heavier, Tucker was easy to spot. Although he was dressed in native fashion, his large white belly stood out like a beacon. Jacques* approached, greeted by Tucker, "Monsieur Allard, welcome to my kingdom."

Jacques* introduced his party and Askin and Tucker left to speak in private. Jacques* could not hear the conversation but noticed that Tucker was becoming quite animated and soon appeared angry. Askin returned to the group and suggested that they leave. When they were away in the canoes he said, "You were accurate in your description of the man, Monsieur Allard. Jacob, I don't think he will be of any use in our plans."

They rounded the point and entered the large bay at the northern extent of the lake. They camped for the night after exploring the area inland. Harsen noted even heavier marsh than in the south. "John, I believe the area of the L'Anse Creuse will better suit your purposes." The next day they entered the Saint-Clair Flats. Harsen was very taken with the area and spent the day exploring islands and channels. Askin asked Jacques* to take him further up the Saint-Clair River. When they returned they made camp at the location of the winter trapping camp of Jacques* and Henri-Pierre.

That evening Askin told the group. "If true commerce is to occur in these parts, sailing vessels must be used. Sailing up this river with its strong current will be quite difficult save for a southerly wind. The fortunate thing is it would be easy to anchor in the shallow protected bay and wait for the proper breeze. In fact, that's what we should call it, Anchor Bay."

The next day they paid a visit to the local Sauteuse tribe before beginning their return voyage down the eastern shore. South of the Flats was a very large, very shallow bay. Henri-Pierre explained, "This bay is marsh for many miles offshore. The land is extremely wet. Good for fish and game, but poor for farming. The southern shore is long and straight. The land is low but almost as good as L'Anse Creuse for farming." At the end of the day they made the mouth of the Détroit River and parted ways. A few days later at Rivard's store, Jacques* heard that the three men had been to the governor attempting to obtain rights to land along the lake.

Life on the farms returned to normal, and little news of the far-off war was heard. Crops were good and the French continued to expand their farms and their families.

Chapter 34

Fort Lernoult, Détroit - Late Summer 1780:

Captain Lernoult and Major DePeyster stood on the southeastern turret of the new fort. DePeyster looked down the river, "Well, Captain you have certainly left your mark here. I will miss you, but I know you look forward to action closer to civilization."

Lernoult replied, "Yes, I will. However I'm sorry I did not have the opportunity to face that rascal Clark. What I will not miss are these odd people. Between the Indians, French, and now a few Germans and Spanish, I do not know whom to trust. They are all so aloof."

An orderly came up the stairway, "Major DePeyster, a group of our men has just arrived. They were taken captive with Governor Hamilton at Vincennes but have been paroled."

"Excellent. Have them assemble in the courtyard."

"Yes sir. They were carrying this letter addressed to Captain Lernoult."

Taking the letter, Lernoult said, "Thank you, soldier." Then inspecting it, "Nothing but my name, what could it be?" He opened it and removed a short letter, reading aloud,

My Dear Captain Lernoult:
I wish to thank you personally for the excellent work you
have done refitting the fort at Détroit. It will certainly save
the colonials a good deal of trouble as soon as I take it
from you.
Yours truly,
Colonel George Rogers Clark
Militia of Virginia

Lernoult handed it to DePeyster, "Arrogant bastard! My only regret is that I will not be here to personally kill him if he ever does arrive."

Lernoult did depart and Clark did not arrive, being occupied with greater problems in the east. The city in the wilderness went about its business as usual.

Sainte-Anne Détroit - Summer 1781:

Father Simple Bocquet was aging. Never a great orator, he had taken to reading the mass from his book and skipping his sermon altogether. Today he was accompanied by a younger priest, and in lieu of a sermon, Bocquet said goodbye to the parish that had occupied a good portion of his long life. "With the unfortunate death of Father Pierre Potier at Assumption earlier this month, we are severely in need of new blood. Father François Xavier Hubert has arrived to do just that. I have married or baptized almost every person present today. I wish to humbly thank you for allowing me that privilege."

At the picnic later that day, more news arrived in the form of Samuel Price. "Washington sent Clark again to take Détroit. Unfortunately he was turned back by Brandt near Pittsburg. But the news from the east is good. Our old friends Francis Marion and Thomas Sumter have used French and Indian warfare to chase Cornwallis out of South Carolina. He is now on a collision course with General Washington. This could settle things once and for all."

The Allard Farm - October 19, 1781:

Summer had changed to autumn as the British kept watch for Clark and his militia. Residents on both sides of the dispute waited for news. For the French, life went on as usual. Returning from the fields, Jacques* entered the house. It was immediately apparent something was up. Jennie* had prepared a meal suitable for *Noel*. She greeted her husband with a passionate kiss. She poured them both a glass of Calvados at which time Jacques* asked, "Is there something I should know?"

"I have been to see Madame Campau," referring to the local *sage-femme* who provided the services of physician, nurse, midwife and pharmacist in the city in the wilderness. "We expect our son in May."

Suddenly the importance of the farm and the result of a faraway conflict took on a greater and more personal meaning for Jacques*. "Are you certain?"

"It's right here." patting her still flat abdomen. The young couple could not know and would not know for some time, this was not the only great news of this particular day.

271

It was not until Christmas day 1781 that news from the colonies would reach Détroit. Due to a mild early winter the French were able to attend mass at Sainte-Anne with their carts still on wheels. Father François Xavier Hubert gave sermons that were not as boring as those of his predecessor, but he lacked the warmth of old Simple Bocquet. He did have a more liberal mind and some of the English citizens, lacking their own church, would attend his service from time to time. Following the mass, Baptiste Rivard stood outside the church and told selected parishioners to meet at his farm on their way home.

After the group had assembled, Rivard took the floor, "Important news from the east. It seems in October, General Washington caught Cornwallis with his back to the sea. The French fleet had arrived and taken control of the harbors. On the nineteenth of October, Cornwallis was forced to surrender and has left the colonies with his army returning to England. Details are not clear, but the report indicated Détroit will soon be part of the new American nation."

A great commotion followed. As the people invited were all non-loyalists, there were calls for celebration and Rivard's liquor stores were suddenly in jeopardy. Jacques* said to Jennie*, "Perhaps our child will be born outside of the British influence!"

Inside Fort Lernoult, the same news was being received differently. Major Arent DePeyster paced furiously. "Unbelievable! How could such a thing happen?"

His aide de camp who had just delivered the unhappy news said, "It is not an official report, sir. Perhaps it is a rumor."

DePeyster replied, "I appreciate your naiveté corporal, but I have seen the same information from three different sources. We must, however, proceed as though it is false until we have official word from Haldimand. Fortunately he told me early this year to make more Indian alliances and stop trusting the French altogether. Those inscrutable bastards!"

Turning to the seated Captain McKee, "McKee, I want you to organize a small group of men. Take them to Sandusky. The Virginians are holding the fort there. See if you cannot unseat them. Take our Shawnee friends. They and the five nations Iroquois are the only Indians still worthy of trust. I wouldn't give the time of day for those rascal Delaware, Ottawa or Wyandot. We should have never have trusted any of the tribes once friendly with the French."

Then back to his aide, "Get me a scribe. I must send a message to Haldimand while the roads are still clear."

Sir Frederick Haldimand was now the Governor of Québec. He had replaced Guy Carleton. Where Carleton was a skilled military leader and strong governor, Haldimand was a mediocre soldier and life-long bureaucrat. He had, however, been a strong supporter of DePeyster's use of Indians in the conflict.

Shortly after, DePeyster received word that McKee's men had successfully routed the Virginians from Sandusky. The report, however, did not include the fact the Shawnee Indians had killed many of the colonialists and burned their popular leader, Colonel Crawford, at the stake, an act of hostility that would have influence on the future of the city in the wilderness.

Official word reached DePeyster in April of 1782:

Major Arent DePeyster, Fort Lernoult, Détroit
Sir:
I am in receipt of official confirmation of the unthinkable surrender of Lord Cornwallis to General George Washington October 19 last. You are reminded that no treaty has been signed nor any boundaries changed. Governance of the territory of Québec will remain the same. I encourage you to continue to use your savage allies as you have in the past.
Sincerely
Sir Frederick Haldimand Governor of Québec

Chapter 35

<u>Milk River Settlement - May 6, 1782:</u>

Jacques* Allard sat nervously on his porch. It was going to be a spectacular spring day. The breeze was offshore and the water of Lake Saint Clair was a mirror as the first crescent of sun appeared on the horizon. The sun was greeted by the usual cries of the birds. These were suddenly broken by a more shrill cry and Jacques* leapt from his seat. As he approached the door, Agathe came through it. "A boy! A beautiful, big one!"

Soon Monique appeared, "You can come in now, Papa." In spite of the ordeal, Jennie* looked wonderful. Still two weeks shy of her eighteenth birthday, she had carried the pregnancy without difficulty or the weight gain typical of the younger mothers.
"What do you think, *Mon Cher?*" showing the infant to his speechless father, "I have already named him Jacques."

The next day, Father Hubert baptized the first Détroit-born Allard, Jacques-Georges Allard. His family would call him "Jacquot'" with the "ot" often used in French for a younger namesake. Jacques* returned to his farming with an additional vigor and plans for future expansion of both farm and family.

Life in Détroit returned to normal in the summer of 1782. The population awaited further news on the ultimate settlement of the war, but it would not come this year. Activities between colonists and Indians in the Ohio country remained hostile, but the city in the wilderness remained unaffected. In fact the only news of that summer arrived in the form of William Tucker.

<u>Détroit, The Pontchartrain Tavern - Late Summer 1782:</u>

Jacques*, Toussaint, and Henri-Pierre were enjoying a beer with their neighbor, Pierre* Yax. He was the son of Michel* Yax, who ransomed to Détroit by Indians many years before had become its first German citizen. Pierre* Yax was planning to marry Marie-Josette* Fréton, daughter of the late Julian* Fréton.

The door opened and William Tucker entered with three strangers. It would be unusual for a British citizen to frequent the Pontchartrain Tavern, but Tucker went where he pleased and held all groups in equal disregard. Going to the table, he said to one of his companions, "You see, Zeisberger, we do have Germans here. Young Monsieur Yax is the son of a family brought to us many years ago by the natives." Then he addressed the group, "Gentlemen, allow me to present David Zeisberger, John Heckewelder, and Richard Connor. They are moving next to my kingdom. I'm not certain I will invite them to be my loyal subjects, but for now they will be my neighbors."

They sat and Tucker ordered a beer. The other three declined. Zeisberger seemed to be the spokesman, "Brother Heckewelder and I are missionaries. We come from the western lands of Germany and are called 'Moravian'. We have been working some years with a group of Christian

Delaware Indians in the Pennsylvania colony at a place called 'Gnadenhutten', after a place in our homeland.

"Last year a group of British soldiers from Détroit attacked the Virginia Militia at Sandusky. They were accompanied by a group of Shawnee pagans who burned the Virginia leader brutally at the stake, a man called Crawford. Sometime later, a group of American militia came to our village. They had no knowledge of who we were or the fact that our people were a peaceful, Christian group friendly to the Americans. They attacked us without mercy and killed many of our flock including women and children. The tribal leaders feared staying in Pennsylvania. Having heard of the Chippewa tribe living with Mr. Tucker, we left Pennsylvania to begin anew here."

Richard Connor finally spoke. In his sixties, he was older than the others. "I was born in Maryland and worked as an interpreter with the Delaware for some years. My wife had been kidnapped by Indians and lived with them from the age of four. After our marriage, we continued my work with the tribe, and fell in with the Moravians. We have joined their band and are moving with them."

Tucker continued, "I thought I would introduce them around. We'll go see the priest, Rivard, Campau, and Saint-Aubin. I think we'll skip DePeyster. He started their trouble. They might lose their Christian zeal and scalp the bastard. He said he didn't want me wearing my red coat anymore," referring to the old tattered British jacket that he always wore in town. "But I told him, 'I got my own kingdom and I do and wear as I please'. Well, we better be on our way."

After they left, Henri-Pierre said, "I hope they know what they are doing. I wonder how Tucker's band can exist on that swampland as it is."

Jacques* added, "I'm not certain Tucker is frequently burdened by thinking."

Détroit - Summer 1783:

Rumors began to arrive that an agreement had been reached in Europe that would cede all of the Québec Territory south of the upper Great Lakes to America. This would include Détroit, but official word had not come. The Milk River Settlement, however, had a big year. Julian* Fréton II had married Therese* Lesperance from Assumption and planned to move back to his father's old farm. His sister, Marie-Josette* Fréton, had married Pierre* Yax and they started a farm near the senior Yax.

Jacob* Thomas III arrived in Détroit. He was the son of the Jacob* II who travelled with Jean-Baptiste Charbonneau and grandson of the Jacob* Thomas I who had been captured in Québec by Jacques* Allard's grandfather Jean-Baptiste* and Toussaint's father, Joseph. Jacob* III had married Josette* Robert-Jean, daughter of Robert-Jean* Jeannes, in New York. They also took up residence in the settlement near her father. The settlement grew annually with new children and this year it included Jacques* and Jennie*'s second child, Suzanne Allard.

Meanwhile Benjamin Franklin, John Adams and John Jay had gone to Paris and had finally concluded the Treaty of Paris which ceded the American colonies and land east of the Mississippi and north through Lakes Erie, Ontario, Saint-Clair, Huron and Superior to the new Confederation of American States. The remaining territory of Québec would remain British and be divided into two areas: Upper Canada being upstream from Montréal and Lower Canada being downstream. To the residents of Détroit this seemed relatively clear cut, and they began to await the Americans.

They first came with Major Ephraim Douglass who was sent by General Washington with a small group of men to take control of the fort. He was, however, summarily dismissed by DePeyster and threatened with force if he did not leave. So he did.

Fort Lernoult, Détroit - late 1783:

DePeyster addressed his officers, "Gentlemen, I am pleased to say the Crown is not going to give us up so easily. We are ordered to stay in place and continue to obstruct any occupation of the fort. I have a recent communication from Governor Haldimand.

Major Arent DePeyster. Fort Lernoult, Détroit
Sir:
I am in communication with Sir Richard Oswald in London. He assures me the agreement with the Americans is only provisional. He believes, as do I, the Americans cannot hold their western frontier from the Indians. In addition, the Montréal fur merchants fear they cannot survive without trade through the straits at Détroit. I am encouraged to use our native allies to continue to disrupt the Americans .Eventually they will be weakened to the

*point we may return and assume our full rights on the
continent of North America. As a precaution, I would
advise you to move key documents and personnel, as well
as any British citizen or loyal colonist who wishes, to the
area of Upper Canada at Amherstburg. I would also not
make expensive improvements on the facilities in Détroit.
Again I warn you, do not trust the French or their Indian
allies.*

*For His Royal Majesty,
Sir Frederick Haldimand, Governor of Québec*

During the next two years, Washington sent more
envoys both to Détroit and to Québec to secure the city.
They were always turned away. Busy with the work of
building a new government, Washington did not have the
men or supplies to make a serious military attack. His
resources were being strained by hostile moves in the Ohio
country by the Shawnee and Iroquois Indians with some
help and encouragement from the British at Détroit. The
city in the wilderness continued in a limbo, a French
population in a new American land still administered by the
defeated British.

Chapter 36

Lake Saint-Clair - Summer 1785:

Jacques* pulled the line. The sun glistened on his back as his muscles strained to bring it up. Soon he had retrieved it, bringing the line onboard to unhook the fish. Henri-Pierre worked the other side as they made it fast work, removing the fish, re-baiting the hook and returning the line to the water on the other side of the boat. Young Jacquot sat quietly and passed his father bait for each hook. Jennie* had objected to taking the four-year old on board to run the night-line, but she agreed when her husband convinced her of the value.

"He needs to learn the ways of the land and the lake. Don't forget, the new boat is more stable than the canoe you used." He referred to the flat bottom rowboat with a small sail they now used to fish and work the lines. It was not as fast or maneuverable as the canoe and a challenge to portage, but it was more stable and easier to maintain and repair.

As he worked mechanically, Jacques* told his friend, "Askin has asked me to take him up to Tucker's tomorrow, so you will have to do without me."

"What is he trying to squeeze money from now?"

"I'm not certain, but he's going to squeeze some of it to me for the service."

Both men laughed as Henri-Pierre noted, "With the way fishing has been, I wonder why we waste our time on the dirt."

Jacques* replied, "Some days I also wonder, but I think the value of the land is the issue. That is certainly what men like Askin think."

Tucker's Camp and the Moravian Village – The Next Day:

On the trip up the coast, Askin showed Jacques* some of the land he and Robert-Jean had acquired or hoped to acquire. "You know, Harsen has bought that island of yours from the Chippewa. He calls it 'Jacob's Island'. I don't know what the government thinks of it, but he has moved his family up there, at least in the summer."

When they entered the clearings that contained Tucker's land and the Moravian Village, Jacques* could see what he had feared. Without adequate know-how and tools, they were not making a successful farm. Most of the inhabitants with the exception of Tucker looked like scarecrows. Tucker came to greet them, "These Indians can't farm for beans." Then laughing his bizarre laugh, "Or corn for that matter. But I have the solution, come over here."

He walked the men to a hidden corner where a prosperous field was growing, tended by a black couple and two children. "I bought the woman and the two little ones two years ago. Just bought the man this year. If I can get them to breed, I'll be set. Wouldn't hurt to get some colored blood into the Indians. Get them to work better. These Africans sure can work."

Jacques* had to admit Tucker had achieved some results. Askin was off looking at something entirely different. Richard Conner came by and greeted Jacques*. "Our people are starving, I hope Tucker's workers can get us a harvest this year. If not, we will be forced to leave."

Askin returned, "Connor, what you need is a road."

"A road, sir?"

"Yes, a road. If you begin one heading to Détroit, it can join the road that leads out of the Milk River. If Tucker gets his slaves working, you will have a conduit for trade."

As Jacques* and Askin headed north, Jacques* asked, "What's this about a road?"

Askin laughed, "Look at those people, man. They will be fortunate to survive another winter. If I can get them to start at this end and DePeyster to start at the other, we could connect the two and have a road all the way to the River of the Huron. Robert-Jean and I have claims on land in L'Anse Creuse. Sooner or later this war and treaty foolishness will be over and people will flood to this area. We will have the means to move them here to rent or buy my land." And with a gleeful smile, "At a tidy profit, of course."

They reached Askin's Anchor Bay and the Saint Clair Flats the next day. Jacob Harsen had built a shelter at the point where the middle channel met the lake, the very spot Jacques* had built his winter camps to trap. Jacques* was surprised at the high quality of the house and the dryness of the land.

Harsen came out to greet them and give them a tour. "I have drained the marsh around my house and built a sort of dyke system as we have in Holland. It is like home except the water is fresh and other than my Sauteuse neighbors on the next island, there are no other people. It is all mine! I will call it 'Jacob's Island'." Noting his own over exuberance, "Excuse me, I am beginning to sound a bit like Tucker."

As the men headed back to Détroit, Askin said, "I don't know if any of these Americans, or British, for that matter, have any idea how valuable this land will be. As the West becomes settled, this will be the highway of everything. The possibilities for commerce are endless!"

The next day, Jacques* Allard made his way in to see DePeyster and make a claim for some land in L'Anse Creuse south of the River of the Huron.

Détroit, the Pontchartrain Tavern - Summer 1787:

Jacques*, Henri-Pierre and some of the other farmers sat discussing the affairs of the day. As Askin had predicted, the Moravians had left their village the previous year. His road, though rudimentary, was completed and simply called the "Moravian Road", the first permanent road outside of the city. Jacques* ordered another beer, "Road or no road, not much is happening out there. Tucker and Connor are there with their families and a few of the remaining Chippewa. Two of Robert-Jean's boys have gone out to his property, but neither is married and not much is happening. The hunting and fishing are too good for them to be troubled with farming."

Pierre* Saint Aubin stepped in, "Our problem is this damnable question of government. It is now four years since the Treaty of Paris and the agreement on boundaries

284

and governance. But the British won't leave and the Americans won't... or can't make them. The Americans have declared this the Northwest Territory and drawn boundaries around the Great Lakes. They even have a governor, but the British are still in control of the strait. As long as that is the situation, they will be in control of everything."

Rivard broke in, "There is no growth in commerce as everyone is uncertain of the future and not willing to invest. Askin is right that people will come, and many, but not until this is settled. As it is, our only growth is from the fertile ones like Allard here." The men all laughed at Jacques* who like many French-Canadians had been able to produce an offspring every year or two. He and Jennie* now had four with the birth of young Pierre this winter.

"This new commander, William Ancrum, is hard to read. I am afraid he is going to continue to stir up the Shawnee and Iroquois in the Ohio, and keep the Americans at bay. Washington continues to try to stop it but can never be decisive."

The door to the tavern burst open and a disheveled young man entered with two young Indian women. The women were not of a local tribe and all three were obviously intoxicated. One of the women was naked to the waist. As they staggered to the bar, Henri-Pierre said, "Toussaint Charbonneau, just what we need." Charbonneau leaned across the bar and shouted, "Marsac! Get me a jug of corn."

Paul Marsac came over and said quietly, "Toussaint, I think you have had enough, and you know we only allow women on special occasions."

"Hell, Marsac, these ain't women, they're squaws."

Marsac remained calm, "Toussaint, you know better than to talk to me like that," reminding him of Marsac's own Indian wife.

"Well, they ain't like yours. These ones is whores," as he snuggled his grizzly face between the breasts of the disrobed one. He then walked over to the table and up to Jacques*. "Hey, Allard. You know where I been?"

Jacques* did not look up but replied, "Drinking I suspect."

Charbonneau put his face in Jacques*'s, and said with his foul breath, "I been THERE! I been to the ocean. I seen it and I'm going back this year. I found the damn passage."

Jacques* arose calmly, "That's good, Toussaint. Why don't you and your friends find somewhere to sleep?" And he began to usher him out when Charbonneau caught him with an unexpected punch that laid Jacques* on his back. Jacques* was a good head taller than Charbonneau, but Toussaint Charbonneau was a formidable character, even drunk. Jacques* arose and hit Charbonneau who landed collapsing a table. Jacques* then grabbed him and threw him out onto the street. The two Indian women followed without a sound. Jacques* returned and picked up the table, "I'm sorry, Paul."

Marsac laughed, "You saved me some trouble."

A man who had been sitting in the shadows came to the table. It was Jean-Baptiste Charbonneau Jr., Toussaint's older brother. "I'm sorry, men. I thought I should remain out of it. I would have only made it worse." He sat down and ordered a beer. "This is killing our father. Toussaint is the most capable man in the wilderness, but he cannot control his wild ways. Half the white men and Indians in the west would like to kill him for one indiscretion or another."

Henri-Pierre asked, "Has he really reached the sea?"

Jean-Baptiste Charbonneau, Jr. replied, "That's the best part. It appears that he has. He took father's maps and spent three years. My father believes from his stories he has actually been there." He arose, "I had better get home. If he comes home like this before I arrive, either he or father will be dead."

Chapter 37

<u>The Cathedral of Sainte-Anne - Détroit, October 1791:</u>

Father François Xavier Hubert stood before the congregation, "Born in Québec and raised in Montréal and on the frontier of New France, Jean-Baptiste Charbonneau has been a member of our community for many years. As strong and rugged as any voyageur, he was yet tender, thoughtful and kind." Following the service, the body of the old voyageur was carried to his grave in the cemetery yard by his old comrades, men whose lives he had helped shape: Jacques* Allard, Henri-Pierre de Baptiste, André* Peltier, Jacob* Thomas II, Louis* Renaud, and Jean-Baptiste* Laforest.

Even his wayward son, Toussaint Charbonneau, came clean and sober to the service. As they placed Jean-Baptiste in his grave, Toussaint came forward with a leather sack. "These contain shells from the Pacific Ocean, the route to which he discovered but was never permitted to see." Then he placed them in the grave. It was the first and last time the city ever saw this strange man cry.

Leaving the service, Jacques* and Jennie* stopped at two nearby wooden crosses. Today they came with the entire family, Jacquot now 9, Suzanne 8, Marie-Louise 6, Pierre 4, and Archange* 2. The crosses marked the graves of Guillaume and Joseph Allard, twins born in 1788 who died one month later, a fate common for multiple births of this era. Jennie* Laforest-Allard looking younger than her age of 27 had given birth to seven children. Jacques* Allard was as strong and rugged as ever. His different colored eyes were still bright, but his graying hair did suggest his 45 years.

The congregation gathered at the grand farm of old Pierre* Saint-Aubin. The north wind brought ashore beautiful white-capped waves as well as a cool, pleasant breeze. The men gathered to toast old Charbonneau and tell endless tales of the frontier. Eventually the conversation turned to politics. As usual, Baptiste Rivard started, "Here we are, ten years after the surrender of the British and they are still living in the fort. We are supposed to be part of a territory and even have a governor... somewhere. Connecticut, New York and Massachusetts all claim this territory, but no one wants to explain it to the British. If General Washington doesn't take control of this strait, he's going to again find himself under British rule."

Jacob Andrews added, "Speaking of General Washington, I understand the Americans have changed the confederation into a united country. It is called the United States of America, and they have elected Washington President. In addition there is a new Constitution with a Bill of Rights."

Pierre Drouillard had come with his son, Georges, now 18 years old, "Stolen from Rousseau, I might add. And on the topic of France, I hear they are having their own revolution against the King. This may cause difficulties for England and force her attention away from the Americas."

While the French citizens of Détroit discussed affairs they could not control but that were bound to profoundly affect them, another event, half a world away, was occurring which would also greatly affect the future of the city in the wilderness.

<u>The Church of Saint-Sulpice, Paris, France - The Same Day:</u>

The gothic cathedral was grander than that visited one-hundred twenty years earlier by young Jeanne* Anguille when she stopped with her brother on her trip to Dieppe and the boat that would take her to Québec to marry François* Allard. Renovations then beginning had since been completed, and it stood as one of the grandest churches in the capital. The neighborhood, however, was deplorable, a cesspool of poverty, crime, and violence. Recent activities of the revolution had done little to change it.

Today's ceremony (the ordination of a few new priests) was subdued, mainly due to the prevailing attitude toward the church. Following the ceremony the new priests were dismissed to be greeted by their families.

Gabriel's father was his only family member present. They embraced and began to walk into the warm autumn day scarred by the smell of nearby fires and the daily stench of Paris. The square was littered with ragged beggars, women with small starving children and all manner of scoundrels looking for ways to relieve passer-bys of belongings. Gabriel's father said, "Let us remove ourselves quickly from this place. There is a man nearby I would like you to meet."

Gabriel had been born in Saintes in the region of Charente-Maritime. A studious undirected boy, he had chosen to attend the seminary at Angers in the Loire Valley, where he blossomed, joining the order of Saint-Sulpice. Tall and gangly with a long crooked nose, Gabriel was the son of a government official in the French Navy. He wore spectacles which rode on the end of his curvaceous snout. Had someone known them both, they would think him a younger version of Simple Bocquet.

Entering an upper class hotel, Gabriel's father spoke to a man who directed them to the upper floor. When his father knocked at a door, they were bid to enter. Two men in priests' robes stood before a desk where an older man in the robes of a Bishop was seated. The man stood and shook hands with Gabriel's father, "Monsieur Richard, how nice to see you." His French was good but his accent decidedly Irish. He turned to Gabriel, "This must be the new Father Richard. Congratulations, Father."

Gabriel blushed at being called "father" and by a Bishop at that. The man continued, "Let me be direct. I met your father through affairs with your government. He told me of your work and asked me to speak to you. My name is John Carroll. I am a native of Ireland but now live in the Americas. I have recently been appointed Bishop of Baltimore in the state of Maryland. As you may know, the former British Colony of Maryland was the sole Catholic colony in the Americas. As the sole Bishop in the new United States of America, I am here recruiting priests for our work. We have many positions in the offices of the Archdiocese as well as some parishes in Maryland. I understand you are considering a teaching position."

"Yes, your Excellency, at the Sulpician Seminary."

"Well, this would be somewhat different. I understand you are fluent in French and English."

"Yes, Excellency, as well as Latin."

The Bishop laughed, "Our position would be somewhat different and I suspect more exciting."

"Isn't America filled with savages, Excellency?"

"Yes, indeed." Then laughing, "And Frenchmen. But they are in the frontier. The frontier is an odd situation at the moment. The United States has claim to the land as far west as the Mississippi River, but the British continue to control it through the fort at Détroit. This and the rest of old Québec, now called Canada, are under the Archdiocese of Québec. We have one mission, however, in a far-off land called Illinois, although most of our work is in Maryland,"

"Well, Excellency, I am not certain, though I am honored by the offer."

"I will be in Paris two more days. Give it some prayer and thought. Discuss it with your father and I will await your answer."

Gabriel and his father walked back to his father's hotel. Once inside his father said, "Son, I have fear, and fear based on good information. This revolution is about to turn very ugly and very violent. There is already public outcry about the abuses of the Church and the clergy. Frankly I fear for your very life. This is a wonderful opportunity that will not present itself again."

Gabriel simply replied, "I will ask God tonight."

Gabriel's father then presented him with a box. When the young priest opened it he gasped, "Father, this is much too fine for me and too expensive for you."

As he lifted the beautiful silver chalice from its container, his father replied, "I wanted you to have something to remind you of your mother and me, and the immense pride you have given us. Think of it not just as a gift from us, but as the property of God." Gabriel embraced his father for the second to the last time in his life.

The next day young Father Gabriel Richard, only one day a priest, visited John Carroll, Bishop of Baltimore. Five months later he again embraced his father as Gabriel Richard boarded the ship *La Reine de Coeurs* at the port of Le Havre and sailed for the New World. They knew they would likely never see one another again.

Shortly thereafter, the revolution did turn bloody and the Reign of Terror began. In August that year, the king was deposed. Five days later, the Sulpician Seminary was invaded and the priests marched to Paris for trial. Many were sent to the guillotine. Gabriel Richard, only 24 years old, had been saved by good fortune, good timing, and the love of a father.

Baltimore, - June 17, 1792:

As a priest, Gabriel was frequently thanking God. He had, however, never given such heartfelt thanks as the day *La Reine de Coeurs* touched the dock in Baltimore Harbor. The voyage had been three weeks of storms and rotten food. Gabriel, who was normally extremely thin, had lost at least thirty pounds.

His companions had been two other young priests named Ciquard and Maréchal. Where Ciquard was quiet and pious and never spoke, Maréchal was gregarious and open talking constantly. He knew more about the Americas than Gabriel knew about France. "Everything is new and exciting. Liberty is the king. The people are wild and full of life and the frontier is filled with Indians, pagan souls waiting to be saved. I can scarcely wait to begin."

The city of Baltimore was beyond anything Gabriel had anticipated. That night he wrote a letter.

Dear Father,
The City of Baltimore is beyond belief. It teems with all manner of people, and things I have never seen. The harbor is a long and wonderful deep river which extends well beyond the boundaries of the town, much like the Seine, but cleaner. The industry is sugar manufacturing from cane brought from the southern islands. The people are active and industrious and movement never stops. The smells are different, newer, and difficult to explain. The most impressive thing is an apparent lack of class consciousness. All men carry themselves as though they were the master of their own fate. I hear the population is not as faithful as those in France and many Catholics do not regularly attend mass. But that is a challenge I am ready to meet. My companions aboard ship were Fathers Ciquard and Maréchal. My new mentor is Father Michel Levadoux, a Sulpician only two years my senior. He has been here one year. Tomorrow I meet with Bishop John Carroll on the subject of my assignment.
Your Loving Son
Gabriel

The morning found Gabriel seated with Levadoux outside the Bishop's office. They were asked to enter and found John Carroll at his desk writing furiously. Carroll looked up from his work. "Ah, Father Richard, I pray you had a pleasant voyage."

"Yes, sir." As Gabriel catalogued his first sin in the New World.

"Well, then, there is currently no teaching position in town, but Father Levadoux has asked that you be assigned as his assistant in his new position. What do you say?"

"Certainly, sir. That would be splendid. Might I ask what Father Levadoux's new position is?"

"Pastor."

"Pastor of?"

"Of the entire Illinois Territory. You leave in the morning. Good day, Fathers."

In the morning the two young Sulpician priests boarded a rudimentary carriage and headed west.

Chapter 38

Milk River Settlement - August 18, 1793:

"Another boy!" Monique escorted Jacques* into the bedroom where his young wife held his latest son.

Agathe, who was enormous with child, waddled over to take a look, "Two brown eyes."

Jacques* picked him up, "This one is a squirmer. Look at those hands. I think he is ready to go fishing."

Jennie* took him back and held him to her breast, "Maybe next week."

The next day Louis-Pierre* Allard was baptized at Sainte-Anne. Louis* Renaud who had accompanied Jacques* Allard when both were boys to Détroit and whose great grandfather had accompanied François* Allard to the New World from Normandie, stood as godfather.

Two days later, Agathe gave birth to twin boys. Unlike the ill-fated Allard twins, these were not identical but quite different from one another. Also unlike most twins of the era, these two were healthy and robust. Henri-Pierre named them Lucien and Michel.

The Pontchartrain Tavern - Two Weeks Later:

Life in Détroit continued as usual. The British flag continued to fly over Fort Lernoult. Although many British merchants and businessmen had moved offices to the south side of the river, trade and commerce continued. French families remained the great majority, but maintained their aloof attitude.

Jean-Baptiste Rivard called for another round. At 64, although he had given control of the store to his son, he remained current on all local affairs. "This town is never going to prosper unless one side or the other can prevail. Washington has had no success in controlling the Indians and their red coat allies, and the British can't prevail against the Americans. No one wants to start a new business here and new settlers are either not welcome or unwilling to come."

Jean-Baptiste* Laforest was now 47, the same age as Jacques* Allard. As head of the mills at Windmill Pointe, he had great interest in business and expansion, "We have excess capacity and could enlarge easily. If only we had new people and more need for lumber and grist. All I have heard from the east is recurring defeats of General Saint-Clair and his Americans."

New York – The Same Day:

Now 61 and in the fourth year of his presidency, George Washington continued to be tormented by the continued British occupation of his western territory. He stood with General Arthur Saint-Clair who had served as his commander in the west for the past three years. "Arthur, if we cannot control the Indians in the Ohio country, we are never going to control the straits at Détroit and never have total control of our country. France, Spain and Great Britain are all eyeing this territory and may decide to take it if they feel we cannot hold."

"I could not agree more, Mr. President, but these Indians are so amorphous and their style of battle so unconventional and, well, uncivilized." Saint-Clair had been born in Scotland and rose through the ranks of the British Army in the Seven Years War. He was now Governor of the Northwest Territory and held the rank of General in charge of American forces in the west. His recent war with the Indians had produced a number of utter failures.

Washington continued, "I have sent George Rogers Clark to Sandusky to negotiate with the leaders of the various tribes. If he has anything less than resounding success, I fear we must attack in a much more aggressive fashion than previously."

"You can count on me, Mr. President."

"I know I can, Arthur, but that is not why I asked you here today. Last year I sent General Wayne and his men to the south of Ohio to train for an all-out battle."

"Anthony Wayne?! That fop!" Wayne was a native-born American and considered odd and unconventional at best. From the early days of the revolution, no love had been lost between him and Saint-Clair. "You cannot be serious, sir. He is the worst manner of loose cannon; even his men call him, 'Mad Anthony' for his fits of outrageous temper."

"Arthur, you're a good man and a good leader. But let us face facts. Your military ventures in this area have been something less than spectacular." Saint-Clair quietly agreed and left as quickly as he could within the bounds of decorum.

<u>Fort Recovery, Ohio - June 1794:</u>

General Anthony Wayne stood looking at a map of the area. His three junior officers stood at hand as they did regularly to rehash the plan. Colonel John Hamtramck was the most senior at 36, next was Captain Moses Porter, and an impetuous young Lieutenant, William Henry Harrison. All were born in the new world and all experienced in Indian fighting. Hamtramck and Porter were reserved and found Wayne's style brash to say the least. In fact, he frightened them. Harrison, on the other hand, regarded "Mad Anthony" as his hero.

Wayne had spent the past several months training his men at Fort Washington at a place now called Cincinnati and had established a string of small forts along the Ohio region, and was now at one called "Fort Recovery". His lesson was always the same. "When we were the British Army, we were overwhelmed by the Indian style of warfare. When we were the American Army fighting the British, we used Indian style to our advantage. However, we are now the American Army fighting the Indian. We cannot prevail with either former method. We must understand the Indian way but only use the tactics that suit us. In the end, we must rely on our British style of discipline, not forgetting the lessons of the past."

Tonight he was more intense than usual, "I have received communication that General Clark has achieved only limited success in the peace negotiation with the tribes.

The Chippewa, Ottawa, and Wyandot have agreed to peace. Other tribes have not. Our scouts tell us that a band of Shawnee are approaching and will greatly outnumber us. If we stick to the principles with which we have trained, we shall prevail."

The attack came and the Americans did prevail. By afternoon, the much larger Indian force had broken ranks and retreated in confusion. This represented one of the few American victories in the Indian war. That evening Wayne met again with his officers. "At dawn we will proceed to Fort Defiance near Lake Erie. Several Indian camps are in the area. It is there we will make our stand to victory."

Fort Defiance Ohio - August 17, 1794:

After meeting with the officers, Anthony Wayne addressed his troops. "Men, the enemy is gathering close by and tomorrow I propose we go and take them. Our scouts tell me there is already dissension in their ranks due to the defeat at Fort Recovery. There is a large clearing nearby where a tornado knocked down many trees. The natives call it 'Fallen Timbers'. We will engage them there. Do not forget how you have been trained. Stay in cover, be patient and disciplined, and use your superior aim. We will prevail."

The next morning Wayne's men did prevail. The battle lasted less than two hours and the Indians retreated in chaos. The Americans did not hold tight as had been typical, but pursued them with relentless vigor, burning each village they encountered until they seemed to run out of villages. Although a formal peace would not be signed for some months, it was clear the Indians had been decidedly defeated.

Once he received the news, George Washington immediately dispensed his Chief Justice, John Jay, to London. Jay returned some weeks later with the elusive document Washington had been wanting, a firm agreement to vacate the Northwest Territories including the strategic fort at the Straits of Détroit.

The news was received in the city in the wilderness with relative calm. Citizens who wished to remain loyal to Britain began to move their households to the south side which the British now called "Sandwich" after the famous Earl. French citizens on either side of the river saw little reason to uproot themselves and stayed where they were. The farms and families continued to grow and the Allards added their fourth son, Joseph Allard.

As always politics moved slowly in the west, and it was not until July 11, 1796, that Captain Moses Porter arrived with a small group of men. He formally accepted control of the fort from Lt. Colonel Richard English and raised the American flag on what was now renamed Fort Détroit. Two days later, the first American Commander arrived in the form of Colonel John Hamtramck who immediately dispatched a letter to the President.

Two weeks later George Washington, with only a few months left in his presidency, held the letter for which he had waited many years, the letter that would assure his presidency would not end in defeat.

July 13, 1796, Fort Détroit
Sir
I have the pleasure to inform you of the safe arrival of troops under my command at this place which was evacuated on the 11th instant and taken possession of by a detachment of 65 men commanded by Captain Moses Porter who I detached from the foot of the rapids for that purpose. Myself and my troops arrived on the 13th.

J.F. Hamtramck
Colonel, Army of the United States of America

Détroit was finally in American hands, at least for a while.

Chapter 39

<u>Détroit, Northwest Territory, United States of America -
August 1796:</u>

The British did not leave Détroit quietly. They broke
the windows of the fort offices, filled the wells with stones,
and even destroyed one small grist mill by the fort. They
chose not to tamper with the mills on Windmill Pointe for
fear of falling afoul of the Tremblay boys who were reputed
as men not to engage in battle.

It had been assumed Anthony Wayne would become
commander of the fort, but his health was failing, so
Colonel John Hamtramck stayed on. If someone had
studied the possibilities, which they did not, they could not
have made a better choice. Hamtramck had been born in
Canada, spoke French with ease and related well to the
habitants. In 1796 five-hundred people lived between the
Raison and the Milk Rivers. Almost all of them were
French. Colonel Hamtramck realized how critical it was for
the Americans to hold control of the strait and was wise
enough to understand this could not be done without the
cooperation of these French citizens.

Once the control of the fort was in order, Hamtramck
began to call on the citizens. Jacques*, Henri-Pierre and
Toussaint were coming from the fields at midday when the
cart of Joseph Campau turned into their lane carrying the
new commandant. Joseph Campau was the great grandson
of one of the original Campau families. Although only 27,
he had a definite talent for business and was turning the

affairs of his father and grandfather into a thriving enterprise. Because he had been cordial with the British, it was even thought he might move to Sandwich with the loyalists, but it was apparent his cordiality was for the convenience of business. He planned to prosper on the north shore of Détroit as an American.

Campau climbed down and introduced Hamtramck to the men, "Colonel Hamtramck has asked me to introduce him to local farmers and leaders." Jacques* made note of how soft Joseph's hand was, compared to Campaus of the past.

After some pleasantries, the men were seated indicating that this would be a serious discussion. Hamtramck got to business, "I understand you men were instrumental in fighting in Québec and Saratoga."

Remaining aloof, Jacques* casually replied, "We acted as seemed to serve our purposes."

"Well, we Americans were fortunate your purposes coincided with ours. I must say in the east, people were not certain how to regard the French and where their allegiances lay. I may add I am surprised that virtually no French citizens left for Sandwich with the loyalists."

Jacques* replied, "You may also note none of the French on the south coast have left for the north. For the most part, Colonel, I believe the French are more neutral than you may think. We do not favor the British, it is true. I remember when I was a boy, the British sacked our villages with the Iroquois. I remember when they burned Québec and how my father died as a result of their war. Our concern has always been how are the Americans different? I must say I am favorably impressed by your visit today."

Turning to Toussaint and Henri-Pierre, Hamtramck continued, "As you must know, one of our greatest concerns is our future relations with the natives. Monsieur Campau tells me that you men are *métis* and have some insight."

Henri-Pierre jumped in before his father could be impolitic. "The Indian has always wanted the same thing, to be left alone, and if not, to be treated well. I must say they have seen little of each from the British or the Americans. There are many tribes in the area and many *métis*. Our neighbors Marsac and Andrews have Sauteuse wives and *métis* children. I hear you grew up in Canada, Colonel. Treat them as the French did and you will have no problem."

Changing the subject, Hamtramck said, "I am impressed by the articulate nature of our conversation, I understand you men speak French and English."

Jacques* replied, "My great grandmother was an educated woman. We have tried to teach the children some reading and writing. As you know, my friends are part Algonquin and we have learned that language as well. As young men we travelled with the great voyageur, Jean-Baptiste Charbonneau." Quickly crossing himself, "May he rest in peace. He encouraged us to learn English for trade. We also speak Iroquois, Blackfoot and some Sioux, Shoshone, and Spanish." Then laughing, "And of course, all Catholics know some Latin.

"The British had no schools for the citizens. There is a man, François Girardin, who has a small school in town. We try to send the older children when it is possible but it is not often so. I hope the Americans will be more interested in education."

On that note Hamtramck bid them good day, "Feel free to call on me if you have the need. I have a feeling I will be calling on you again."

Sainte-Anne, Détroit - April 1798:

The city in the wilderness was beginning to grow slowly; both French and American families began to appear and the locals continued to produce their own additions. Jacques* and Jennie* had added their eighth living child, Felicité, the previous spring. Father François Xavier Hubert, on the other hand, was failing, and his replacement was due at today's mass. It was rumored he had traveled from the parish of Vincennes in the south where he had worked in the Indian Missions.

As the parishioners filed into the church they noticed the frail Father Hubert speaking to the new young priest. Sitting by the altar was a third man, tall and gangly with glasses sliding onto his nose. Jacques* gasped in jest, "My God! Simple Bocquet has arisen from the dead and it is not yet Easter."

Father Hubert introduced Father Michel Levadoux who took the floor. "I have implored on Bishop Carroll to allow me an assistant. May I introduce Father Gabriel Richard."

Father Levadoux was a tolerable priest, pleasant enough and not long-winded. He went about his duties with a mechanical efficiency. Gabriel Richard, on the other hand was lively, animated, and likeable to a fault. He began to visit the parishioners and did it with a tireless zeal, visiting everyone: Catholic, Protestant, Indian or whoever. He even visited Tucker and his Chippewa and slaves. He had the uncanny ability to store and recall names instantly. As would be typical, the priests alternated celebrating mass. When it was Levadoux's turn, the more pious members and people living near the church were in attendance. When Father Gabriel Richard spoke, the church was filled.

Hamtramck was smart enough to know he must engage the priest in such a community, so he visited with Levadoux from time to time. As the trend became apparent, the soldier asked the priest how he regarded the situation. Levadoux replied, "I became a priest because it was my station in life and position in my family. I believe I serve God well and to the best of my abilities. I met Father Richard when he came to Baltimore from France. We travelled to the mission at Kaskaskia together and worked there for six years. When I requested he accompany me, I knew what I was asking for.

"Father Richard has a higher calling. His skill and energy are more than I have seen in any man. He is bound for greatness that I am not. I understand and accept it. I may for a time be the head of this church, but he will be its heart and soul."

Gabriel Richard had enough energy for three priests; he immediately drew up a list of needs for the parish. He planned to start a small school, recruited François Girardin to bring his small school to the small church hall and began to scour the community for literate ladies capable of giving instruction. When he realized most of these would come from the small Protestant contingency of the city, he rationalized, "It will be good for all. The students can have an education and the ladies can have the benefit of a Catholic atmosphere."

He catalogued the weak points and needs of Simple Bocquet's aging church building. He immediately called on Jean-Baptiste* Laforest to plead for free lumber for his renovations and help from the strong Tremblay boys in putting it in place. When Levadoux celebrated mass at Sainte-Anne, Gabriel would ride south toward the River Raison or north toward the Milk River to say mass at one of the larger homes for those "unable" to get to the city. Colonel Hamtramck remarked, "The men would say 'Mad Anthony' Wayne never slept. It appears the new assistant priest suffers the same affliction."

Father Gabriel Richard was tireless in the task of saving the souls of his flock. He made a point to visit every couple who had been married by the magistrate or almost as bad, not married at all, and asked them to come to church, ask forgiveness and be properly married. He prevailed on Jacob Andrews and his Sauteuse wife to come and be baptized, then married, and also baptized their daughter, Therese.

The young priest's gaunt face and long hooked nose gave him a stern façade, but he did have a sense of humor frequently sprinkled with a small amount of sarcasm. One day a young American soldier, a Protestant, asked him if he believed Protestants would go to Heaven. Gabriel regarded the young man sternly and said, "My boy, if you lead a good and Christian life, I am certain you will be welcomed in God's church." Then with the hint of a twinkle, "Of course, you may be seated toward the back."

Sainte-Anne, Détroit - September 23, 1799:

The throng of well wishers filed from the church. Jacques* and Jennie* greeted them as they left. Jacques* had always thought Susanne would be the first to marry, but her younger sister, Marie-Louise had surprised them with the proposal of Nicolas. Jacques*had reflected on her young age. At 15 she was even younger than Jennie* at the time of his marriage. Nicolas Patenotre was 31, about the age of Jacques* at his marriage. Nicolas's father had come from Montréal in 1759 and married the sister of Josie* Duchesne-Fréton.

Also greeting the parishioners was Father Gabriel Richard, who had taken great interest in one of his first Détroit marriages. He had visited the Allard farm on a few occasions in preparation. Father Richard was very clear on the sanctity of marriage. He was not so worried about the age of the participants as long as the ceremony was in the church.

Chapter 40

Grosse Pointe - early October 1799:

Father Richard had finished mass at the home of Jacques* Saint-Aubin. The large home and spacious grounds, one of the grandest on the northeast side of Détroit, lent itself well as a place to gather for mass. The farm was one of the first areas in the city in the wilderness to be settled by white men. Later it would hold many grand homes and ironically be named "Indian Village".

As Jacques* and Jennie* were leaving with the children, now nine with the recent birth of François Allard, Father Richard hailed them and ran to catch them, "Monsieur Allard, I am planning a trip to visit our parish at Michilimackinac. I visited with Pierre Drouillard in Assumption as I am told he has considerable interpretation skills and has been to the north many times. However, it seems his age is creeping up so he volunteered his son, Georges, also skilled but not so well travelled. He suggested I contact you as you have considerable experience."

Jacques* hesitated as his wife gave a disapproving look, "Well, Father, you know I have my farm and my family…"

Gabriel Richard took charge, "We will not be long. I am certain the de Baptiste men can help in your absence. The harvest is all but complete."

When Jacques* hesitated further, Father Richard continued, "Good then, we shall leave from the docks tomorrow at dawn. Bring your oldest son", motioning to Jacquot. "Bless you, Sir." And he was off.

Jacques* shrugged at his wife who replied, "He is a difficult man to deny. I will give you that."

The Détroit River - the next day:

The orange glow had only reached the horizon when the group was ready to push off. True to his word, Gabriel Richard was ready well before dawn and ready to pull his own weight. He had some experience in canoes during his travels to, from, and around Kaskaskia, although much of the time he travelled by road and generally Indians or voyageurs did the work. Father Levadoux was not above being waited on, but Gabriel Richard wanted to work and learn.

A perfect early autumn day, the mild breeze was offshore. The sky was clear and the sun warmed the men and the lake. Jacques* had put Gabriel Richard in the front of his canoe anticipating he would be little help, but the priest was full of questions and took direction well. By midday he was almost adequate by non-voyageur standards, never complained and rested only when the others did.

Although now 18, Jacquot had never been on a voyage this long, he had accompanied his father to the north of the lake to fish, hunt and trap on several occasions and was well versed on the ways of the wild. Georges Drouillard had also travelled with his father who worked as an interpreter on many occasions. At 26 he was more skilled than most men his age. So the two handled their canoe with ease.

The lakeshore up to the Milk River was beginning to look like civilization. Although there was much vacant land, there was almost always a farmhouse in sight. After the Milk River, the wilderness quickly returned, only five farms in all of L'Anse Creuse and two were vacant. When they reached the flats, they made a brief visit to Jacob Harsen and the Sauteuse Camp. Because Gabriel Richard was interested in everything seemed to notice everything: the plants, animals and terrain. He produced a string of questions always wanting to know more.

When they reached the Saint-Clair River, the strong current made the going slow and difficult, but the scrawny priest held his own. On the second day he remarked, "I only hope that God will have the same current in the same direction for our return trip."

Jacques* laughed, "God has always been quite consistent in this river, Father."

When they reached Lake Huron, things improved. The winds were calm, and the weather had turned rather hot. Because it had not rained since a few days before their departure, Jacques* was careful to make camp with the fire on the beach and close to the lake to avoid igniting the foliage which was changing hues daily. At midday as they approached the tip of the thumb of the Michigauma Peninsula, now called "Michigan" by the Americans, Jacques* noticed a growing darkness to the northwest.

"Father, I believe we should land here for camp. I suspect relief is coming to the hot and dry weather, but it may arrive violently." They beached their canoes and brought them farther up the beach than normal fearing a north wind directly onshore. Gabriel saw a strange bird and followed it into the woods. Jacques* told the boys, "Stay and make camp. I had better keep him in sight."

The bird moved directly south, and fast, but the priest kept up. They were more than half a mile into the woods when he lost sight of it. He turned to say something to Jacques* when he was interrupted by an enormous bolt of lightning to their north, followed immediately by thunder. "We had better get back, Father. I think the storm is upon us." Just as Jacques*'s words were out, the wind shifted violently to the north. Soon they smelled smoke. "We should make haste to the beach. I'm afraid the lightning has caused a fire."

As they began to head back they were met with a wall of wildlife. Birds, rabbits, squirrels and even three deer, fleeing to the south. Jacques* could see the smoke and knew the flames would not be far behind. "This calls for a change of plans." He looked about quickly and soon found what he wanted. Although it was not apparent to the priest, Jacques* had found an Indian road which he sincerely hoped led to what he wanted. "We have to move fast, Father, try to keep up with me."

They ran for what seemed an eternity. The north wind which had started cool was now hot from the fire. The smoke was more intense and the flames were more visible and definitely closer. Jacques* had to move more slowly than he would have liked as the priest was having considerable difficulty keeping up. Gabriel Richard was hard to rattle but he was becoming very concerned, so concerned that he did not notice what Jacques* Allard certainly did, the animals were all travelling in exactly their same direction.

The heat became intense, and sparks were flying in front of them. Jacques* was also becoming very concerned, thinking, "Maybe God doesn't care about me, but hopefully he won't want to burn the priest." Just as he was losing hope, he saw it. "Here it is Father, quickly!" He pushed the priest ahead, and he began to tumble down a ravine. They landed at the bottom where a large stream gurgled ahead, "Thank God, there is still water." He threw the priest into the stream and shouted, "Get as submerged as you can only bring your head up to breathe and put your robe over your face and breathe through the wet cloth."

Gabriel obeyed. He was amazed at the number of animals keeping them close company. They had much more respect and fear for the fire than they had for the men. The ordeal lasted about an hour. The heat became unbearable and the water felt as though it was about to boil. When it seemed they could breathe no more the rain started and it came with the same ferocity as the fire. Soon the fire was extinguished and the forest stood in ashes. When he felt it safe, Jacques* said, "We can get up now."

Gabriel arose, "Oh dear, I fear I have damaged my leg in the descent."
Jacques* helped him to a rock where he could examine his ankle, "The skin is intact and it is not deformed. Hopefully a bad sprain. Wait here." In a few minutes he was back with some charred sticks and vines. "The black will match your robe."

314

As he bound the priest's leg, Gabriel remarked, "This will give me a whole new insight into describing the flames of Hell."

Laughing, "Father, you are one strange man for a priest."

Helping him up, he showed him how to use another stick as a crutch. They began to make their way back much more slowly than their trip in. Gabriel was amazed by the devastation, the charred forest and the large number of dead animals. They came upon a nest with a mother fox, burned trying to protect her young. In spite of his leg, the priest bent to touch it. Jacques* could see a tear form in his eye. "I almost feel as though we should give them all a burial."

When they reached the beach, the boys were obviously relieved, although Jacquot told Gabriel Richard with some pride, "I knew you would be alright with my father." The fire had started about 100 feet inland and moved straight south. As a result, the forest around the beach was spared. The lake was roaring like the ocean with huge rollers hitting the beach.

Jacques* said, "We will be here for a day or two until this dies. Fortunately this is still a good camp in spite of the fire."

Like all good priests, Father Gabriel Richard was inflexible on the subject of mass attendance and took the opportunity to celebrate the sacrament each Sunday for his current miniscule congregation. Jacques* had been on other voyages where a priest was along, but these were much larger groups and true voyageurs could find some errand of urgency when necessary. Here attendance could not be avoided. Fortunately Father Richard had a blessedly short form and saved the sermon for after dinner. He had brought his own communion set which included his brilliant silver chalice, the ordination gift from his father. As he stood at an altar of a fallen tree with colored leaves falling about him, he declared, "Only God himself could make so wonderful a cathedral."

During a voyage such as this with limited company, the men began to know each other well. By the end of the trip they would have all heard each other's stories and have had an excellent opportunity to take a true measure of their companions. Gabriel was only 32 years old, merely six years older than George Drouillard but twenty-one years the junior of Jacques* Allard. Gabriel had read the writings of Father Jacques Marquette and his companion, the voyageur Louis Jolliet. He was very interested in learning about the life and ideas of his voyageur companion and began to regard Jacques* as his Jolliet.

Northern Michigan – October 1799:

The men had crossed the wide bay called "Thunder Bay" for its behavior in storms. As they made camp north of the bay, Jacques* declared, "We should reach the fort in one good day or two at the most. Gabriel had become accustomed to the ritual of setting camp and tried to be as useful as possible. As he gathered sticks for the fire, he found a large pile of dry wood just inside the forest. When he pulled it up, he was startled to see a nest with two furry creatures appearing to be raccoons. To his dismay, he then heard the most fearsome growl he had ever heard.

316

He turned to face a creature unlike anything he had ever seen. It had the contour of a raccoon but was as large as a small adult black bear. Gabriel had never before thought of an animal as evil, but this one came close to it. He tried to back away and made the mistake of replacing the sticks. The mother became enraged and Gabriel could only think she was deciding how much to make him suffer before his death. As he whispered his final words to God, he heard God reply, "Don't move Father."

He turned slowly and saw that it was not God, but Jacques* Allard. Thank goodness he could shoot the creature. To his horror, the priest realized Jacques* did not have his rifle. Both would now die. Jacques* moved slowly and calmly, approaching the animal who remained quiet. He softly touched her long snout and to Gabriel's amazement, took one of the cubs and carefully set it in front of the mother. She in turn took the cub and returned to the nest. Jacques* and Gabriel were allowed to return to beach unmolested.

When they returned to the camp, Jacques* said, "I believe it would be prudent for us to move the camp farther north." Gabriel moved like lightning reloading the canoe and they soon pushed off from the shore. The priest remained silent until they made their next destination.

Once they had made camp, Gabriel was calm enough to speak, "What in the world was that?"

"The English call it wolverine. There are not many by Détroit any longer although they are still common around here. The Indians say it is the fiercest animal on earth. I have seen one kill a bear easily more than twice its size."

"And whatever did you do to it?"

"For some reason I do not understand, animals do not fear me, and I do not fear them. It has always been so."

"A gift from God."

Jacques* laughed, "An old Sioux guide once told me that. He called it animal charming. Apparently there are others with the 'gift', but I have never seen one. One suggestion, Father, when you see sticks as though someone has stacked them for you, leave them be."

Father Gabriel Richard did not know that some years hence, an action of his would cause this odd and rare animal to be immortalized.

Fort Michilimackinac – Two Days Later:

At the end of the American Revolution, the British deemed the fort on the south side of the strait too difficult to defend. As a result they moved it to Mackinaw Island, on a hill overlooking the harbor and the strait. The very spot where Cadillac over 100 years before had noted as the ideal spot for such a fortification. The old fort on the southern peninsula lay in ruins. Farms were scattered among both sides of the strait and on the island. Since Pontiac's revolution, the trade at the straits had suffered, first with Pontiac, then the American Revolution and then the uncertainty that accompanied the ongoing British occupation. The Americans had taken control of the fort a short while after the liberation of Fort Détroit. Trade was now increasing, but the population had shrunk to fifty families.

There was a small chapel near the new fort that Father Gabriel Richard made his base. There had been no priest for a while and many French citizens came to have their children baptized or their marriages sanctified. A small cabin next to the chapel served as shelter for the four men. After dinner, Jacques* and Gabriel sat smoking on the porch, watching the sun set on the western strait with its backdrop of magnificent color. "I must say that in France, and in Illinois, autumn pales compared to this."

"It's true, Father, there is nothing on earth to compare to the color of October in the north woods."

"Where have the boys gone this fine evening."

"I believe they went to town," referring to the small village at the foot of the fort. "Looking for some excitement, probably women."

"And what would they want from women?"

"I suppose the same thing men are always looking for from women."

"You cannot mean fornication?"

"Well, that's some more direct than I would put it, but I believe it is on the list."

Then the priest asked Jacques* something that surprised him more than anything to date, "Jacques*, what is it like to make love to a woman?"

Jacques* almost swallowed his pipe. When he recovered, "Well, Father, it depends on the woman and the circumstance. Always it's exciting, fun I guess. At its best it is sharing something as special as anything in life."

"More special than prayer?"

"Well, I think there is a competition there, Father."

Gabriel reflected for a while and continued, "I believe in this new world, relations outside of wedlock seem to be more prevalent than in France."

"I have never been to France, Father, but I have always expected it is the same everywhere. It is just things here are more open, wild and uncertain. Take the voyageurs. These men are gone for months on end, sometimes years. Both the man and the wife can become lonely. You know yourself, we have children born and baptized when the father has not been home for a year. There are children born four months after the return of the father. Then there are the widows, lots of young widows around here. What about these folks you have been marrying this week? Were they living in sin because there was no priest? And what about young Georges Drouillard here? His mother was a Flathead woman. She died and his father had to go beg Simple Bocquet to baptize the boy. Let me tell you a secret, I had a Flathead woman at the same time. I loved her as much as I love my Jennie*. She died, too. We were never married; I have a difficult time seeing that as bad."

Having encountered more than he had expected, the priest excused himself and left for bed. In the morning they left for Détroit.

Southern Lake Huron – November 1799:

Father Gabriel Richard was celebrating his last outdoor mass of the voyage. As he raised his silver chalice in the air, two men suddenly emerged from the forest. One held a gun on the priest and the other guarded the three-man congregation. The man at Gabriel's side said in

English, "We don't want no trouble parson, just that cup there."

Gabriel turned quietly and answered, "It is not mine to give, my son. It belongs to God."

The man hit him in the stomach with his rifle butt. "Soon it's going to belong to us."

Gabriel regained his posture, "Again it is not mine, but God's."

Seeing the priest was defenseless, the man set his rifle down and struck him in the face laying him flat. "I'll show you God, you papist son of a bitch."

Gabriel again crawled to his feet and picked up the cup. "Sir, I think you had better leave."

This time the man knocked him down and kicked him mercilessly several times in the mid-section. "I ain't going without that cup." And the man picked it up along with his rifle.

To everyone's shock, Gabriel managed to get to his feet. He straightened his spectacles and came to the man. Grabbing the man's wrist and looking deeply into his bloodshot eyes, "Once more, please go, and in peace."

The man looked at this straggly man whom he outweighed by at least 100 pounds. Something happened, he looked at his companion, then at the three parishioners. He handed the cup to Gabriel, turned and ran off.

A relieved Jacques* Allard quietly replaced the knife he had secretly taken from his boot, "Well, Father, I guess you showed him."

Gabriel dusted himself off, "Let us finish mass."

At the conclusion of the sacrament, Jacques* Allard remarked, "Gabriel, I guess I can charm animals, but you can charm men." With that Jacques* became one of the few

people in Détroit, who would ever call the priest by his
Christian name.

Chapter 41

The Saint Clair Flats – Winter 1800:

    Jacques* Allard now realized he was never so happy as when he was in the "flats". He enjoyed life as a farmer, family man and citizen of old Cadillac's city in the wilderness; but hunting, trapping and fishing were in his blood, and they would never leave. More than being in the flats, he enjoyed teaching his boys the ways of the wild. His father had tried to teach him as much as he could, but now Jacques* knew it was Toussaint and Jean-Baptiste Charbonneau who had taught him the most. At 54 years he had only recently come to the realization his own father had died at the age of 43.

    Jacquot had accompanied him for some years, and Pierre, now 13, had come the past three years. This year he and Henri-Pierre had brought the younger boys, Louis-Pierre* Allard and Henri-Pierre's twins, Michel and Lucien. All three of the younger boys were but 7 years old. What they lacked in strength and experience, they more replaced with enthusiasm. The first ones up and always ready to go, they never complained about anything. Their fathers had been introduced to the wilderness at an early age, and they believed the same would benefit their boys.

    Jacquot found the life in the wild now routine and he spend many evenings at the Sauteuse camp in the company of young women. He had even brought young Pierre with him on occasion. Jacques* knew their mother would hardly approve, but also remembered his own life at that age.

Louis-Pierre* by contrast, was interested in learning everything and knowing how to do it best. He had the zeal and concentration that made his father want to teach him more and more. Louis-Pierre* was also a strong lad. He was a head taller than the twins and almost as strong as Pierre who was 6 years his senior.

One month into the adventure, as the other boys were tending the traps, Jacques* and Louis-Pierre* fished though the ice on Anchor Bay. A more avid fisherman than his older brothers, Louis-Pierre* listened intently to his father and always remembered the lesson. "Just as we do at home, make the hole in the ice round, a sharp corner is more likely to crack. If you can see the bottom, sink a bright stone. If it seems to move, get off the ice quickly as this means the whole ice is shifting. If you cannot see bottom, like today, take two bearings on the shore and remain conscious of them. Some days, even in the middle of winter, something you cannot see or hear, perhaps something very far away, can cause the ice to crack and began to move."

As if on demand, when Jacques* stopped speaking Louis-Pierre* had an enormous pull on his line. The youngster fought for some time before he pulled a giant walleye from the water. "Look, Papa. It must be eight pounds." As he struggled to unhook his prize, it jumped away and slid along the ice.

It was the sort of day perfect for *ah-key* as a recent crack in the ice had flooded the surface and made it smooth as glass. As a result, the monster fish was able to flap his way for quite some distance. Louis-Pierre* took off after his great catch. When he was thirty feet into the chase, he tripped on a ledge of ice and fell flat. To his father's horror, he fell into the ice and disappeared through a very small hole.

Jean-Baptiste Charbonneau had long ago taught a young Jacques* Allard that panic was the worst thing to have in the wild, "The graver the situation, the more important calmness of thought and action become." Jacques* now realized the strip of ice where his son had fallen was caused by a recent separation and refreeze. The ice here would not begin to support his weight and rushing to his boy's aide would only cause them both to share the same awful fate.

He grabbed his wooden pole and a length of rope he always carried and proceeded slowly toward the black hole in the blue ice. When he came to the edge of the thin ice he lay on his stomach and began to crawl so his weight was more distributed. To his dismay he realized the ice would not hold him even in that position. He began to carefully consider other means of rescue when to his amazement; the young boy's head popped through the hole, "Papa!"

"Louis-Pierre*, I am throwing you a stick, take hold and do not let go." He quickly tied the rope to the stick and slid it to the hole. His son took hold and he carefully began to pull. Louis-Pierre* was almost back on the surface when the ledge of ice broke and he again submerged.

"Papa, help!"

"Keep holding on! You'll break through the ice until I get you to where it's strong again." This process occurred three more times. When the boy was less than five feet away, he again disappeared. His father said the most sincere prayer of his life. It was soon answered as the boy's head reappeared. He again took the stick and this time Jacques* brought him to safety.

"The water is really cold."

His father grabbed him and headed quickly to shore, being ever conscious of not stepping on any more thin ice. When they reached camp, they were alone. Fortunately Jacques* had a habit of always keeping the fire smoldering in a permanent winter camp. Within minutes he had a blaze. He removed the boy's wet things and wrapped him in a skin blanket. He was no longer breathing. Jacques* did not know how long he had been without air, but he knew people in cold water could remain alive for very long times. He began to squeeze his chest and suddenly he coughed up water and began to cry. His father held him even tighter.

He started to breathe more regularly and suddenly looked up at Jacques*, "Did you remember my fish?"

Jacques* laughed and said, "Of course." He made some soup for the lad and by the time the others returned from the trap lines, Louis-Pierre* was alert and talking. Just before dark, Jacques* took a careful walk out onto the lake. At the scene of the excitement he found the monster walleye that had not had the good fortune to fall in with Louis-Pierre*. As the boy nearly drowned in the water, the old fish had drowned on the surface. Jacques* took his boy's frozen prize back to camp.

That night Pierre asked his young brother, "How did you get out?"

The youngster replied calmly. "I did what Papa had told me. He said when you fall through the ice, stay calm and turn over and look up. I did and saw a black hole just like he told me. I went to the black hole and it was the way out."

Pierre asked, "Were you real scared?"

"No, Papa says when things are bad is when you must stay calm."

Late that night when everyone was asleep, Jacques* Allard sat by the fire and smoked his pipe, alone with his thoughts. He remembered another winter night forty years earlier. His father had taken him out in the woods. That night he told him the family legend of the medallion and Indian wampum necklace that now hung from Jacques*'s neck. His father told him it was to be passed on to the son determined to be the most adventurous. Jacques* asked his father, "But how will I know which it is?"

His father simply replied, "You will know." His father died that very night, forty years ago.

Jacques* put his hand over his medallion, and he felt a slight but definite tingle on his chest.

Chapter 42

Détroit - Summer 1802:

Sitting alone on a fallen tree, Jacques* watched the storm approach. Particularly hot weather had made it a rather violent summer. In fact, the very tree on which he sat had been uprooted somewhere up the lake during a recent tempest. Now it lay on the Allard beach providing a convenient place to rest.

Jacques* loved to watch lake storms when he was on or close to the shore. He had great respect for them and always feared the sudden squall when he was far out in the lake. The day had been unbearably hot. The air was deathly still, and the dark northern sky was becoming as black as night. Lighting bolts appeared in the northern lake, but there was no thunder, indicating the storm was still far away. Then ripples from the North interrupted the still water; a blessed north breeze began.

Jacques* could now see the squall line in the northern lake as it approached from Anchor Bay. This squall came quickly. Nowhere could one watch the approach of a storm like on the Great Lakes. The wind became strong and soon violent. Jacques* grabbed his hat as it threatened to abandon his head. Now the lightning was close and the thunder deafening. The rain began in big drops and turned to torrents driven by the magnificent north wind. A giant bolt of lightning struck an old oak in front of Toussaint's house splitting the old monster in two.

Rain turned to hail and Jacques* took cover under a large pine. He knew he should go inside but this show was too wonderful leave in the middle. As quickly as the rain had started, it stopped, but the sky did not begin to clear. Rather it stayed dark and the air became again warm and heavy and still. The wind began anew with a greater level of violence. The sky was an eerie yellow. Jacques* heard the sound of rushing water and he saw the funnel of water rise over the lake.

Jacques* Allard had seen several water spouts in his life but never one as grand as this. Toussaint had told him that a water spout would rarely harm a boat, but this one certainly had the capability. It moved south toward the Détroit River and as suddenly as it had appeared, it disappeared into the lake. Now the wind died and the sky cleared suddenly as it is like to do after such an event. The air became still but much less muggy. Steam rode from the ground as the baked earth welcomed the relief of the cool water.

Jacques* turned to the house lost in his thoughts. The Allard family continued to grow. Suzanne had married Etienne Duchesne the year before and young Reine Allard had been born in April. Now in June Détroit was incorporated into a town, an actual municipal entity of the United States. Things began to have a stability not seen in his lifetime, but affairs half a world away were taking shape of something that would have much more far reaching implications on old Cadillac's city in the wilderness, and Jacques* Allard in particular.

Talleyrand paced nervously about his grand office, wondering how he would avoid the next crisis for his country. Born with a deformed leg that would mark him his entire life, Charles Maurice de Talleyrand-Périgord had exceeded anyone's expectations for a crippled lad, even one from a wealthy family. There would never be any doubt he was a survivor of the first order. Ordained to the priesthood in 1779 at the same seminary of Saint-Sulpice that would ordain Gabriel Richard twelve years later, he had gone on to become the Catholic Church representative to the French Crown.

Serving in the reign of Louis XVI, he was made the church representative to the Estates-General in 1789. There he met another crippled aristocrat, Honoré-Gabriel Riqueti, Comte de Mirabeau. Mirabeau convinced Talleyrand to support the revolution and together they helped write the Declaration of the Rights of Man. From there he quietly became the Foreign Minister of the first French Republic.

Fading from the scene during the reign of terror, he had now resurfaced to become Minister to Napoleon Bonaparte. As Talleyrand often said, "Treason is a matter of dates." The door opened and Talleyrand's aid escorted Robert Livingston into the room. The two men exchanged greetings and were left alone to negotiate. Livingston had been sent by the new President of the United States, Thomas Jefferson.

Livingston began, "Monsieur, as you know, my government has a genuine interest in purchase of the port of *la Nouvelle Orléans,*" using its French name. "We are ready to pay a handsome price. As you must realize, for you it is a port to nowhere but a great wilderness."

Talleyrand countered, "Mr. Livingston, as you know, we have recently acquired the whole of Louisiana from the Spanish. General Napoleon has great plans for this territory. I doubt any price would be acceptable."

Talleyrand knew that although Napoleon once had great plans for a territory in the Americas, he had lost his interest due to more pressing issues in the Eastern Hemisphere. Talleyrand considered this a folly but could only stall and hope to improve the price. Negotiating continued into the night.

Washington, D.C. - Four Weeks Later:

Thomas Jefferson gazed from his office window. The United States capital for only two years, this small southern town had a long way to go to become a New York City, Philadelphia, or Boston. His aide ushered Robert Livingston to the room. "Well Robert, what do you report from our old allies in France?"

"Mr. President, I have been negotiating with this odd little man, Talleyrand. He is an inscrutable sort and personally has no interest of losing France's territory in the new world. However, his little Corsican boss seems to have other thoughts. Apparently he needs the money to pursue his goals in the old world."

Jefferson came characteristically to the point, "Do they have a proposal?"

"Actually yes, sir. They have no interest in the sale of the port alone, but for a slightly higher number, they are willing to sell us the port of New Orleans along with the whole of the Louisiana Territory."

Jefferson turned, stared, and sank into his chair. "The whole thing?"

"So it seems, Mr. President."

"Why in the world would they consider such a thing?"

"As I see it Mr. President, They must sell the port of New Orleans to get the money they need. Without the port, they have no access to the Louisiana Territory. Spain and England would both dearly love control of this land and have a chance to take our land as well. Without a true French occupation, the land would be up for grabs. France has no fear, however, of the United States. It actually makes the British and Spanish threats less dangerous from Napoleon's viewpoint."

Jefferson thought and sketched on a sheet of paper. "I'm a farmer and know the value of land. This will… my God, this will double the size of the nation, but with wilderness. Money is tight, and there are those in Congress who will holler bloody murder. On the other hand, how can we pass it up?"

Chapter 43

Lake Saint Clair – August 1803:

Jacques* and Henri-Pierre pulled the line together until they had the great fish at the side of the boat. Henri-Pierre cleated the line to the boat while Jacques* took a great club and hit the monster on the forehead, stunning it temporarily. Taking a large gaff hook, he hooked the creature and the two men brought him aboard.

Wiping his forehead, Henri-Pierre sighed, "Not bad. Over one hundred pounds." Catching his breath and uncleating the line, he added, "Let's bring in the next one."

The men were working a night line over "the sturgeon bank," as they called a drop-off six miles from the United States shore and six miles off the Canadian shore, about eight miles from the mouth of the Détroit River. In the hot days of August, the immense fish lay at the bottom and were easy prey. On a good day they could bring in two or three such giants which would feed their families for weeks or could be sold to some of the inns newly opened in Détroit.

Normally two or three of the boys would come to help, but today they were at a lesson by Father Gabriel Richard who continued to give what education he could to the local youngsters. They met almost every week, even in the summer, although this would stop when the harvest began.

Jacques* observed, "We seem to have one more. Once he is in the boat, we will head in before the wind shifts." Henri-Pierre had predicted a change in the hot weather earlier in the day. Jacques* knew his friend's Indian weather instincts were usually accurate. As the men brought the line along, they baited the empty hooks so the line would be ready once they had emptied it.

Once their third and last catch was aboard, they finished sinking the line and headed home. Henri-Pierre gave a nod to the northern horizon, and Jacques* noticed the clouds gathering, "We'd better make some time." The boat was rigged so two men could row at once although usually only one did. Both men took their positions and they sped toward shore.

Soon thunder was apparent in the north and early ripples appeared. The wind shift was pleasant on this hot, humid afternoon, but the men realized they may not reach shore before the storm reached them. Soon rain began bringing more relief but also more concern. As the waves built they began to worry. The rain came so hard visibility ceased to exist. Jacques* brought out his old military compass and secured it where he could see it but it would not be lost overboard.

Conditions deteriorated further but the men knew they were making good time as they rowed with the wind and the current which would become greater as they approached shore and came closer to the mouth of the river. Eventually it became bad enough they considered getting rid of the fish to make more speed, but they rejected this not only to keep the valuable fish but also to keep more ballast in the boat and make the craft more stable.

The rain began to abate, and the wind had died when they heard the funnel. Soon they saw it, certainly the largest water spout either had ever seen. They sat exactly in its path. Before they could react, it hit. Old Toussaint's assumption that spouts never hurt boats was disclaimed as they became airborne and the world went black.

Jacques* awoke. He was disoriented but soon remembered the storm and realized he was clinging to a piece of wood, probably a piece of the boat. He called to Henri-Pierre, but there was only silence and the sound of the driving rain. He called and called again to no avail. Although he was a strong swimmer and generally able to stay afloat easily for hours, he felt himself failing and knew he was soon to loose his grip and submerge. Suddenly he saw something swimming rapidly toward him. "Henri-Pierre!" No answer. The swimmer came closer. It could not be his friend as it was too large. Then he realized, it was his bear! The old bear came to the wooden float, "There are still things to be accomplished, young Allard."

Immediately Jacques*'s eyes opened. The bear was a dream, but unfortunately, not the storm. Jacques* was lying on a broken side of the boat which was still afloat. The storm was clearing and he could see shore. He knew with the current and wind direction, he would eventually be taken to the mouth of the river. He began in vain to call for his friend, but there was nothing to hear but the sound of his voice and nothing to see but the lake.

Jacques* made shore shortly after nightfall. He went to the mill and Jean-Baptiste* Laforest took him home. Immediately he went to see Agathe with the bad news.

335

Henri-Pierre's body came ashore south of the city the next day. It was brought home. Agathe wanted him buried in the cemetery of Sainte-Anne but Toussaint insisted he be buried near his home in Indian fashion. This caused a divide between Henri-Pierre's father and wife which would never heal. Jacques* did not take a side but quietly agreed with Toussaint.

Eventually Agathe moved to Assumption with the two girls. The twins stayed with Toussaint. The old Indian's wife, Monique, had died the year before and he had taken to living in a camp in back in Indian style. He gave his house to Jacquot Allard. Of the twins, Lucien who had always favored the Indian ways, stayed with his grandfather, but Michel chose to move in with the Allard family.

The Allard Farm – Late Autumn 1803:

Having finished the harvest, the Allard family had a less hectic schedule. Months had passed since the disastrous day on the lake, but Jacques* still could not come to grips with the absence of his life-long friend. All of Henri-Pierre's ancestors had outlived their Allard counterparts, and Jacques* had always expected it would be the same with him.

Jacquot, though still single, had moved in to Toussaint's old house next door. He was, however, always present at the dinner table. At twenty-one he had taken an interest in the affairs of the community and planned to remain fixed in the city in the wilderness.

"I tell you, father, it is enormous, the most important thing since the revolution. It will double the size of the country and push the boundaries clear to the Great Falls. Rivard says the Louisiana Purchase is going to cause Détroit to grow beyond all expectation. Saint-Aubin says people and goods will flow through the straits, and Joseph Campau says the business opportunities will be endless. I have decided to try my hand in some of this and possibly start to increase the family land holdings. Pierre is going to join me."

Pierre, now sixteen, joined in, "That's right. We are going to make our living here. The life in the fur trade is soon to end as more people cross the frontier."

Jacques* half listened and nodded, but his thoughts were far away in the west with his old friend, Henri-Pierre. His dreams and the boys' conversation were quickly interrupted by a loud knock at the door. "It must be something important to call after dark with snow in the air."

Jacques* opened the door to young Georges Drouillard. Now twenty-nine, he was frequently absent from Détroit as he continued to translate for the government in the Indian territories. Jacques* had not seen his old companion's son for some time. Jacques* bid him enter.

"Jacques*, I'm sorry to call at this hour, but I have an urgent need of Toussaint Charbonneau. Do you know of his whereabouts?"

Jacques* pondered, "I haven't seen the rascal for years. I figure he probably pushed himself too hard on someone who finally killed him. Either that or he is permanently drunk with some Indian woman."

Drouillard looked disappointed. "I have been everywhere, as far as New Orleans and the Great Falls. You were my last hope of finding him."

"Sorry I couldn't be more help. Come in for a while."

As he closed the door, Drouillard continued, "You can be helpful. In fact without Charbonneau and with the death of Henri-Pierre," as he crossed himself, "You are the only one who can help me."

The two men were seated in the front room and Jacques* poured two glasses of cider while Drouillard continued, "Almost a year ago, I received this letter."

He handed it to Jacques* who could not read much English but thought he knew the signature, and with some astonishment asked, "Is this who I think it is?"

"That's right, Thomas Jefferson, the President himself. I need your help on the greatest adventure of all time."

Jacques* looked over to the table where his wife was seated, "Perhaps we should continue this conversation on the porch."

TO BE CONTINUED

EPILOGUE

When I conceived of writing the history of the Allards, it was the story of Jacques* Allard I was most anxious to tell. A young boy who leaves his family at a critical junction in history becoming a true voyageur and later the first Allard citizen of Détroit. His lifetime encompasses a vital period in the development of Cadillac's city in the wilderness as well as that of the American nation.

Lake Saint Clair and the Saint Clair Flats: An area that has always held a special meaning for me. There is hardly a memory of my youth that does not contain it. It was equally special to my Allard ancestors. As a youngster, trips to Harsens Island were always a high point of the summer. Reachable only by ferry, it retained a tranquility which I remember to this day. We would always stop at Brown's landing, home and business of my mother's first cousin, Earl Brown. We visited his establishment often, and before his death a few years ago he was very helpful in my research of the Allards.

Pontiac's War: After the fall of French Canada to the British in 1760, the native and French people of Détroit were uncertain of their future. As the British presence became more prominent, the Indians began to lose the standing they once had with the French. Pontiac was a shrewd leader and at one point during the conflict controlled most of the Great Lakes Region. There were Frenchmen in Détroit with loyalties to each side. Most had sympathies with the Indians but realized the ultimate outcome. As a result most remained aloof. I believe my description of events is fairly accurate.

The American Revolution: This was another source of ambivalence for the French citizens. Many did have American sympathies and took part in the ill-fated Battle of Québec, as well as other successful battles such as Saratoga. As shown in The Allards Book Three: Peace and War, the Americans learned a great deal from both the French and Indian styles in battle, and men such as Thomas Sumter, Andrew Pickens and Francis Marion used it to their great advantage.

1781-1796: Most Detroiters are unaware of this interesting period of fifteen long years when Détroit was theoretically part of the United States but remained under British rule. The British believed as long as they controlled the vital straits, the Americans could not sustain the Indian war, and the new country would eventually fall back to British hands. Had it not been for the persistence of Washington and Anthony Wayne along with their French-Canadian allies this could have been the case.

The American Government: This presented another ambivalence for the now French-Americans which will play into book five. As Jacques* Allard told Hamtramck, most French stayed where they were: either in Détroit or Sandwich (now Windsor) with little regard to the government. Again they remained aloof.

Sunday Picnics: Always a part of French life in the new world, these affairs continued to the time of my youth. My mother and grandmother told wonderful stories about them. They were ongoing forums for gossip, socializing, news, discussions, eating, drinking, and the occasional "friendly fights" so common to the French culture in the new world.

DESCENDANTS OF PIERRE* ALLARD
TWO GENERATIONS

1. **Pierre* Allard**, b. Apr 28, 1716, Charlesbourg, QC,
   (son of Jean Baptiste* Allard and Anne Elizabeth*
   Pageot) baptized May 1, 1716. He married Marie
   Angélique* Bergevin, Nov 5, 1743, in Charlesbourg,
   QC, b. Oct 10, 1722, Charlesbourg, QC, (daughter of
   Ignatius* Bergevin and Genevieve* Tessier) d. Mar 18,
   1788, Isle Dupas, QC. Pierre* died Dec 27, 1759,
   Quebec.

   Children:
   2.   i   **Pierre** b. Dec 23, 1744.
   3.   ii   **Jacques*** b. Oct 14, 1746.
        iii   **Marie Angélique Allard**, b. Oct. 02, 1749.
   She married (2) Antoine Amable Dutaut
   Vilandre, Oct. 27, 1777, in Isle Dupas, QC,
   (son of Pierre Dutaut and Marie Louise
   Hus). Marie died Jun 16, 1832.
        iv   **Joseph Allard**, b. Apr 12, 1752,
   Charlesbourg, QC, d. May 04, 1752,
   Charlesbourg, QC.
        v   **Marie-Anne Allard**, b. Sep 16, 1753. She
   married (1) Noel Penisson, Aug 18, 1777, in
   Isle Dupas, QC, (son of Jean Marie
   Penisson and Catherine Monet). She
   married (2) Raphael Desorcy, Jan 30, 1786.
   Marie-Anne died Feb 17, 1839.
        vi   **Louis Allard**, b. Feb 11, 1755,
   Charlesbourg, QC. He married (1) Marie
   Levron, Aug 18, 1806, in Quebec. He
   married (2) Marguerite Malbeuf, Aug 14,
   1780, in St Cuthbert QC, (daughter of Jean

Baptist Malbeuf and Dotothee Cloutier). He married (3) Louise Masse, Feb 25, 1790, in St Cuthbert QC, (daughter of Jean Baptist Masse and Louise Larose). Louis died Apr 02, 1825, Quebec.

vii **Michel Allard**, b. Nov 20, 1756, Charlesbourg, QC. He married Marie Louise Plouffe, Jul 25, 1785, in Berthierville QC, (daughter of Pierre Plouffe and Angelique Hamel). Michel died Sep 28, 1832.

viii **Louis Allard**, b. Oct 12, 1758, Charlesbourg, QC, d. Aug 29, 1759, Charlesbourg, QC.

Second Generation

2. **Pierre Allard**, b. Dec 23, 1744, Charlesbourg, QC. He married Elizabeth Lariviere Chapdelain, Feb 03, 1772, in Quebec, (daughter of Jean Seraphin Chapdelain and Josephte Brisset). Pierre died Oct 26, 1795, Quebec.
   Children:
   i   **Francoise Allard**, b. Jul 27, 1777.
   ii   **Marie Ursule Allard**, b. Jan 10, 1779.
   iii **Marie Genevieve Allard**, b. Oct 06, 1780.
   iv   **Antoine Allard**, b. Feb 16, 1782.

3. **Jacques* Allard**, b. Oct 14, 1746, Charlesbourg, QC. He married Marie Genevieve * Laforest, Feb 7, 1780, in Detroit, MI, Ste. Anne, b. June 16, 1764, Detroit (now Windmill Pointe GP), (daughter of Guillaume* Laforest and Marie Marguerite* Tremblay) baptized Jun 17,

1764, Detroit, MI, Ste. Anne. Jacques* died 1814   ?, Detroit, MI.

Children:

i   **Jacques George Allard Jr.**, b. May 6, 1782, Detroit, MI. He married Therese Marsac, Jul 15, 1811, in Detroit, MI, b. 1792, (daughter of Jean Marsac and Therese Andrews).

ii **Suzanne Allard**, b. Sept 14, 1783, Detroit, MI. She married Etienne Gatignon dit Duchesne, Jan 25, 1801, in Detroit, MI, b. May 25, 1776, Grosse Pointe, MI, (son of Pierre Jean Gatignon dit Duchesne and Josette Lacelle).

iii **Marie Louise Allard**, b. Feb 19, 1785, Detroit, MI. She married (1) Nicolas Patenotre, Sep 23, 1799, in Detroit, MI, b. 1768, Grosse Pointe, MI, (son of Nicolas Patenotre and Catherine Gatignon dit Duchesne) d. 1808, Detroit, MI. She married (2) Anthony Salois, Feb 19, 1811, in Detroit, MI, b. Yamaska, QC, (son of Micael Salois and Marie Denis).

iv **Pierre Allard**, b. Jan 28, 1787, Detroit, MI. He married Agatha Laperle, Oct 06, 1812, in Detroit, MI, b. 1780, Detroit, MI, (daughter of Joseph Laperle and Frances Brillant) d. 1854, Grosse Pointe, MI. Pierre died Mar 1 1856, Grosse Pointe, MI, buried: Mar 1 1856, St Paul's GP.

v   **Guillaume Allard**, b. Aug 01, 1788, Detroit, MI (twin), buried: Sep 09, 1788.

vi   **Joseph Allard**, b. Aug 01, 1788, Detroit (twin), buried: Sep 09, 1788.

vii **Archange* Allard**, b. Oct 16, 1789, Detroit, MI, baptized Oct 17, 1789, Ste Anne, Detroit, MI. She married Gabriel* Renaud, May 02, 1808, in Ste. Anne Detroit, b. Nov 23, 1775, Grand Marais, Detroit, MI, (son of Louis* Renaud and Marie Anne* Casse dit St. Aubin) baptized Nov 23, 1775, Ste. Anne, Detroit, d. Nov 22, 1844, Assumption, Sandwich (Windsor), ONT. Archange* died Aug 04, 1810, Grosse Pointe, MI, buried: Aug 04, 1810, St. Paul GP.

viii **Louis Pierre* Allard**, b. Aug. 18, 1793, Detroit, MI, baptized Aug. 19, 1793, Ste Anne, Detroit, MI. He married Therese Godfroy* Balard, Feb 18, 1822, in Ste Anne, Detroit, MI, b. Dec 17, 1805, Detroit, MI, (daughter of Etienne Godfroy* Balard and Elizabeth* Thomas) baptized Dec 18, 1805, Ste Anne, Detroit, MI, buried: Oct 9, 1853, Mt. Clemens, MI. Louis died Jul 1832, Grosse Pointe, MI.

ix   **Joseph Allard**, b. July 29, 1795, Detroit, MI. He married Magdeline Tremblay, Oct 06, 1818, in Detroit, MI, b. Oct 13, 1798, Detroit, MI, (daughter of Francis Tremblay and Mary Louisa Crequi) d. Aug 08, 1881, Erin Twp., MI. Joseph died Jun 18, 1878, Erin Twp., MI.

x   **Felicity Allard**, b. May 8, 1797, Detroit, MI. She married Jean Evangelist Tremblay,

Apr 30, 1822, in Detroit, MI, b. Oct 28, 1784, Detroit, MI, (son of Francois Tremblay and Magdeline Meny).

xi **Francois Allard**, b. May 29, 1799, Detroit, MI. He married Margaret Marsac, Sep 07, 1824, in Detroit, MI, b. 1806, (daughter of Jean Marsac and Therese Andrews).

xii **Reine Allard**, b. Apr. 28, 1802, Detroit, MI, buried: Mar 18, 1807, Detroit, MI.

xiii **Adelaide Allard**, b. July 10, 1804, Detroit, MI, buried: Sept 27, 1805, Detroit, MI.

DESCENDANTS OF HENRI
FIVE GENERATIONS

1. **Henri**, b. 1630, Quebec. He married Angelique, b. Quebec.
    Children:
    2.   i   **Philippe** b. 1650.

Second Generation

2. **Philippe**, b. 1650, Quebec. He married Marie, b. Quebec.
    Children:
        i   **Henri**.
    3.   ii **Joseph** b. 1676.

Third Generation

3. **Joseph de Baptiste**, b. 1676, Quebec. He married Monique de Baptiste, b. Quebec, (daughter of ... de Baptiste and ... Algonquin).
    Children:
    4.   i   **Toussaint** b. 1716.

Fourth Generation

4. **Toussaint de Baptiste**, b. 1716, Québec. He married Monique Thomas, (daughter of Jacob* Thomas and ... Roy).
    Children:
    5.   i   **Henri-Pierre** b. 1746.

Fifth Generation

5. **Henri-Pierre de Baptiste**, b. 1746, Québec. He married
   Agathe Saint-Pierre.

       Children:
      i **Michel de Baptiste**, b. 1793, Detroit.
      ii **Lucien de Baptiste**, b. 1793, Detroit.
      iii **Lucille de Baptiste,** b. 1780, Détroit.